The
Aw
by

"This is not only a fine read, this is an important novel by an important new voice in the art of blending fiction and fact and making sense of it all." — *Grady Harp, Literary Aficionado*

"This is a fine, fine novel for all ages. Youth should read it to be inspired; those of us past youth should read it to be reminded of who we were meant to be." — *Hubert O'Hearn, By The Book Reviews*

"Narrative and dialogue contain picturesque prose that opens the story in the mind of the reader. Highly talented and skilled writer." — *Judge, Writer's Digest Self-Published eBook Awards*

"Klann-Moren gives a true history lesson and her inclusion of historical events in her novel makes the book more vivid. I personally loved it and recommend it to anyone looking for a light, fresh, and cultural (historical) read." — *Kelly Santana for Readers' Favorite*

"*The Clock Of Life*, by Nancy Klann-Moren is one of those books where everything feels right." — *Candi Sary, author of Black Crow White Lie*

"An ideal novel for a book club. *The Clock Of Life* is a strong and thoughtful exploration of a truly American experience."
—*Frank Mundo, L.A. Books Examiner.com*

"Brought to life by a first rate storyteller, *The Clock Of Life* is a book I was sad to see end." —*Edie Crabtree, Newport Beach Independent*

"Giving the gift of experience is one of the most important functions of literature, as is conveying important moral messages and lessons. *The Clock Of Life* does both extraordinarily well. You gotta love a book that lets you walk in the shoes of the characters, feel their hearts and souls and live their lives. This is just such a novel."
—*Sandra Shwayder Sanches for Book Pleasures.com*

"Technically, as far as I could see, this novel is flawless. It has a strong voice, well-drawn characters, a realistic and moving plot, and important, well-expressed themes. I highly recommend it." —*Tahlia Newland, Awesome Indies*

"A must-read. The story is a reminder of a significant time in history when American protests changed the status quo. We watch Jason Lee struggle to come of age while haunted by the past, and finds his voice even though thwarted by the realities of injustice and inequality." —*MaryAnn Easley, author of I am the Ice Worm, and Knuckle Down*

"This story is poignant and real. I highly recommended."
—*Nicole Trwst, author of The Belvedere Club and Bayou Nights*

The Clock Of Life

ALSO BY NANCY KLANN-MOREN

Like The Flies On The Patio

The Clock
Of Life

A Novel

By Nancy Klann-Moren

AnthonyAnn Books

THE CLOCK OF LIFE: Copyright@2012 by Nancy Klann-Moren

All rights reserved. No part of this book may be used or reproduced, distributed, or transmitted in any form or by any means, or stored in a database or retrieval system, without the prior written permission of the publisher.

AnthonyAnn **Books**

ISBN: 978-0-9884944-1-1

This is a work of fiction. With the exception of Emmett Till, CORE activist William Moore, the Civil Rights luminaries, and the not so luminous individuals who placed their mark on the historical Selma to Montgomery march, the characters in this book are all fictitious and are the product of my imagination.

Certain newspaper clippings referenced in these pages were articles, or portions of, originally published in the *Selma Times-Journal* during those tumultuous days in March, 1965

www.nancyklann-moren.com

To Richard—whose belief never waivered
With all my love and thanks

And my sons, Scott and Bryan

1

1974

On that first day of school Mama wrapped her hand around mine as we walked together into the classroom at Cobb's Creek Country School. I'd been so sheltered about our family's past—not to mention the small-minded ways of Hadlee, Mississippi—that I was completely unprepared for what would come.

Mama leaned down and whispered, "No need to worry, Jason Lee. Everything'll be fine, son." I breathed in the familiar almond-cherry scent of her lotion. "Be brave like your daddy was," she said. "He was a hero."

Straightaway a lump caught in my throat. Those were the first words she'd spoken of him to me. Until then, I never even wondered about the man.

With that she tucked a strand of hair behind her ear and moved toward the door. She turned back and smiled at me before leaving.

Despite my initial eagerness to attend school, when I looked around I felt alone and uneasy with the surroundings—the enormous room, the five rows of desks, the green chalkboard along the front wall, the rowdy voices, and the children's faces, dirty and clean, black and white. They were unfamiliar faces, and as different from each other as the eggs collected from our chicken coop, except for the two boys leaning against the back wall. Their faces were the same, with wide foreheads and pointed chins. But one had a head of hair that looked like it'd never seen a comb, and the other's hair was shaved to the scalp, exposing three round sores along the side of his head.

The one with hair burrowed his dirt-stained hands into his pockets and set his eyes on me. His piercing glare caused my mouth to go so dry I licked my lips, then turned toward the windows, pretending to study the white magnolia flowers bouncing on the branches of the trees that lined both lanes of County Road 38, the one thing I knew connected me to my home three miles away.

When I turned around, a colored boy wearing green sneakers pointed to a desk in the middle row.

"Sit there."

"Me?"

He nodded. "Keep clear of the chair behind it."

The boy pushed a noisy cart with uneven wheels through the aisles and placed one dog-eared school book on each desk. He was the blackest colored I'd ever seen, and for some reason I wanted to reach out and touch him.

"I'm Jason Lee," I said.

His shoulders shot up. "Samson Johnson."

I set myself down in the smooth seat and looked at the book on my desk, but couldn't read the words stamped on the cover, and didn't want to let on.

"Incomin," someone yelled.

The children scurried to get to their seats and the room quieted down some. A sound similar to footsteps worked its way down the center aisle. Click-scrape-clack. Click-scrape-clack. A woman with a metal brace strapped to one leg limped her way past us to the big desk at the front of the room. She turned and smiled at us.

"Good morning, class. My name's Miss Hopewell." She set her papers on the desk, plucked a stick of chalk from the drawer, and printed something on the chalkboard. She turned back toward us and clasped her hands together. "I'll be takin over for Miss Iola, teaching grades one through four. Poor lady had quite a fall over the summer and broke her hip."

"Thank the Lord," Samson Johnson said under his breath when he slipped into the desk to the right of mine.

Miss Hopewell pointed to the boys by the wall. "I see we have vacant chairs. You two, take your seats, please." Her finger wiggled when she spoke to them.

The boys made their way to the empty desks behind Samson and me. I turned around to say "hey" to the one in back of me. He glared, same as before, and didn't say "hey" back. Feeling self-conscious, I turned around and focused my attention on Miss Hopewell.

"I hail from the state of Indiana," she said. "Some six hundred miles away."

I didn't have any idea how far away six hundred

miles was but couldn't imagine being *any* miles away from Mama and Uncle Mooks.

"I signed up for a volunteer program that serves rural communities like Hadlee," she said, and went on about all the good the program does. Most of the kids weren't interested in her until she stomped on the schoolroom floor with the shoe on her good leg and yelled, "Attention. Eyes forward, class. Since this is my first day, I'll read your names from the roll call sheet. When you hear yours, stand up so I can see who you are." She glanced down. "Winifred Abbott."

The classroom exploded with laughter. It seemed Miss Hopewell and I were the only two who didn't get the joke.

A plump girl with eyebrows thick as a grown man's stood up. A dingy underskirt poked out beneath her printed dress. She hitched her hands on her hips, the way an old lady does, and said, "My name's Reba. Not nothin else—just Reba."

Miss Hopewell studied the roll call sheet. "Is Reba your given name?"

"Yes, ma'am, I given it to myself."

That time I laughed with the rest of them.

"Thank you, Reba. You may sit down." Miss Hopewell scribbled something on her paper. "Culver Chubb?" She scanned the room.

"Here," the boy behind me shouted loud as a bugle, straight into the back of my head. He didn't stand.

"Thank you, Culver." She looked at the boy behind Samson, the one with the sores on his head. "You must be Eugene Chubb."

Eugene did stand. He pushed his jaw forward and shoved his desk smack into Samson's back. "Here."

Samson's face crunched, but he didn't turn around or say anything. Culver, the one behind me, launched a machine-gun laugh and smacked his desk with the book Samson had left there. Smacked it five times. My insides jumped with each smack.

I looked over to Samson. "You okay?"

"What's it to you, niggalova?" Culver said and punched me in the back with his fist.

I twisted around. "What was that for?"

His mouth curled into a snarl. "Niggalova."

Three or four of the kids in nearby seats laughed. I turned back to see if Miss Hopewell had witnessed the punch.

She was looking up at the light fixture. "Oh, Lord," she said. "Lordy, Lord." Her mouth puckered.

"Miss Hopewell?" I raised my arm to get her attention, to make sure she'd seen what happened. Even with my hand shooting skyward, she looked past me. "Miss Hopewell?"

"Put it down," Samson said. When I looked over, he shook his head like he thought me a fool. "She ain't gonna do nothin, so put it down, and leave it down."

*

Earlier, in the car that morning, Mama had pointed out one particular magnolia within walking distance from the schoolyard. "See that one? The one surrounded by the big patch of itch grass?"

"Uh-huh."

"Meet me there when school lets out. I want to show you somethin."

After the final bell rang I wasn't more than five feet out the door, headed to my meeting place with Mama, when the Chubb boys sandwiched me. They came from behind and put their arms around my shoulders like we were pals, one skinny Chubb on each side of me, squeezing tight. They walked me toward the swings. Halfway there Eugene stabbed his bony knuckles into my stomach. No one had ever hit me so hard before. Stunned, I couldn't believe the pain and I gasped, not sure another breath would come. As if that wasn't bad enough, Culver swung his foot in front of my leg and shoved me. My hands scraped along the ground. Then my chin hit.

The boys ran off, laughing.

While making my way to Mama's magnolia, willing the tears not to come, I picked bloody bits of gravel from my palms. My eagerness to go to school had vanished, and my head throbbed with questions, like how to figure when to say something and when to keep quiet. Who it's okay to talk to and who it's not. And how it is you learn these things. I knew for certain they weren't things Miss Hopewell would be teaching us.

When I got to the tree I looked up the trunk. In the smooth grey bark I caught sight of a heart with initials inside it. I heard footsteps behind me and my chest felt heavy again. Thoughts of what more those two kids might do to me with no one else around flooded my head. Even so, I worked up the nerve to turn and face them.

The girl named Reba ran toward me. "I saw what they did to you," she said, winded. "They got a mean streak."

I stuck my hands in my pants pockets even though they burned like crazy. "They didn't hurt me."

Reba picked at a wart on the back of her hand and talked soft. "All their kin's that way."

I wondered why she ran so far to tell me about the Chubbs, but before I got the question out she was headed back the way she'd come. The skirt of her dress bounced with each step. She turned around and walked backwards. "And stay clear of the Johnson boys, too. My folks say it ain't right to mix with coloreds."

Not too long after Reba ran off, Mama pulled up. She got out of the car and studied the initials scratched in the tree. A surge of recognition hit me. They were the initials JLR + CK. My daddy's initials, same as mine, and Mama's too, before they married.

"Is that you and him?"

"He was eighteen when I met him." She smiled. "A far cry from anyone I'd ever met before. Bold, brash, and full of life."

It was odd to hear her speak of him. I couldn't even think of a question to ask about him.

She touched my scraped-up chin. "What happened here?"

"I fell."

"You sure?" She fixed her eyes on me. "And your

hands?"

"Same."

"Come on, son. Time to go."

The minute I closed the car door and settled in she said, "Tell me everythin 'bout your day, Jason Lee."

I made no mention of what happened with the Chubbs. Instead, I told her about the boy named Samson who gave me a book and showed me where to sit. And how Reba said it ain't right to mix with him because he's colored.

She pulled onto the road. "So, someone named Reba told you it ain't right?"

"Uh-huh."

"It's a tough thing to do in these parts, but you be friends with anyone you want, Jason Lee. Don't let nobody tell you different, you hear?" Her tone sounded like a scolding.

"I won't."

"Your daddy got himself forty-seven stitches across the back of his shoulder. And they threw him in jail to boot, just so you and boys like Samson could be friends."

The air inside the car turned hot as a furnace.

"My d-daddy went to jail?" I stuttered, not knowing if I felt shame, excitement, or something else. The only thing I knew about him was he fought in Vietnam and died there, but I didn't have any idea where that was.

J.L. Rainey died the autumn after I was born, in 1968. He never even set eyes on me, his only offspring, who carries his looks, and more.

"Yes siree, he went to jail. Nineteen sixty-five. Selma." She said it proud, which didn't make sense.

"But this morning you said he was a hero."

"He was."

"Heroes can get put in jail? That ain't right."

"Sometimes it's the only way you can get heard."

"How come you never told me about him goin to jail? How come you never told me nothin?"

"Thought you were too young. Besides, the jail's not the point. And, I'm tellin you now." She took a deep breath. "Your daddy wasn't a perfect man by any means, and sometimes he was downright frustratin, but strong willed people can't help but do what's right in their hearts."

"Whaddya mean?"

"He demonstrated alongside the coloreds for equal rights."

I nodded like I understood.

"It was a time when such behavior was frowned on around these parts. And, truth be told, still is by some. Back then, tempers were on high alert and you never knew what to expect. Participatin in the movement was a dangerous thing to do. Lord knows I didn't want him to get involved, but that wasn't his way."

"So, Mama, I got a question. Is someone whose friends with coloreds a niggalova?"

"Oh, my, Jason Lee." She looked at me and gave a huge smile. "Someone called you that on your first day of school?"

"Uh-huh."

She laughed. "I guess the apple don't fall too far. They called your daddy that same thing, all the time. My, my." She laughed some more. "Despite what I just said, that mindset isn't so accepted as it used to be. Attitudes are beginnin to change slow but sure. Time's provin he was the one thinkin straight, after all." She nodded a few times. "We'll put some salve on those hands when we get home."

With that, our conversation was over and, as it turned out, most any other mention of him for quite a few years to come.

I thought about the proud look on her face when she said my daddy was a hero, and my mind swirled with thoughts of the likes of Superman and Captain America being thrown in jail. Then I thought about the word, *niggalova*, and decided it didn't seem so bad.

During recess the next day I stayed in the classroom, pretending to read a book, to keep clear of the Chubbs. In due time, Miss Hopewell shooed me outside to get some fresh air. Like hounds on a rabbit, Culver and Eugene found me, got hold of my arm, bent it behind my back, and wouldn't let go until I yelled out.

The following day they hit me on the side of my head so hard my ears rang. The day after that they pulled on my underpants until they were so far out of my jeans it took a great deal of maneuvering to get them back where they belonged.

The Chubbs didn't show up for class on Friday, but I still cowered in the doorway and ducked behind bushes, expecting a surprise attack anytime.

I couldn't let Mama in on any of this after it dawned on me that she needed me to be brave like my daddy had been, and I wasn't.

2

Our property measured thirteen acres, and we lived in the house my grandparents built from the ground up. It sat on a mound of sand and fine yellow clay in the shade of twenty-three Napoleon cypress trees, all over a hundred years old.

The corrugated tin roof crackled and groaned and popped each day when the heat from the sun rose and fell. During the rainy season, that same roof shot water down its furrows onto Mama's Pride of Mobile azaleas bordering the front porch. In spring the azaleas thrived with watermelon-colored blooms for the better part of two months. Her blue asters took their turn later in the year.

On Sundays I spent a good amount of my time on the front porch with Uncle Mooks. His favorite place to sit was under the living room window on the lumpy brown couch stuffed with springs and tree moss. I liked to sit on the birch swing that hung on chains attached to the porch beams.

On lucky days a funeral parade passed by, being as we lived dead-center between the Faith Deliverance Holy Church and the graveyard. We always waved when the cars, with their headlights set on high beam, drove past, slow and steady as a family of box turtles.

Never once did anybody wave back.

The Sunday after my first week at Cobb's Creek School, Uncle Mooks settled himself outside on his couch before the sun burned its way through the morning clouds. I carried out our two bowls of grits drenched in melted butter and yelled out, like always, "True grits, more grits, fish grits, and collards." It was our custom for Uncle Mooks to finish with, "Life is good where grits are swallar'd."

But that morning he just stared off in the distance and rubbed his prized possession, the gold pocket watch he always carried with him.

"Time for breakfast," I said, holding one of the bowls out to him.

"Time for breakfast," he repeated and put his watch on the couch. Instead of reaching for the bowl, he continued to stare out past the yard.

"Uncle Mooks?"

He rocked forward and back, causing the couch springs to chirp like a nest of irate crickets. "When's it that bastard's time?" He looked at me as if I knew what he meant.

"What bastard?"

"That bastard, that God damn bastard." He pointed to the road. I watched a faded green truck roll out of sight, just ahead of a cloud of dust.

"Who was it?"

"Peek," he said. "The bastard Peek."

Sometimes scattered memories about his time in Vietnam sprouted from Uncle Mooks' mind and caused him to have an agitated spell, but I was sure it wasn't the case that day.

"Who's Peek?"

He rocked faster and I knew not to ask more questions. The bowls of grits began to weigh my arms down as I continued to stand there.

"Here, take this." I forced one toward his lap so he'd reach for it. He stared into the bowl of grits, then began to eat. We sat together in silence, smothered in the stillness of the morning, thinking our own thoughts.

Sure as summer clouds bring rain, it wasn't long before a funeral parade rolled by—a hearse that led a procession of two sedans and five pickups.

"There's nothin wrong with takin a ride in a hearse, so long as you're sittin up front." Uncle Mooks said.

"You say the same thing every time we have a parade."

We sat in place and waved until the last of the taillights were so far away they looked small as red marbles. Uncle Mooks glanced my way.

"Jason Lee, the clock of life's always tickin towards the funeral parlor."

"Whaddaya mean?"

"I mean, whatever you do, make sure you stay one step ahead of the second hand. You hear what I'm sayin, son?"

I looked into his flecked blue eyes and bobbed my head up and down. "You okay, Uncle Mooks?"

"Damn right I'm okay." He pointed to the dent in his left temple. It was more of a hole the size of a quail egg and the very reason for all his troubles. His voice rose. "Don't never go fight a war drummed up by politicians who don't have the balls to call it a war. They never send their own kin there. Vietnam conflict, my ass. Conflicts are for talkin out. You hear me, son?"

He rocked some more, picked up the watch, and stroked his fingers across its face. Mama opened the screen door and stepped out, the worry line between her brows pinched.

"Thing's okay out here?"

"Funeral parade went by," I said. "And he started talkin bout Vietnam."

"He don't mean to get upset," she said. "It's not his fault."

"And someone called Peek. Who's Peek, Mama?"

She put her finger to her lips. "Shh. Not now, Jason Lee."

If you weren't family, you'd be hard-pressed to see Uncle Mooks and Mama were brother and sister, let alone twins, unless you caught them smiling at the same time. Both their mouths turned downward and their chins puckered, and they both had thin, brown hair. Mama's rested soft against her shoulders. Uncle Mooks pulled his back in a scrawny ponytail, and he only shaved his sparsely haired chin about twice a month. He always wore overalls and his Mississippi State Bulldogs ball cap.

Their size was what really set them apart. Mama didn't weigh more than a hundred pounds and Uncle Mooks was, in simple terms, real big. When Mama needed something from the top shelf of our cupboards she'd call out to him, "Hey Mountain, can you reach somethin for me?" He'd answer, "Sure enough, Anthill."

Mama settled next to him on the couch. The small veins on her cheeks stood out against her pale face. She pulled off his cap, stroked his hair, and massaged the scar on his temple. Uncle Mooks shoved his hands under the bib of his overalls and stared off with an unsettled look, as if the answers to his questions stood out there—somewhere beyond our simple parcel, a twenty minute drive from the heartbeat of town.

They didn't need words. Mama and Uncle Mooks seemed to understand the thoughts that passed between them. She began singing, *Oh, I went down south for to see my Sal, singin Polly-Wolly-Doodle all the day.* Uncle Mooks' far-off look went away. He smiled and sang with her. *Fare thee well, fare thee well, fare thee well my fairy fey. . .*

After a few verses my attention turned to the field on the other side of the road, where an extended family of fox squirrels, the same color as the dirt, had laid claim. When they scurried through the trees, the foliage seemed to rearrange itself into a churning sea of conflict. For all the times I'd studied their ways, that was the first time I realized the aggressive ones called the shots. They fought dirty and got what they wanted. Rivalry and plain old meanness seemed to power those squirrels, same as it powered Eugene and Culver Chubb. The timid ones stayed clear, and didn't challenge their fate.

"There's more grits on the stove," Mama said. "How about I get you another bowl?"

"Sure," I said, but my mind was still on the Chubb boys. How I hoped to someday summon up the nerve to stand up to them. To be brave.

"Put some marshmallows on top," Uncle Mooks said.

According to Mama, he rushed into this world five minutes ahead of her and was, of course, twice her size from the beginning. Being her big brother was a responsibility he attached great importance to. When they were sixteen, tragedy hit. Their folks were on their way to the Lake of the Ozarks for a family wedding when their rattletrap of a Ford station wagon plunged off the side of the road and took them with it.

After the accident, Uncle Mooks assumed full responsibility of his and Mama's future, persuading the authorities to look the other way for two years so they could stay together and hold on to the house until they were of legal age.

"It's that bastard's time," Uncle Mooks said, staring out at nothing from the couch on the front porch.

*

Come Monday morning, the kitchen radio was on while I ate my breakfast and Mama slathered pimento-cheese spread on two slices of white bread.

"Mama, what's a midnight train to Georgia?"

"That's simple son, it's a train leavin at midnight, goin to Georgia." She placed the sandwich in a waxed bag with a double fold-over top and set it, a crabapple, and two butter cookies in a brown paper sack for me to take to school.

"Listen here, Jason Lee," she said when she handed me the sack, "I thought about this all weekend and decided today's the day you can start walkin to school on your own. It's been a week, and you know the way."

The morning air felt crisp and smelled of a burn pile somewhere in the distance. Proud of Mama's confidence in me I kicked up pebbles along the road, filled with my first taste of independence. A mockingbird on the crossbar of a power pole was imitating the song of a thrush. I stopped to watch him. Pretty soon he did a little flip and then went right back to singing. I smiled and thought, *He feels good as me.*

"Hey, Jason Lee." Samson Johnson ran up from a side trail off the highway. He stood a head taller than me. "You walkin?"

I looked up to answer him. "Mama figures I'm ready."

"I walk every day. Blueberry?" He opened his fist. Six berries sat cradled in the pink of his palm. I took three and popped them into my mouth.

"They need more time. Kind of sour."

"Kind of," he said.

We headed down the path past a thick tangle of honeysuckle vines. I pulled off two flowers, handed him one, and we sucked on the nectar.

"How old are you?" I asked.

"Almost eight."

"I'll be eight year after next."

He laughed and said, "What was you lookin at back there?"

"A crazy mockingbird doin summersaults. I like 'em, but my Uncle Mooks don't. Says they're thieves, takin the songs of other birds. He says it's the same as stealin."

"What kind of name's that?"

"What, Mooks?"

"Yeah."

"Short for Melvin Orville Oswald Kaster. But no one calls him by those names."

"Mooks." He nodded like it made sense, then glanced back up at the bird. "My pa says they should be our national bird. Says they the best jazz musicians anywhere."

"You think so?"

He hiked one shoulder to his ear like I'd seen him do in school when answering a question. "I don't much care, but you're right about the berries. Tomorrow I'll pick from the bottom of the bush. They're sweeter down there."

"I got a question for you."

"What's that?"

"On the first day of school, how'd you know Miss Hopewell wouldn't do nothin about the Chubbs?"

"Just knew. You'll know things like that, too, when you're almost eight."

Our friendship happened in an instant and felt as comfortable as an old pair of sneakers with no need to match. Even so, I slowed when we got close to school, thinking the Chubbs might spot us. But then I remembered my daddy got forty-seven stitches across the back of his shoulder so Samson and I could be friends. I mustered up the courage to run and catch up, to walk beside him.

Turned out the Chubbs never spent more than a week's worth of time at school each year.

*

As usual, Uncle Mooks was on the porch when I got home, constructing one of his wind spinners. He used tin snips to cut his own unique design into empty Falstaff cans, and then he stretched them into spirals.

He called his empty beer cans dead soldiers, and kept them in a steel drum in the corner, beside his couch.

He fastened his wind spinners to coat hanger wire and attached them to the limbs of the cypress trees throughout our property where they twirled whenever they caught a breeze.

I plopped myself in the swing. "Uncle Mooks, it seems most all the kids in my classroom can read the clock on the wall, but I'm havin trouble."

"Can't learn nothin more important."

"I figure since you're an expert on time, you should teach me."

I never knew Uncle Mooks before he suffered his head wound, but there was no doubt he still knew things from back then, like how to recognize the calls of the first purple martins to arrive in spring. He showed me how the birds fashioned their nests and laid one pure white egg each sunrise for five days. He showed me how to scoop up the spiders and mosquito hawks and carry them outside before Mama got to them with a fly swatter. And even though he never went fishing himself, he knew where to dig for the best worms.

We played stare-down, no blinking, no flinching. The trick was, don't look at your opponent's eyes. Focus on the eyebrows. He taught me that a stare-down is part of the basic training of life and not to rush it because time's either for you or against. He'd say, "Time makes the decision, not you."

He patted the cushion next to him. "We can start right now." Uncle Mooks took his watch from his pocket and flipped the face cover open. "When you learn to tell time, you'll come to know how special it is." He rubbed his leathered fingers over the crystal.

"Now put your hand over your heart."

"Why's that?"

"Go ahead. Feel it?"

"Yes I do, but what's this got to do with learnin to tell time?"

"Each beat's a tick of time." He put the watch in my hand. "Look here, Jason Lee, there's hands and numbers. The hands move clockwise, just like life."

I focused all my concentration on the watch.

"This here, the number on top's the most important of all. It's the twelve. It means noon and midnight."

"Midnight's the time the train goes to Georgia."

"I reckon."

I leaned against his arm and breathed in the smell of beer on his shirt, ready to master the mysteries of time and all its wisdom.

3

1978

By my tenth birthday, our cypress trees were chock full of Uncle Mooks' wind spinners. The older ones had ceased to move and took on the look of rusted leaves hanging loose. Mama felt he'd constructed enough of them and put her foot down, insisting he find a different pastime.

He switched to whittling pine scraps into monkeys no bigger than salt shakers. Monkeys with their hands over their eyes, or ears, or mouths. After sanding them he carved his mark on the bottom, then placed them on the porch ledge, facing out.

Things at school had gotten better, too. Acceptance was slow to come, but over the four years I'd been there, most of the kids had grown tired of bullying Samson and me for being friends. Except the Chubb boys.

One afternoon they caught up to us by the pond near Wilders Grove Road. Mama allowed me to fish there with Samson so long as his older brother went with us. She knew Noah and believed I'd be safe in his care.

We came across a discarded bottle opener along the way and stopped to scar the bark of a cypress with our carvings. We set our poles against the tree while taking turns with the opener. Noah had about finished his when the distinct rattle of bike chains worked its way up the path.

Looking like a pack of ferrets on bicycles, Culver, Eugene, and their pint-sized brother Lil' Floyd pedaled toward us. They stopped in the road about twenty feet away and straddled their bikes.

Dried mud streaked both Eugene's and Culver's faces. One of them, I'm pretty sure it was Culver, looked at me, spite in his eyes. "Here niggalova, niggalova, niggalova," he sang out, like he was calling for a pet.

"Ain't that timely," Eugene said. "We don't got to wait for nightfall to catch us some coons and skin 'em. There's two right in front of us."

Lil' Floyd, no more than seven, yelled with full force. "Three of 'em."

"No, Lil' Floyd," Eugene said, the dutiful older brother imparting his wisdom. "That there's two coons with a sack-a-dung between 'em."

"No need for name callin." Noah squeezed his hand around the churchkey. "We'll be movin on."

The Chubb boys laughed. Eugene said, "You ain't goin nowhere."

"We ain't lookin for no trouble," Noah said.

"Trouble? How 'bout I whoop your ass?" Culver dropped his bike.

Noah snatched his fishing pole from against the tree and clutched it like it'd turned into a spear. "You two stay put, you hear me?" Samson and I nodded.

He took three steps toward the Chubbs, with the church key in one hand and his fishing spear in the other.

Culver walked three steps toward Noah. He spit in the dirt and brought his fists up to his face like a boxer. Eugene and Lil' Floyd dropped their bikes, too, and went over to flank their brother.

Samson and I looked at each other. My mind went numb with fear and sweat collected in my armpits. By the time I got my wits back I realized I'd grabbed my pole and clutched it like a baseball bat, up to my shoulder in position to take a swing.

Samson whispered, "Come on, he needs us." We took a half-dozen slow, cautious steps toward Noah. The three of us, standing under a tree holding bamboo fishing poles, faced the three Chubbs on the side of the road, their bare fists raised in position for hand-to-hand combat. The strength of the hatred in their faces pierced me. I could hardly breathe.

Culver hocked up a loogie and spit it at Noah, but missed. Noah lunged forward and poked him in the chest with his pole.

Culver gripped the end. "You're dead, nigga."

Noah tossed the opener to Samson, wrapped both hands around the fishing pole and yanked it back, like when snagging a big one. The hook burrowed into Culver's palm. His eyes widened. He looked at his hand. "You mother fuckin piece of shit."

Eugene and Lil' Floyd both went for the pole and the three of them pulled on it until it flew from Noah's grip. The Chubbs began to fight each other for it until Culver hollered, "Let go. It's mine." The hook was still clamped deep in his palm, blood dripping.

Lil' Floyd backed off, looked around, and locked his eyes on me. I yelled—not words but more like a war cry. With a strength I'd never known before I charged with my pole still cocked to take a swing, and whacked him in the side. The pole bounced back with a tremor. Lil' Floyd wailed like a baby, a sound I wanted more of. I gave him another, harder smack in the ribs. He screamed louder.

Before I could take my next swing, Eugene knocked the pole out of my hand and got hold of the front of my shirt. I pushed him, but he fastened one of his legs around me. We fell in a heap, him all skin and bones, on top of me. He sat on my chest and squeezed his knees against my ribs. He grabbed a fistful of my hair with one hand and thumped my head on the dirt. His other hand hovered above my face in a bony ball, and then he slammed it into the side of my cheek. The pain exploded.

I wriggled to break free but his knees pressed harder. The expression on Eugene Chubb's face was filled with mud-streaked satisfaction. He pulled his fist back again, but the deafening squawks from a flock of angry crows stopped him cold. What seemed like a cloud of black angels swooped in and circled the tree we were under—their nesting tree. One bird dive-bombed the back of Eugene's head and plucked out a clump of hair. His expression changed from satisfaction to panic, and he jumped off me, slapping at his head like it'd caught fire. He wailed, same as Lil' Floyd had done earlier. I didn't realize it at first, but the fear on Eugene Chubb's face was proof positive he was scared stiff of those birds.

A second, bigger flock swooped in to form a jagged shadow that darkened the ground around us. I crouched, hands over head, heart racing, while the birds cawed and screeched and dove at us—protesting the intrusion on their homestead.

Culver must have forgotten the hook was still dug into to his palm because he dropped Noah's pole and all three Chubbs scrambled toward their bikes with their eyes to the sky like they were witnessing the end of the world.

"That's mine, you chicken-shit." Noah ran forward to rescue his pole and swung it over his head, forcing the hook to break free from Culver's hand, along with a chunk of flesh.

Culver cussed his lungs out as the Chubbs rode off, bikes cranking faster than before. Noah, Samson, and I ran to the road to watch.

"You scared a birds?" Samson yelled at them.

"Hush up," Noah said. "Just hush up." He picked the flesh off the hook and slowly reeled in the tangled line before heading toward the fishing pond.

"I ain't afraid of no Chubb," Samson said.

Noah stopped walking and turned around. "First of all, I said hush up. And second thing, you make damn sure you give thanks to every black crow you see from this day on."

4

I thought about crows a lot after that. I thought about Samson and Noah, too, and how I was proud to be their friend, and at times even wished they were my brothers. I thought about the hollow spot in my heart that needed to be filled with more than the boundaries of our thirteen acres and Uncle Mooks' fixation with time ticking too fast or too slow, for you or against. And I wished for more than our weekly Saturday drives in Mama's Buick Skylark into Hadlee to deliver eggs to Hershey's market.

Since Uncle Mooks never left our property, it was just Mama and me who went to town. The drive was so familiar I knew exactly where to spot the jackrabbits darting through the chickweed and which fields to search for deer grazing.

When we passed the Hadlee town plaque next to Boden's Tack Shop I'd recite the words by heart. *Hadlee, founded in 1802, when Josiah Hadlee migrated from Louisiana to set up his sugar plantation.*

The story was, Hadlee had been rebuilt four times because of God's hand or Mother Nature's foul mood. The most notable time was the twister that stormed through and next to flattened everything in 1939. Our house and most every other building standing, dated back to then.

Our first stop was always the Grinnin' Catfish Cafe. Three long windows stretched across the front, facing County Road 38, and three more overlooked the parking lot. Like most of the buildings in town, the cafe was built of wood, but its distinct orange color set it apart.

The largest catfish ever caught in all of Mississippi dangled from ceiling hooks behind the lunch counter. It faced the front door, and its beady eyes studied the comings and goings of the place. Its mouth hung half open, with whiskers that reached out a foot on either side.

On each table were orange placemats cut in the shape of the ugly beast, with all its record-breaking statistics listed across the belly: Blue Catfish (Ictaburus Furcatus). Length from lower jaw to tail: 58 inches. Girth at widest point: 44 inches. Weight: 119 pounds. Nickname: Felix.

Mama's friend, Miss Therese, waited tables at the cafe. They'd been friends all my life. She originally hailed from a town called Blue Mountain, up in Tippah County, but moved to Hadlee for a "no-good son-of-a-bitch man who drank himself to death." - her words, not mine. That was about the same time my daddy died. Being the two youngest widows in town sealed their friendship.

When finished visiting with Miss Therese, we'd drive toward Main Street, past the old, dilapidated Hadlee Mill. A faded Coca-Cola logo stretched across the one remaining brick wall, so faint it seemed more like a thought than an advertisement.

During one of our trips to town I started singing "California, Here I Come" for no particular reason except it was on my mind. We'd been studying the miners of 1849 and how they'd left everything behind to head west and follow their dreams of California gold. We were rounding the curve by the town water tower when Mama said, "Learn to be grateful for your roots, Jason Lee. California's a long way off. Won't do you no good to wish for more." The name Hadlee came to view, painted on the side of the tower's rusted tank panels high above the wooden framework.

"I was just singin, Mama."

"I know, but don't get any big ideas of leavin. Your daddy used to talk about leavin all the time. A garden is only as good as you make it. If you want more, nurture it with a shovel of manure and hard work."

"What do you mean?"

"Think of Hadlee as your garden."

She wasn't making much sense, so I stayed quiet and kept on daydreaming about how brave the miners were to leave everything behind and take a chance on the unknown. After awhile I worked up the nerve to ask, again, a question she'd never answered.

"Remember a long time ago, the first time I asked you about the man named Peek, and you told me we'd talk about it when I got older?"

"No, I don't believe I remember that."

"You said that very same thing the next time I

asked."

"Did I?"

"Yes. And then the next time, too. Why don't you tell me about him now?"

"Peek?" She shook her head like she couldn't make out what I'd asked.

"Peek," I said forceful. "Drives a green truck. Gets Uncle Mooks upset every time he goes past."

"Today's so fine I don't want to talk about Grover Peek." Mama kept her eyes focused on the road.

"I figure I'm old enough now."

"See those dogwoods shimmerin in the wind? Dogwoods remind me of happiness."

"What happened between him and Uncle Mooks? Did somethin happen?"

"Jason Lee, stop pesterin."

"I ain't pesterin, just want to know."

"Grover Peek's a man to stay away from."

"Why?"

"He's the devil's seed," she said. "A monster that people put up with because of his position in the Klan, and I'd be grateful if we didn't have to talk about the likes of him again."

It was the strongest talk she'd ever used with me and I knew to go no further.

*

Our weekly trips stopped being about selling eggs the day the big brown envelope arrived.

"Look here," Mama yelled, standing next to the mailbox at the the end of the drive. "Look here." She waved the envelope above her head and began to run toward the house. I leaped off the porch and ran to meet her. "What is it, what?"

"Our future. Our independence." She kissed my cheek. "Jason Lee, I'm ninety-nine percent sure I passed my correspondence courses. Look at me, I'm shakin.'" Her eyes filled with tears.

"What is it?"

"I'll bet my bottom dollar it's a diploma. Look here, the return address's from the Allied School of Legal Transcription."

"That's good, right, Mama?"

"Better than good, Jason Lee. It's everything." She tugged at the flap, tore the envelope open, and held up a sheet of paper with a gold border and fancy writing. I couldn't fully grasp what had happened. Even so, I felt infected with her happiness. I'd never given much thought to the way she stayed up reading until all hours of the night. Only then did I realize she'd been studying.

After the dinner dishes were cleaned and put away, Mama asked Uncle Mooks and me to join her outside. She slipped her arms through our elbows and marched us out to the old milk house.

Before she opened the door she looked at Uncle Mooks. "Mr. Kaster," she said. Then she smiled at me. "And Mr. Rainey. May you two be the first to lay eyes on my new office."

The milk house had been vacant for years. It served as a shelter for rodents and old farm tools, but when she opened the door and ushered us inside you could have knocked me over with a pinky finger. She'd painted the walls a pale yellow, the color of butter, and covered the windows with green lace curtains. On the far side of the room were two rockers with spindles across the backs.

"Never saw those before," I said.

"I brought 'em down from the attic. They're my folks' porch chairs." She looked at Uncle Mooks. "Remember these? I figured enough time's passed, so I put them back to use."

He walked over and sat in one.

"Remember?" she said. "That one's Daddy's."

He nodded while stroking the chair's arms, as if trying to feel a memory. He closed his eyes and leaned his head back. I knew his simple touch on that simple chair meant more to him than Mama's diploma.

"Come over here, Jason Lee." Mama led the way to the desk she'd put together from an old door stretched across two low file cabinets. The plate of chocolate chip cookies and pitcher of Kool-Aid on the desk caught my eye, but Mama pointed to a frame on the wall above it.

"Look, son, my diploma. Come on over here, Mooks." He didn't move. Sometimes he could suck the good mood out of a room, even though he didn't mean to. "Mooks, come celebrate with us." Her voice sounded hopeful, but he didn't budge from the chair, just stroked the wood.

She poured the punch and raised her glass toward the frame. "Now that it's official, I pronounce this old milk house to be the new headquarters of the Rainey Transcribing Company of Hadlee, Mississippi."

From that day on, after dropping off the eggs at Hershey's Market, we drove to the Diversity Coalition of Legal Assistance League to exchange Mama's finished transcripts for the next week's assignments. The jobs were small at first, but she didn't mind.

"I think I'll take 'em an Amalgamation cake," she said one day. "A little employment insurance. Somethin to sweeten 'em up. It can't hurt."

"Funny name for a cake. What's it mean?"

"Amalgamation means combinin things that don't usually go together, for the better."

So began her Friday evening ritual of baking two cakes. The first thing she did was remove the handed-down recipe card from its place in her mother's cookbook and set it on the counter. She had no need to read it but kept it there anyway.

The wall phone hung to the right of our long, shallow sink. She secured the receiver under her chin and cradled the yellow mixing bowl in her arm while talking with her friend, Miss Therese. She creamed the butter and sugar as they discussed the week's gossip, never letting the phone slip from her ear while mixing the plump batter. I came to realize their conversations were as important to the outcome of the cakes as any of the other ingredients.

When they were done talking and the cakes were safe in the oven, she mopped the linoleum floor that dipped toward the back door and curled at the edges.

Before long the house filled with the sweet aroma that came to put its mark on Friday nights. After she spread the meringue on top, she'd decide which cake to take to the coalition. Uncle Mooks and I ate on the other one all week.

5

1981

The thing that set our family apart from the others around Hadlee was we didn't belong to a church. I'd never set foot inside one in all my thirteen years.

Mama'd have nothing to do with them. It wasn't only church. She refused to be a part of any organized gatherings or community groups or even the quilting bee. Private as she was, she felt it more important for me, her, and Uncle Mooks to stay to ourselves than to fall prey to the scrutiny of others. Dropping by the Grinnin' Catfish on Saturdays was her exception, and I'd grown to look forward to our trips into town.

Hadlee carried the chatter and bustle of people with things to do and say, and our time there gave me a weekly dose of freedom. One morning we walked into the Grinnin' Catfish to find the place booming with commotion, and the pitch of the conversations higher than usual. Mama and I sat at a table along the windows facing the parking lot, where we could keep an eye on the car and its precious cargo of Amalgamation cake and transcripts.

Miss Therese set two cups in front of us. "Coffee's

hot." She filled mine halfway to leave room for my mounds of sugar.

"What's goin on?" Mama asked.

"Haven't you seen the newspaper?"

"Not yet. Just got here."

"Big news. This place's been buzzin like a hornet's nest all mornin." Miss Therese took the *Clarion-Ledger* from one of the empty tables and slapped it down on ours. Across the top of the front page, in gigantic letters, the headline read, "DARWIN WINS, CREATIONISM IS NOT SCIENCE."

Mama smiled. "Well I'll be damned."

Miss Therese pulled a chair from an empty table over to ours and sat down. She perched her glasses on top of her rust-colored updo.

"A judge in Little Rock, Overton's his name, ruled against teachin creation in the schools." She pressed her finger on the article, "According to this, he said it's constitutionally improper."

"Hot damn," Mama said and popped her fist on the table.

"What's that mean?" I said, not following why the news put her in such high spirits.

"Means Judge Overton. . .uh. . .what's his first name?"

"William," Miss Therese said.

"Means Judge William Overton's a smart man."

I still didn't get it.

"You might want to lower your voice," Miss Therese whispered.

Mama didn't. "What he's sayin is they can't teach the church's mumbo jumbo in the classroom, Jason Lee."

"What's mumbo jumbo?" I asked.

She didn't answer. Just clicked her fingernails against the table and looked over at her friend.

Miss Therese said, "You know I go to church most every Sunday."

Mama nodded.

"And so does every other human bein in this place."

Mama kept nodding.

"But I gotta admit this Darwin thing might have some merit, 'cause if you glance up my ex's family tree, all you'll see is orangutan backsides."

I laughed. "That's a good one."

"I thought so," Miss Therese said, and went back to being serious. "But, you bein the exception, Cassie, it's for sure Overton didn't make any friends around here."

"Mumbo jumbo," Mama said again.

"But how can a judge up and overturn a decision after—what?" Miss Therese pulled her glasses down to her nose and looked at the paper. "Twenty years?"

"Come on," Mama said. "Judges wear black robes over their clothes so folks can't see the payoff money bulgin from their pockets."

"What's come over you?" Miss Therese laughed. "You usually hold your tongue—not like me."

I took a sip of coffee and looked out the window to check on the car. The warm brew slid down my throat.

"I got *some* opinions," Mama said.

Miss Therese brought her elbows onto the table and crossed her arms. "Yeah, but you usually keep 'em to yourself."

"I know. But lately I've been feelin like a pressure cooker with a stuck lid workin its way loose. It ain't healthy, and I'm gonna stop bitin my tongue. At least I'm gonna try."

A man yelled out loud enough so everyone in the place could hear him, "You see this garbage?" He held the newspaper above his head. "This ain't right!"

Miss Therese leaned in and lowered her voice. "That group's a pack a trouble makers." Her head bobbed in the direction of the loud one. "They come in close to twenty minutes ago. From Alabama. Headed down to Natchez. They hadn't seen the news until they got here, and now all three of 'em are mad as hell 'bout Overton's decision." She made pretend quote marks with her fingers. "Because it ain't the Christian way."

Mama laughed.

"By the time I got back to 'em with their food, they'd decided to scrap their plans in Natchez and head for Little Rock to hogtie the judge and string him up, not to mention strike a match to the courthouse."

One of the men tapped the side of his coffee cup with a teaspoon, to let the world know he wanted service. "Excuse me." Miss Therese stood up and tucked the order pad in her apron pocket. "Gotta go shut that one up. Time for refills."

"Okay Mama, answer me this," I said, watching Miss Therese leave.

"Shoot."

"With so many churches around here and everyone belongin to one or another, how can they all be so bad?"

Mama checked her watch, took a dollar from her wallet, and set it on the table. She hiked her purse strap on her shoulder. "Time we get goin, son."

On the way out she stopped in front of the men from Alabama, set her jaw and scowled. Something I'd never seen her do before. It set my nerves on edge.

"Hey, Mama, don't you think it's time we get goin? I need to meet Samson."

She didn't move.

The man who had held the newspaper up aimed a smile at her and said, "You want somethin, ma'am?"

"Come on, Mama, let's go." I tugged on her sleeve.

She shook her head and frowned. "You're right, Jason Lee. Besides, it's startin to smell in here." She turned and headed toward the door.

The three men burst into a fit of laughter. One of them yelled, "Hey, Mama, come on back and I'll give you somethin that smells real good. Tastes good too." He made a sucking, kissing noise. "Somethin for you to smile about, Mama."

She'd always made a practice of paying no heed to the likes of those men, so I was at a loss to understand why those three got to her. It felt like I should do something. Stand up for her—something. But, of course, I didn't.

"What's goin on?" I asked in the car. "Why'd you

stop at their table?"

"Beats me." She blew a puff of air out of her mouth. "I'm sorry I did that. It was stupid. I coulda put us in harm's way. I've been on edge lately and somethin just came over me."

"Is it 'cause they said it ain't Christian?"

"That's not it."

"And how come you don't like Christians, anyway?"

"I just don't like bein told how to think or how to live my life by a bunch a hypocrites."

"Hyp-a-what's?"

"People who talk one way and act another. Like those men in there." She put the key in the ignition. "If you live your life right, you don't need no church."

"Okay, don't get mad, but I got another question."

"I won't get mad."

"Why do they call it The Good Book?"

Mama shook her head and laughed. "Beats me."

I sat back and thought about someday sneaking off to a church to sit through a sermon and see what it was all about. I figured it had to be good.

*

We parked nose to the curb in front of Koman's bakery. Gracing the front window were Styrofoam reproductions of Mrs. Koman's white frosted cakes in the shape of trumpet swans. Six years worth of Dunlap County Fair blue ribbons for the specialty cake category hung from their necks.

Mama headed to the Diversity Coalition, and I took

off for Pinks Five and Dime to meet Samson, like I did most every Saturday. Pinks had the distinction of being the only two-story building in town with an escalator, and it had a lunch counter in the back that charged twice the prices of the Grinnin' Catfish.

Three vending machines hugged the store's front wall: an old Pepsi machine with a pull handle, a Tom's toasted peanut machine, and one shaped like an old fashioned gas pump with jawbreakers in the glass top. Mama knew she could always find me either at Pinks or at Wally's hardware store.

Samson walked up to me wearing his big quarter-moon grin. His last growing spurt had added a foot to his height. His flat nose had widened and blended into the smoothness of his skin. His long arms hung loose like they were attached with rubber bands.

"Hey, Jason Lee."

"Hey, yourself. You got slugs?"

One of Samson's uncles fashioned electrical boxes out of scrap metal. On occasion he bestowed the round punch-outs on Samson and his brothers. They were close to the size of a quarter—close enough to fit into the Pepsi machine.

"Three, but before we use 'em, I got somethin to show you. Best we do it in private."

I looked around. "Private? Why?"

"I came across somethin slick as grease. Somethin even better than these here slugs."

"What?"

"Gonna show you but don't want no one else to see.

I figure the corner phone booth'll be private enough."

We were halfway to the booth when Samson slowed down. "See there? Grover Peek's comin this way."

"Where?"

"Straight ahead."

A scrawny man in a grimy Peterbilt cap shuffled in our direction. Grey stubble covered his bony chin. He was no taller than a boy. I couldn't believe it was the same man Mama called the devil's seed.

"That old man? *That's* Grover Peek?"

"Uh-huh," he said, walking ahead of me.

"What you doin?"

"Gonna stare him down."

"You crazy?"

The old man's eyes locked on him. When they passed, Peek lunged and shoved his shoulder into Samson, forcing him off the curb. Samson's foot slipped in the muddy gutter and he landed on one knee.

"Learn your place, boy," the old man growled.

An ear-splitting whistle came from the shoe repair shop across the street. Sure as stink follows garbage, it was one of the Chubb twins cheering for Grover Peek.

The burn of shame filled my chest. Since the beginning of our friendship, I'd held on to the idea that my daddy looked over Samson and me from above. *Please don't be watching now.*

I offered my hand.

"I don't need no help." Samson shook his head and scraped the soles of his green shoes against the curb. "I can take care of myself."

Someday, I said to myself, watching that poisonous insect of an old man inch his way down the sidewalk. My shame deepened.

"Dickhole," Samson said, brushing at the dirt on his pant leg. "Caught me by surprise."

"Thought he'd be big."

"He ain't big. Just mean."

"Big like Frankenstein," I said.

"Nope. Just mean. Makes Frankenstein look nice. Forget about the dickhole. Let's get to the phone booth. It's more important."

We stepped inside and closed the door, sealing in the humid southern heat.

"Smells worse than cabbage farts in here," I said.

"Quit whinin." Samson took the receiver off its cradle and gave it to me. "Pretend you're makin a call."

He grabbed the phone book hanging from the sturdy chain attached to the small metal shelf, ripped off its front cover, and dropped the book back down to dangle.

"What's goin on?" I said.

"Hush up and watch."

He set the cover on the shelf and pulled a jackknife from his pocket. "Check the street. See if anyone's lookin this way."

I pressed my back against the windowed door and looked down the street past the town clock. "All clear. And it's 10:45."

He held up a shiny quarter between his forefinger

and thumb and flashed an excited grin. "We're gonna make more of these. Watch this." He positioned the quarter in the middle of the cover page and worked the knife blade around it. The result, a perfect cutout circle.

"Now, watch this." He pulled a wad of aluminum foil from his other pocket, tore a piece off, worked it around the cutout, then rubbed it with the side of his knife. Before long it took on the likeness of a real coin.

"Simple as syrup," he said and set it on the shelf.

"Looks real good. Can you make one for me?"

"Course I can. I can make a hundred, that's the point. And now, so can you." He made two more and handed one to me. "Just need to start collectin foil scraps outa your ma's kitchen."

I couldn't stop smiling.

Samson put the supplies back in his pockets. "Let's put 'em to the test."

"Pinks?"

"Course."

We left the booth and made our way back to the five-and-dime, pumped with anticipation.

"Phone quarters, that's what we'll call 'em," Samson said. All three of the Johnson boys had a need to name most everything. "Get it?"

"I get it."

"The phone booth and all?"

"I said I get it."

Not a soul was near the vending machines when we got back to Pinks.

"Try one of your uncle's slugs first," I said. "If the

phone money jams the machine, we'll have at least one drink."

The Pepsi bottle rattled through the machine and rolled into the holding bin.

"Maybe one more slug," I said. "It's a sure thing."

"Chicken."

Before I could respond he took a foil quarter from his pocket and slipped it into the coin slot. It went in smooth, but when he pulled on the lever nothing budged.

"Pull harder," I whispered.

"You pull it. Maybe you got the magic touch."

"Me?"

I gave it a try, and with the help of a grunt the bottle shot down to the opening.

"Soda jackpot," Samson said and grabbed it.

My mind spun with the notion we could manufacture our own money.

"There you are." Mama's voice shattered the moment.

We both stood at attention.

"What're you two doin?" she asked.

"Nothin," I said.

"Nothin?"

"Just buyin a soda." I pointed to the bottle in Samson's hand.

She glanced at his muddy shoes.

"Don't let me find out differently. You goin to Wally's after this?"

"Uh-huh."

"Do me a favor 'cause I won't have time. We need light bulbs. Hundred watts. Two'll do. I gotta get back to the Coalition." She handed me a dollar and went for the door.

"That was close," Samson said, undaunted. "Go ahead, try yours."

"You crazy? What if she comes back?"

"Buck, buck, chicken cluck." He flapped his elbows. "I dare you, double-dare you."

"That's not fair."

"Double, double dare you with a cherry on top."

"Okay, but I'll get you back. Keep an eye out for her."

I stepped in front of the peanut machine and put the phone quarter in the coin slot.

"Hurry up."

"Don't rush me."

I wrapped my hand around the knob and pulled. A hand-sized bag of goobers spun down the metal coil and landed in the tray.

We shook the peanuts into our bottles and watched the foam rise, then we clanked them together in a toast of triumph. The only thing better than the taste of Pepsi and peanuts is the taste of *free* Pepsi and peanuts.

We'd outsmarted the powers of the vending world on our own, and we no longer needed to depend on Samson's uncle.

Three flat-pitched beeps from Noah's truck sounded out front of Pinks.

Samson tossed the last phone quarter to me. "Try

this one at Wally's place."

"I don't know."

He tucked his hands under his armpits and flapped his elbows. "Buck, buck, chicken cluck." He ran out the door, still flapping.

6

Wallace's Hardware, Teapots, and Tobacco.

"It's a mouthful," Wally would say. "But if it was good enough for my folks, I reckon it's good enough for me. Besides, don't know what I'd change it to."

The first smell to hit your nose when entering the store was the tangy scent of WD-40. He kept a tester on the bench next to the front door for anyone who needed a squirt. No matter what his customer's project, it was his first recommendation.

"Jason Lee Rainey, it looks like you grew another inch this week." It wasn't true but I smiled and nodded just the same. "And you're lookin more like J.L. every day."

I was named after my daddy, but no one ever referred to him as Jason Lee. Wally and he'd been boyhood friends.

"Where's everybody?" I said.

"Gator Face's holdin a meetin about the water tower."

"Who's Gator Face?"

"The mayor."

"What about the tower?"

"Needs paintin. A waste of time if you ask me."

"I like it the way it is." A rusted tower was all I'd

ever known.

"It's likely to fall down before the paint dries."

"It ain't so bad," I said. "Hey, Wally, we need light bulbs."

"You know where to find 'em."

I poked down the middle aisle past the fishing gear and galvanized washtubs and retractable clotheslines. The light bulbs were stocked along the back wall, past the bins of nails and bolts and nuts and washers.

An old grocery scale with a bent needle pointing to half-a-pound, and a stack of small paper bags were next to the bins. A sign above the scale read, "Honor system. Weigh and leave money in the box." The metal box stayed unlocked.

I picked up the lone pack of Sylvania 100 watts on the shelf and headed back past the bulletin board. A big orange note was fastened to the corkboard with a fish hook. *Remington .308 with scope. Good for boar. $75.00.* Another note, handwritten with a blue marker said *FREE, two pair of used boots, size 14.* I looked at my feet, knowing they'd never see the insides of a fourteen.

It was odd seeing Wally behind the counter instead of Darla. She'd taken charge of the hardware portion of the business years before. Since Wallace's Hardware, Teapots, and Tobacco was part store and part meeting place, Wally gravitated to the latter, as the greeter or ambassador of goodwill to anyone who'd rather visit than get anything done. He also patched up differences the regulars might have with Darla.

Miss Therese told me that after Wally's folks passed

on he closed the store for the winter and drove north to Lake Superior to try his hand at salmon fishing. He came back before the season ended with a promise to never leave the South again. To the surprise of everyone around he brought a hard-working new bride with him. Miss Therese said Darla was nicer back then, before her disposition turned dark as night. And prettier, too, with hazel eyes, and hair spun like golden cotton candy.

I set the Sylvania's on the counter. "This is your last box."

"I'll tell Darla."

"Is she at Gator Face's meetin, too?"

"No. She went to give one of our suppliers a piece of her mind. At least it's not me she's after this time."

I reached into my pocket for the dollar and my fingers brushed against the smoothness of my newly minted phone quarter. I glanced at the gumball machine in the corner—*Buck, buck, chicken cluck*—but knew I'd never try one at Wally's place.

I tossed the bill on the counter. "This is for the lights."

"Tell you what." Wally picked up the dollar and took his time scrutinizing it. "The bulbs are on the house if you'd care to wager this here dollar on a game of checkers, man to man."

"Sure."

"Man to man means your mama don't need to know about it."

"I know."

He came out from behind the counter. "It's been a while since we played. Fetch yourself some sunflower seeds."

"Don't mind if I do." I rushed to the oak barrel full of seeds stationed next to the oversized checkerboard. Wally'd painted black and red squares on a slab of plywood and fastened it to two sawhorses. The years had faded the paint on the playing area down to little more than an outline of itself. A five-pound Folgers can packed with a year's worth of bottle caps sat on top of it. Two milking stools were shoved underneath.

We pulled the stools out and sat down. Wally laid the dollar on my side of the board.

"Virgil the Vanquisher." His voice boomed. "Versus Jason Lee the Contender."

Wally's real name was Virgil Ulysses Wallace. His nickname could have been Curly because of his hair or Rusty for the same reason. Mama told me they called him Half-a-Shake Wallace after he lost the last three fingers on his right hand in a mill accident. But he wasn't too partial to that one.

"I call Pepsi," I said and began to pick twelve bottle caps out of the coffee can.

"Grape Nehi for me." Wally took off his glasses and set them down. His round face and frizzled hair reminded me of pictures I'd seen of koala bears.

We arranged our caps to start the game.

"Who goes first?" I said.

"I do." He paused and looked at me. "I swear I can't look at you without thinkin about him." He raised the two fingers on his damaged hand toward the ceiling. "He's up there with God."

"Don't let Mama hear you say that. You know she's not too keen on God."

"That's right." He laughed.

"I can't figure out why, and you know she ain't about to tell me."

Wally slid a bottle cap forward. "After your daddy died she lost trust in most everything. The government, religion, people's good thoughts, but especially religion—why God let it happen and all. She crawled into her own shell and hasn't been quite the same since. You never know, though. One of these days she might come back around."

"I doubt it."

From a previous talk with Wally, I knew that when the fighting in Vietnam turned serious he'd planned to enlist. Around that same time his dad contracted black-lung disease and took to his bed. Then his mom busted up both her legs from a misstep on the store ladder and, sure as bad things come in threes, Wally caught his fingers in the saw.

"Got a two-fingered draft deferment," he said.

Wally's pockets bulged with sunflower seeds. He sucked on them when shooting the breeze with the regulars, spitting the spent shells on the sawdust floor.

Since it wasn't Mama's nature to open up to me, I talked to Wally about my daddy. He filled me with stories. It felt like being served a brew of the very blood that ran through me. They generally turned into history lessons, too. Those stories helped me stand straight and proud. Our time together seemed good for Wally, too, like the memories harkened him back to the best part of his life.

"Did I ever tell you about the time J.L. got thrown in jail, when he and those others tried to finish the march William Moore started?"

"In Selma?"

"No, Selma came later. This one was at the state line."

It'd been years since Mama told me about him going to jail. I'd tucked it away in the *not to be talked about place.* I was surprised that Wally knew about it.

I was old enough to be aware that some of the folks around Hadlee felt my daddy was a disgrace to white people, a no-good son-of-a-bitch, because of the way he rushed to the wrong side of segregation. Others were willing to dismiss his ideas about civil rights, being as he was the only son of Hadlee, Mississippi, since World War II who died fighting for his country. When I was a toddler there had been a short-lived proposal to erect a memorial statue of him next to the Hadlee plaque.

"How many times did he go to jail?"

"Don't know for sure."

"Twice?"

"More than twice."

"So what happened that time? On the Moore march?"

Wally jumped one of my Pepsi caps and threw it back in the can.

"It was plumb loco for a white man to protest against segregation back then. You know that, don't you?"

"Uh-huh."

"There's a fine line between bein brave and bein crazy, and J.L. liked to straddle it."

"Whaddya mean?"

"He was smarter than anyone around these parts even though he didn't think much of proper schoolin, and I'm pretty sure he gave more than one of his teachers an ulcer. Even so, I'd be hard-pressed to remember a time he wasn't carryin a book with him. You probably don't know this, but to this day he's the only person who's read every single book in the Hadlee library."

I shook my head. "Mama don't tell me nothin."

"Anyway, some of his ideas didn't fit. He was like the one piece of a jigsaw puzzle that got tossed in the wrong box. 'I'm itchin to get outa here,' he used to tell me. 'As far as I can go without a passport, maybe California.'"

"Like the miners," I said.

"You know he had plans to get a college degree when he got out of the service, don't you?"

"No."

"Sure he did. A law degree. And he and Cassie planned to leave Hadlee, 'forever or longer,' he'd say."

I stared at the checkerboard with no thoughts of the game. *A lawyer? Leave Hadlee?* Of course, Mama'd never said a word. He'd done so much I didn't know about.

My mind wandered to the idea of going to jail and what it'd feel like to spend time in one.

Wally watched while I thought. He shook his head, then put his glasses back on.

"Anyway, gettin back to Moore."

"Moore?" I'd forgotten what we were talking about.

"William Moore." Wally raised his eyebrows.

"Right."

"Can you imagine? In '63? That crazy bastard intendin to walk from Chattanooga to Jackson to hand a letter to the governor—alone." He laughed. "The goddamned governor of Mississippi—alone. To ask him to accept integration? On top of that—" Wally shook his head. "He was wearin two signboards."

His voice grew louder. "One said, *End Segregation in America*, and the other one said, *Equal Rights for All Men*. Might as well have worn a bull's-eye on his chest. Crazy bastard." Wally stuck more seeds in his mouth. "They murdered him in Alabama, outside Attalla. Two bullets to the head."

"Never learned about that in school." I didn't feel so good about the story.

"Don't suppose."

"But we studied how Governor Wallace blocked the schoolhouse door and wouldn't let the colored kids in."

"Lookin back, it was an upside-down time, Jason Lee. Nineteen sixty-three started with George Wallace vowin 'segregation now, tomorrow and forever in his inaugural, and it ended with President Kennedy gettin himself shot in a state that helped carry him to victory."

Wally jumped another one of my bottle caps and tossed it in the can. "I keep gettin sidetracked. Back to Moore. They found the letter he carried and they printed it in the Clarion." Wally pointed at me. "I'm gonna quote this word-for-word. I haven't forgotten it 'cause I'd never seen anything like it in a Southern paper before. 'The white man cannot be truly free himself until all men have their rights.'"

He leaned in on the checkerboard and jumped another one of my bottle caps.

"Thought this story was gonna be about my daddy," I said, unnerved by what had happened to Moore.

"I'm gettin to that part right now." Wally laughed. "J.L. was sure of himself, and he was cocky, and he liked to shake things up by talkin and, oh boy, could he talk. But that was the first time he acted on his convictions.

"When he heard about the killin, he got so fired up he went to Attalla and joined a handful of others with the same mindset. They're intention was to finish the march to Jackson in Moore's honor. I thought it'd be too dangerous and tried to talk some sense into him. Course I couldn't."

"How 'bout Mama?"

"They hadn't hooked up yet."

"How'd he know those other people were headed there too?"

"Got a call from someone who knew someone. There was a chain of folks—an underground collection of 'em—who kept in touch."

"So, what happened?" I took a handful of seeds from the barrel.

"Turns out the whole bunch of 'em got arrested at the Alabama state line. Never got to march a step. J.L. came back mad as hell. The next day I asked him if he'd learned anything." Wally sucked on his seeds.

"What'd he say?"

"He looked at me, serious as could be, and said, 'We can conquer it—the hate.'" Wally rubbed his head. "J.L. was one of the very few around these parts that understood things needed to change. In another time, in another place, he coulda made a difference."

The feeling came over me again. The one that was certain I'd never measure up.

"What kind of hogwash are you feeding the boy?"

Birdette Foster's voice startled me. I hadn't heard the little bell ring over the front door. I looked up beyond his six-foot-plus, extra long body to the John Deere cap on top of his head.

"Just chewin on Jason Lee's ear about J.L.," Wally said. "Pull up a chair."

"Don't mind if I do. Waitin on the wife. She's at the Busy Bee under one of those dryin helmets. Looks like torture to me."

Bird grabbed a milk stool by the wall and scooted it close to the checkerboard. His spindly legs spread to either side.

"You at the mayor's meetin?" I asked.

"Not me. Can't stand the mullet-head and don't

care what color they choose." He pointed to the checkerboard. "You got a move right there."

"Thanks," I said, embarrassed I'd been staring at it all along.

"So, what kind of lies are you tellin the boy?" Bird said.

"We were talkin about the time J.L. got arrested."

Bird laughed. "Which time?"

"The Moore march."

"Well, well, ain't that a coincidence. Just so happens I was with him the night he got back." He pointed to the board for me to slide another bottle cap forward.

"Where?" I said, then made my move.

"Down at Five Mile. Drinkin." Bird rested his elbows on his knees. "Seems the whole town was there that night. Most had heard about J.L. stormin up to Alabama and gettin thrown in the pokey. Everyone agreed it was a foolish thing he did."

Darla came through the back door carrying a box of plastic flyswatters. "Where's everyone?"

"Mayor's meetin," Wally said.

Her brows pinched. "Forgot. The tower. How much is that gonna cost us?" She headed to the center of the store with the box of swatters.

"Like I was sayin." Bird eyed the direction Darla went. "We were sittin at a table, J.L. and me. He was hell-bent to wash his frustration away with a quart of Jack." Bird looked at me. "Back then there weren't any rules around here about underage drinkin. The owner, Orvis was his name, never gave a squat about liquor laws."

"How old were you?" I asked.

"Bout seventeen, give or take, but that don't matter. Like I was sayin, J.L. chugged from the bottle for the sole purpose of gettin shit-faced. Come around ten o'clock he'd made it. And I wasn't exactly sober."

We all laughed. The three of us men.

"We was passin jokes back and forth when Peek walked into the place," Bird said.

I looked up. "Grover Peek?"

"Only one Peek in these parts. He came in belligerent as a polecat. Back then he was a force to reckon with. Seein him now, it's hard to figure how that shriveled old man used to be so powerful."

The shock of hearing his name brought back all the shame I'd felt earlier on the street with Samson.

Bird continued. "He walked straight to the bar, the whole time staring at J.L. with them hard eyes of his."

"I seen him today," I said, remembering his eyes.

"Peek?" Wally said. "He hasn't been in town for a couple years. Wonder what's the occasion."

"Can't be good." Bird shifted on the stool to get more comfortable and checked his watch. "Like I was sayin, we were drunk as skunks. Soon as Peek bellied up to the bar, J.L. said, 'Figures,' and slammed the bottle on the table. 'Grover Fuckin Peek comes in here tonight of all nights, after the day I had? Just the sight of him makes my skin crawl.' Everyone in the place was on full alert and waitin to see what would come next."

"Was there a fight?" I asked, too eager.

"Not a fist fight."

"Then what?"

"Peek looked in our direction and told Orvis, loud so's everyone in the place could hear, 'Don't waste your good liquor on that nigger lover.'"

I watched Birdette Foster's smile widen.

"Know what your daddy did then?"

I shook my head, forgetting my plan to double jump Wally's two Grape Nehi bottle caps.

"He flashed Peek a shit-howdy smile with damn near all his teeth showin, and in a voice smooth as butter, said, 'You're right. I'm a lover of many things and many people—niggers included.'

"Peek yelled, 'Is that right, you no-good sack a dog crap?" Then he pulls a .32 from his belt and points it straight at J.L.

"Everyone in the place froze. J.L. looked at the gun, then at Peek. 'A faithful lover at that,' he said, cocky as a rooster come Friday mornin. If that wasn't enough, he had the balls to pick up the bottle of Jack and point the neck at Peek, like it could out-shoot the colt."

Birdette Foster took his cap off. "I'll never forget what came next."

"What?"

"J.L. said, 'I'm even a lover of poor, ugly, misguided, hateful hick-bastards like you.' Then he smacked his lips together and blew a kiss in Peek's direction."

"What'd Peek do?" I asked, scared as if my daddy was still alive and about to be shot.

"Everyone in Five Mile laughed their heads off, except Peek, of course."

"What'd he do?"

"He didn't do nothin. Didn't say nothin. Just swigged down his drink and left."

"So, my daddy won," I said.

The bell above the door rattled. Mrs. Foster poked her head in. "You ready to go?"

"Be right there." Birdette got up.

"Not exactly, Jason Lee." His voice went flat. "Five Mile burned down that night. I reckon nobody won. Especially not Orvis."

He looked toward the front door and smiled at his wife. "You clean up good. How 'bout a bite at the Grinnin' Catfish to celebrate your good looks?"

Thinking about what Bird had said, I lost track of the game. Wally captured my last king and raised his arm in victory. "The Vanquisher wins again."

"I'll get you one of these days."

Wally retrieved the dollar.

"Can I talk to you about somethin?"

"You know you can."

"It's about Grover Peek."

Wally's eyes searched my face.

"Like I said, Samson and me passed him on the street. The bastard knocked him off the sidewalk, and I didn't do nothin to stand up for my friend." Wally didn't take his eyes off me. "And that's not all. I didn't stand up for Mama this mornin either."

"Whoa, one thing at a time. Let's concentrate on

Peek. There's nothin you coulda done about him, Jason Lee."

"My daddy woulda done somethin."

"Maybe he woulda, but it's best you keep a level head."

"How come he's like that?"

"What?"

"Hateful."

"He was bred that way," Wally said.

"Shoved him right off the sidewalk," I said. "And I didn't do nothin."

"Stay clear of him."

"Mama says he's the devil's seed."

"That's one way to put it. You ever heard of the White Knights of Mississippi?"

"I think so. They're like the Klan?"

"Yep. There was a time Grover Peek ranked supreme in the White Knights and wielded a great deal of power. People feared him and rightly so. Spite's his middle name. Can't help it."

"Why can't he help it?"

"He was raised that way. Taught to hate anyone different than him, from the time he was in the cradle. Half the South was raised similar. But, on top of that, Peek wasn't treated much better than a dog himself. His hate runs deep as bone.

His folks chained him and beat him. Then they up and disappeared when he wasn't more than your age. They were never seen again. But I suspect they're still on the property. Or under it."

7

Sunday started same as most, with me in the backyard helping Mama tend to her garden and Uncle Mooks on the porch watching for funeral parades.

Mama had planted a row of Queen Anne's lace alongside the old stone wall, not too far from her patch of root vegetables, to attract the black swallowtails when they migrated through Mississippi. The bees liked them, too.

Through the years I'd become proficient with the hose and knew how to position my thumb over the end to create a gentle spray for the dainty white flowers Mama loved so. Then I would move it just a fraction, forcing the water straight and hard to chase away the bees that hovered.

Mama worked further out back, fussing with the golden jubilees and beefsteaks located next to the picket fence. The first thing she did was examine the leaves for hornworms and whiteflies—her mortal enemies.

A breeze caught Uncle Mooks' wind spinners and they twirled in the tree branches. Mama straightened up and stuck her hands in the pockets of her apron. "I'll be a while, Jason Lee," she yelled. "The darn pests are at it again and need a good sprayin."

I wet my bare feet with the hose.

"Okay, Mama. I'll go out front with Uncle Mooks for awhile."

His portable radio squawked from the porch rail, the bottom of the second inning, Atlanta against Los Angeles. Eighty-one was not a good year for baseball. The player's strike carved a two-month chunk out of the season, so it was good to hear the crowd noise again and listen to Skip Caray's play-by-plays. Uncle Mooks concentrated on the calls with a half-carved monkey cradled in his hand and a can of Falstaff between his legs.

He loved baseball. Every now and then his emotions took over when the Braves fell behind, and he'd toss the radio into the yard and swear at it. We'd already gone through three radios that season. The Braves were ahead when I settled on the swing.

"Hey, Uncle Mooks?" He looked at me with a lazy gaze. "See those little chokeberry bushes over there in the field?"

He squinted past the heat of the day. "I see 'em."

"They're new. Where'd they come from?"

"Seeds musta blown in with the winds of time."

"What's the winds of time?"

"Don't remember. Musta known once."

My insides were busting to tell someone about my new secret. Since Uncle Mooks had taught me things over the years, I figured it was my time to finally reciprocate.

"Hey—"

"Hang on. Full count."

I couldn't wait. "I know how to make fake money. Want me to show you?"

He stood up like a shot. The beer can hit the floor. "Show me," he yelled out, as a foamy stream of Falstaff moved toward the back wall.

"Shhh. Don't let Mama hear."

He picked up the can and set it, and the little monkey, on the porch rail. "Show me."

"First thing we need's a magazine or something with a hard cover like that, but I don't dare us any of Mama's."

"Okay, I know," he said and shuffled into the house without another word. He was gone a full half-inning.

"I got it," he said, slapping two magazines on my lap.

An issue of *Popular Science* from August 1964 was on top, with a picture of a small submarine on the cover. The headline—*A Jeep in the Deep: Tiny New Subs*. The other magazine, called *Guns,* had bright green lettering across the bottom of the cover. *Big Boar Competition, pg. 48*. The words were circled in pen, with an asterisk next to them.

"Where'd you get these?"

"They're mine."

A coincidence is a funny thing—*Remington .308 with scope. Good for boar. $75.00.*

"Did you hunt boar?"

"Pigs," he said matter of fact.

"Pigs is boar, right?"

"Right."

"Did you use a Remington?"

"What?"

"What kind of gun did you use?"

He looked over at me. "Gun? M16. Standard issue." My heart skipped.

"A gook getter," he said louder.

The surprise twist in conversation caused my voice to wobble. "That's not what I'm talking about." Quick as I could I said, "You want me to show you how to make that money?"

He poked his bottom lip out. "Show me."

I nodded, relieved, and looked at the magazines in my lap. The notion of him once reading them, or reading anything, had never crossed my mind. My head spun with the idea there'd been a time when he hunted boar and he even liked science.

"Along with the magazine, you need one of these." I pulled a real quarter from my pocket. "And some foil."

I handed him the magazines and the quarter, and left.

"Where you goin?"

"I'll be right back."

I looked out the kitchen window to make sure Mama was still in her garden, then opened the top drawer where she kept the box of Reynolds Wrap. My head buzzed with new thoughts, like the idea of Uncle Mooks actually having a past life.

And I couldn't help but wonder what it'd be like to own a rifle of my own. To go hunting. Or how long it'd take to save up seventy-five dollars.

The Braves were still ahead when I got back to the porch.

I sat on the floorboards, cross-legged. "Just so you know, these coins work good as real quarters. Yesterday me and Samson took 'em for a test drive at Pinks. One in the Pepsi machine, and one in the peanut machine."

Uncle Mooks rubbed his hands together.

"Come on down here next to me," I said. "We're ready to start."

He didn't say a word, just watched me cut, wrap, and smooth. In no time I'd finished off two beauties.

He smiled his approval. "Damn, Jason Lee."

"Told you."

"Damn," he said again and snorted his big donkey laugh.

"You know it ain't real money, don't you?"

"Margarine ain't real butter neither, but folks use it just the same." He held his palm out. "Give me a try."

I slid everything over in front of him. His big hands worked steady. In no time he'd made ten coins and slipped them in the bib pocket of his overalls. I was feeling good about us working together on the coins and about my new knowledge of him and his past, and those feeling got the best of me.

Because I longed for help figuring out why I hadn't stood up for Samson or Mama, I said, "I saw Grover Peek in town yesterday."

Uncle Mooks' eyes turned to slivers.

With all my might I tried to will those words back.

He pointed at me. "I seen him do it." With a grunt he worked himself up off the floor, grabbed the half-carved monkey from the couch, and hurled it into the middle of the front yard. It tumbled head-over-feet and landed next to a clump of dandelions, face-skyward to the sun, hands over its eyes.

Uncle Mooks jumped the porch stairs and ran to it.

"Wait." I took off after him, wanting to crawl inside myself and escape the mess I'd triggered.

He dropped to his knees, picked up the monkey and stroked the carved-out hands. "See no evil," he said and rocked. "See no evil."

"He's okay. Everythin's okay, Uncle Mooks."

The muscles in his jaw tightened. He looked at me. His eyes grew mean, and he said, "Get down. It ain't safe."

He flopped on his belly and crawled like G.I. Joe, his elbows pulling, his knees and feet pushing like frog legs. "Get down," he yelled. "Right now or they'll kill you. GET DOWN." He held the monkey solid in his fist.

The thick air closed in around me. Scared out of my wits, I dropped flat to the ground.

It wasn't long before he stopped crawling and popped his head up. He got himself up on his elbows and looked around. His breath grew faster. "Did you see 'em?"

I stayed as still as I could. "What's goin on?"

"All butchered-up? In the school? Did you see?"

"No, I didn't see nothin."

He scanned our property. "Little kids, dead. All piled on each other?" He sat up, blinked some, and looked at the little monkey in his hand. He confided in it like they were the only two around.

"But it's okay now, little one. I got 'em."

My mind went fuzzy. "Got who?"

He was still talking to the monkey like it had asked the question. "Them who killed 'em."

He looked up and smiled at me, a real crazy smile. His cheeks reddened. I opened my mouth but didn't know what to say. Uncle Mooks wagged the monkey in the air. "Got two of 'em, anyway." Then he dropped it on the grass and plucked out a dandelion puff next to his leg. He blew the fuzz off. "Forty rounds in that bomb crater full a water. They was takin a bath."

"You shot 'em?"

"Platoon brothers, my ass." He laughed. "They won't hurt no more kids."

I felt just as confused as my uncle, and wasn't sure how he got from Grover Peek to platoon brothers.

"Uncle Mooks?" I whispered. "It's me, Jason Lee."

"I know."

I inched over on my hands and knees and sat next to him. "We're gonna be fine."

He nodded.

I began to sing, the way Mama did to calm him. By the time I got to, *With curly eyes and laughing hair,* he began to sing with me. *Singin Polly-Wolly-Doodle all the day.*

My heartbeat settled. "Come on, Uncle Mooks, let's

go back to the porch. We should clean up our mess."

"What mess?"

"Don't want Mama to find out we been makin money."

"Some folks say time is money," he said.

"I know, Uncle Mooks."

"You think that's right? Time is money?"

"Yes, I do." I offered my hand. "I'll help you up. Sounds like the game's still on. Let's get back to the porch and check on the score."

"Okay."

He walked with me.

"One more thing," I said, not wanting Mama to find out any trace of what we'd done. "Can I see them coins you made?"

"Nope. They're mine." He touched his bib pocket.

When I finished cleaning up the porch I watched Uncle Mooks work. His hands moved gently across the wood of the little monkey. His face looked peaceful. The things he'd said out in the yard couldn't be right. My Uncle Mooks would never kill anyone.

The Braves won, six to four, and no funeral parade went by that afternoon.

*

After Mama and Uncle Mooks went to bed that night I snuck into his room and emptied his bib pocket.

In my dreams, Uncle Mooks and I were squashed next to each other on a bench in a small submarine, with our feet against a steel bar under the cockpit. The bar suddenly morphed into foot pedals. We pushed on them and propelled the sub through a school of fish. I tried to talk, but empty bubbles came out of my mouth instead of words. When Uncle Mooks talked, his bubbles had words written inside them.

"Rest," the first bubble said. Then more came. "Don't" "Worry" "I" "Know" "How" "To" "Do" "This."

I stopped pedaling. Uncle Mooks kept on. His strong legs got us past the fish and up to the surface, where we drifted to a sandy shore next to a tree full of wind spinners lit with twinkling lights. Two rifles were propped against the trunk.

We climbed out and got to land. The door slammed shut with a sucking sound and the sub slipped backwards into the water. Before it fully submerged I saw the name *Jeep in the Deep* etched on the side. While it dropped into the lake, I heard something rustle in the brush and turned to see a wild boar rushing toward us. Uncle Mooks grabbed one of the rifles—the one with the orange tag. "GET DOWN," he yelled.

After he shot the boar, Uncle Mooks used his whittling knife to slit its belly open. Dead children oozed out.

My scream woke me.

8

1983

"I come across a way to draw from my pa's still, a little at a time," Samson said, on the walk to school one morning.

"What still?"

"Shine still." He smiled his mischief smile. "Moonshine. Hooch. The devils drink. It's his sideline business."

"Never knew that."

"So, my jar's half full." He leapt forward and stepped on a stink bug that wasn't doing anything wrong.

"What jar?"

"The one I'm fillin."

"Bet he'd tan your hide if he knew."

"Won't find out. Did it real slow. Finally got half a pickle jar." He spread his thumb and forefinger about four inches apart. "That much."

"Where's it at?"

"Safe in a tree. Cut out a hole and covered it with bark. Ain't never gonna be found."

"You gonna drink it?"

"Figure we should."

"We?" I couldn't help but smile.

He snapped his fingers and sang out, "Jason **Lee**, it's for you and **me** to split the shine, fif-**tee**, fif-**tee**."

"When? Where?"

"I'm thinkin our secret spot at the river."

"When?"

"Figure Saturday night, say eleven."

My smile disappeared. "Saturday night?"

"What's a matter? You ain't never snuck out at night before?"

I didn't answer.

"First time's the best. I'll be waitin."

*

That Saturday, at suppertime, my nerves were on high alert. I didn't want to look at Mama across the table so I studied the macaroni and cheese on my plate, and took a second helping to stay busy.

At ten thirty, when the house was quiet with sleep, I slipped out of my bed and climbed down the knotted branches of the cypress next to my window. The half moon ducked behind thin clouds.

I made my way toward the river, clutching an old flashlight with both hands. Its dim yellow beam flickered most of the way, but every now and then it went out and needed a shake. Tree shadows whipped across the night like ghosts, and the snap of twigs echoed under my footsteps. I imagined rabid wolves with red eyes following me. Worse yet, I heard footsteps that could have been Mama's. The only thing I dreaded more than her discovering I'd snuck out was the thought of Samson making fun of me for being too chicken to show up. What really kept me going was the chance to drink shine for the first time.

To take my mind off the crunch of branches, I counted, *one white lightnin, two white lightnin, three white lightning*, with each step. When I got close enough that Samson might hear me, I stopped counting and marched on in silence.

He waited on the flat boulder overlooking Mosquito River, our official meeting spot. I climbed up and parked myself next to him.

"What took you so long?"

"I'm here, ain't I?"

Not wasting any more time, he said, "I call this meetin to order." He pulled the jar from his jacket pocket and held it up to the sky. "On this, our first drinkin meetin, I christen this here important jar with the name, Judy."

"Judy? You goin batty?"

"Punch and Judy, get it? The hooch's the punch—"

"Okay, I get it."

He gave the lid a twist but it didn't budge. He turned the jar over, tapped the lid on the rock, and tried again. It opened.

I looked over the rock's edge at the river as it slithered down its course in the darkness. "You wanna fish at the pond tomorrow?"

"After church and chores, sure."

Samson raised the jar to his lips, took a deep breath,

and tossed back a swallow. He made a sucking noise through his teeth.

"Speakin of church," I said, "I thought you was a Baptist."

"Am. What's that got to do with the price a beans?"

"Didn't that church burn down?"

"Yeah. So what?"

"This shine—it's all right with the church?"

"What?" He handed me the jar.

"Don't churches frown on liquor?"

"Sure they do. You see a church anywhere around here?" He fanned his skinny arms through the air to make his point.

"No, I don't see no church."

"Besides." He brought his arms down. "I reckon it's better to be a Baptist and drink shine than be someone with no church at all."

"Someday I'll go."

"You gonna drink that or what?"

I couldn't come up with one more excuse to prolong my reason for being there. "Sure am." I brought it up to my lips. "This stuff smells like my mama's nail polish remover."

"Just drink."

Not one second after I took my first swig a fire hit the back of my throat, then roared through my chest and settled like smoldering embers in my belly. "Tastes bad as it smells," I said between chokes.

"This stuff's made for the kick, not the taste. Try *not* to taste it."

I wiped my eyes with my sleeve. "White lightnin ain't for sissies."

"No, it ain't, but this here's better'n white lightnin. It's my pa's own brew. Calls it Mr. J's Black Thunder. Get it, black for white, thunder for ligntnin?"

"Course I get it."

I breathed in the humid air to cool my throat and looked at the river again, doing its own thing, paying no attention to us. My mind raced ahead, looking forward to more nights like that one. The feeling of freedom is a powerful thing.

After a few more swigs my tongue felt loose and I thought I should tell Samson he was my best friend and without him I'd only have Mama and Uncle Mooks—and I loved him like a brother. "I got somethin to tell you."

"I already know. You're sweet on Reba."

"No, I ain't," I said, shocked out of my previous thoughts.

"You sure? I seen you talkin at lunch, with her wearin a sweet-on-you look."

"I said no I ain't. No means no."

"You better mean that. She's a bitch."

"Plus, she's too damn tall. I couldn't be sweet on no girl that tall."

"She started out short 'n fat and now she's tall as a giraffe." He made a noise intended to be a giraffe snort. "How's that happen?"

"If she don't stop growin, she'll have to marry Kareem Abdul-Jabbar," I said. "Think he's seven-foot-two."

"That reminds me. Did I ever tell you I'm gonna be a baseball player?" Samson handed the jar back to me.

"What position?"

"Right field, like Frank Robinson."

"The Reds?"

"First the Reds, then the Yankees."

With a belly full of Mr. J's Black Thunder, it seemed anything was possible.

"The Reds is my uncle's second-favorite team. I'll come to your games. And bring him, too." The shine really kicked in about then. I let myself picture Uncle Mooks and me watching Samson hit home runs out of the park.

"What 'bout you?" Samson asked.

"What?"

"What you wanna do?"

"Don't know. But I know what I don't wanna do. Be a soldier. My daddy, he was killed."

"I know."

"I know you know." I nodded. "And Uncle Mooks ain't right in the head 'cause of soldierin. Thinks he killed men in his own platoon, when they was takin a bath. The thing is, ever since he told me 'bout it, I can't help but think it coulda really happened, and I look at him different."

"He's different, that's for sure."

"It's been about two years and I got this dream keeps comin back, over and over, about a submarine and dead kids comin out of a hog's belly."

"He's crazy as a bed bug," Samson said, dismissing the subject. "So, what *do* you wanna do?"

My eyes had adjusted to the dark. I looked up to notice the silhouettes of the treetops against the sky, which caused a small dizzy spell.

"I think I'll build big things, like gigantic buildings. Taller'n these trees." I shot my arm upward.

"Like skyscrapers?"

"Only bigger. Taller. Sky-invaders."

"Or maybe I'll be a fireman," he said.

"Two miles high." I paused. "What'd you say? A fireman?" I thought about it. "Me, too. I could be a fireman. We'll work together in the same station."

Samson drank the last of the shine and wiped his mouth with the back of his hand. "And drive the hook and ladder."

Everything seemed possible. We both looked up and could see our future in the treetops spinning above us.

"Long as we're gonna work together, we ought to be blood brothers," I said.

"You mean cut our fingers?"

"Yeah, and mix our bloods together."

Quick as that, Samson gave a holler and smashed the pickle jar against the boulder. It broke in a thousand pieces.

"You just killed Judy," I said and caught a case of the giggles.

He laughed along. "I got lots a Judys."

When we settled down to the business of our blood

brotherhood, we could only find a few shards on the rock big enough to use. He handed one to me.

In spite of the darkness and the effects of the shine, we managed to poke a hole in our index fingers without going too deep. We held them up, finger facing finger.

"On the count of three," I said, closing my eyes and imagining the two streams of blood flowing together.

Samson said, "Whatever happens, both our bloods'll pump through each other for the rest of our lives."

"Know what we are now? You and me, we're an amalgamation."

"Amalgamation? You make that word up?"

"No. It's puttin things together that shouldn't mix, to make somethin better than it used to be."

"Blood brothers," he said. "For good or bad."

"Ain't gonna be no bad."

An orchestra of crickets filled the night.

*

The path home might as well have been lined with ball bearings, the way my feet wobbled and slipped. Even so, I felt sure of myself—sure enough to laugh at the crunch under my feet and howl at the ghosts that were too chicken to show their faces. In the middle of one of those howls, a giant tree stepped in my way and bounced me to the ground, face down. It took some time to get my breath back and figure out what'd happened. I mistakenly rolled over and looked up at the spinning sky. My stomach lurched. I got over onto my knees, crawled to the base of the tree, and puked up Mr. J's Black Thunder and macaroni until there was nothing more than spit left.

9

Come morning I discovered that somewhere along the way I'd scraped my elbow and smacked my arm. My muscles ached, my head felt two sizes too small for all the pain and pounding that was going on, and my breath smelled like a dead possum. Nausea was close by. I didn't remember getting back up the old trusty cypress or climbing inside my room, but the new secrets I held—sneaking out of the house, having a blood brother, drinking shine—made my misery almost pleasurable.

I knew if Mama took a good look at me she'd know everything I did without me saying a word, same as the way she always knew things. So, I spent most of the day on the porch with Uncle Mooks, doing little more than rubbing my thumb over the fresh cut on my finger. Turned out she was so busy with an emergency transcription, she hardly gave me the time of day.

I hadn't remembered Samson and I were supposed to go fishing until he came by around three, with his pole and a bag of crickets.

"I ain't up to it," I said. "I'm sick as a dog."

"Yeah, yeah, I know." He shook his head. "And tired as a bear in winter. Come on, Jason Lee. A dip in the river's the best cure."

"I barfed my brains out last night. I'm here to tell you, macaroni barf actually looks like brains. Melted brains."

"Come on. A change of scenery'll do you good."

Samson persisted until I got off my butt and went with him.

Heading down Wilders Grove Road we heard the clack-clack of Samson's little brother's old rusty bike. For some reason he'd named it Ruby.

Elijah had fastened playing cards to the spokes with clothespins. The king of spades strummed his front wheel and the king of clubs followed from the back. A pillow of dust sprang up when he passed. He kept pedaling down the road, acting like he didn't see us. Not a nod or a hello. Nothing.

"Where's he goin so almighty fast?" I asked.

Samson looked ahead, studying the dust that settled from his little brother's trail, and he shrugged a shoulder.

"What's that mean?"

"Means what it means."

"Mean you don't know?"

"No."

"What's it mean, then?"

"Nothin. Just close your mouth about it. Means it ain't none of your damn business."

We stopped walking and faced each other. I crossed my arms and spoke slow, right in his face. "Keepin secrets ain't right. Secrets cause the clock of life to speed up and cheat you outta precious time."

"The clock of life, Jason Lee?" He shook his head. "That's what you have to say? The clock of life?" His head kept on shaking. "You're soundin like that crazy old uncle of yours. All he talks 'bout is clocks and time. That's what you're soundin like."

"I'm gonna pretend you didn't say that. Besides, why can't you answer me a simple question? It ain't been twenty-four hours since we mixed bloods. Ain't that supposed to mean somethin?"

Samson's eyes met mine. It was my first stare-off away from the front porch. I knew he couldn't win. My eyes were trained from years of practice with Uncle Mooks. It took awhile, but he finally looked away.

"I think we're havin a conflictation. You know what that is?" I said in my best Uncle Mooks manner.

He shook his head no.

"It's a confrontation and a conflict all rolled into one, and conflicts are for talkin out, not for fightin over. You hear me?"

"Course I hear you. I ain't deaf."

I realized I really did sound like Uncle Mooks. "Okay, it don't matter where he's goin." I walked ahead. "Come on, let's fish."

"He's headed for Peek's place," Samson said to my back.

"Peek's place?" I turned around a little too fast, my head still feeling the full aftereffect of the shine.

"Uh-huh."

"Grover Peek's place?" I practically yelled. "Is he crazy? What if the old man catches him?"

"He ain't gonna get caught."

"He's your brother," I said in frustration. "And Grover Peek's the meanest bastard in these parts. What kind of stupid is that?"

"I couldn't do nothin." Samson smacked the ground with his fishing pole. "He's turned ornery lately and stubborn as a mule in a corncrib. Said he's gonna pee in Peek's pond."

"Pee?"

"I told him he was on his own. But I didn't think he'd do it."

My insides turned.

"We gotta get him."

Peek's property was a good quarter mile away. I threw down my fishing pole and ran. Samson caught up to me. Signs saying NO TRESPASSING were posted all around. With each step closer I became more fearful for Elijah, and once we crossed into Peeks property I feared for all of us.

"I see him," Samson said and pointed.

Elijah stood on the edge of the pond staring off in the distance, with one hand holding on to Ruby's handlebars.

We moved in.

"Elijah," I said. "You gotta get your butt outta here."

He turned and looked at us. "I ain't doin nothin wrong. Just lookin at a hole in the dirt what's filled with water."

"You askin for trouble?" I said.

"What's it to you, Jason Lee? Mind your own business."

"You do what you came here to do?" Samson asked.

"Uh-huh." Elijah gave a satisfied nod.

"Good, now let's hightail it out a here."

We were almost off Peek's property when gunshots cracked through the air. Grover Peek walked out from a grove of kudzu-smothered trees. His cap sat backward on his head.

He pointed his rifle toward the sky and stared at us with eyes that could have been the bullets themselves.

"This here's my property." The old man was no more than ten feet from us. "You don't deserve 'em, but them was warnin shots."

Elijah was on one side of me, Samson on the other. My chest was pounding so loud I wondered if they heard it.

Peek pointed the rifle directly at us. I looked into the face of the shriveled man, not much bigger than me, and knew if any of us moved we'd all be killed.

He looked at me. "I know who you are. I knew your sorry excuse of a pa." Then he shifted his eyes between Samson and Elijah as he spit out chaw juice. His focus came back to me. "The nigger-lovin apple don't fall too far now, ain't that right?"

Elijah's hands began to twitch. The old man pointed the gun barrel at him.

"Be still," I whispered, trying not to move my lips.

Fast as I said it, he jerked the gun back at me again.

"Shut up, kid. You got that son-of-a-bitch's mouth.

Never knowin when to shut up or who to talk to." Sweat collected on his forehead and a drop of tobacco juice seeped from his mouth. "You know what he did, your no-good pa?"

"No, sir."

"He helped that scum-dog nigger boy escape before the trial."

I stood still, fixed in my shoes, not an eyelash moving.

"You know that?"

"No, sir, I don't know nothin 'bout that, sir."

The old man spit again. He shook his head and blinked like his eyes had gone bad. He frowned and teetered for a minute. "He wouldn't never shut up 'bout the niggers havin the same rights as us real Americans." Elijah twitched again but Peek didn't see it. "The only right a nigger should have's the right to go back to Africa on a boat—in a pine box."

He shook his head and blinked again. "I fgrue yur tooooo rreaal . . ." It sounded like some foreign language. Then he collapsed to his knees.

The gun barrel kicked skyward as a shot went off. The bullet hit an upper branch of the oak beside us and ricocheted back down to the hard-packed soil. It skipped over Elijah's left foot and stopped. We scrambled out of the way. After the rush of adrenalin settled, I looked at Grover Peek laid out in the dirt. One of his arms slapped the ground a couple of times, like a hooked fish struggling against the shoreline. Then it stopped.

"Is he dead?" Samson said.

Elijah inched toward the old man. He picked up a stick and poked him in the stomach. I'd seen him do the same with dead jack rabbits. The old man's eyes opened.

Elijah jumped back. "Look," he yelled. "They movin. They blinkin and movin."

Peek's eyes seemed to be the only part of him still alive, but they didn't look like bullets anymore. They looked like glossy blue marbles gliding back and forth. Then they blinked and blinked and blinked.

"Look there, he pissed his pants," Elijah said and poked him in the groin. A tear ran toward the old man's ear. Elijah poked him again.

"Stop doin that," I said.

"Why?" he said and pointed the stick at Peek eye.

"Stop." I yelled and looked around, feeling the weight of responsibility come over me. "This ain't right. I'm gonna get help."

"We don't need no help," Elijah said.

I started to run toward home, then remembered Elijah's bike Ruby was in the dirt close by. I grabbed it and started pedaling for home fast as I could.

"Mama," I yelled at the top of my lungs all the way up our drive. "Mama, Mama, Grover Peek's dead." Her Skylark was nowhere to be seen. Uncle Mooks ran down the front steps.

"What'd you say?"

I dropped the bike to the ground. My lungs burned. "Grover Peek's dead, except for his eyes. Where's

Mama? I need help."

Uncle Mooks laughed like I'd told him the funniest joke he'd ever heard. "Hot damn." He moved his hips and did a stomping dance. "You sure?"

"Where's Mama?"

"Gone to town to deliver somethin."

"I need her now," I screamed. "I need Mama."

Uncle Mooks looked like he might fall into another agitated spell, but after what I'd been through, it was the least of my worries.

"He ain't dead, dead. Just almost."

"Where?"

"On the ground by his pond."

He processed what I'd said and frowned. "What was you doin there, on his land?"

"I need a hand, Uncle Mooks."

He made a sour face and shook his head. "No, not my hand."

"Come on, you gotta," I whined.

"What was you doin there, on his land?"

"Quit askin questions and help me."

"Why was you there?"

"Getting Elijah. Samson and Elijah's up there with him, now."

"Samson and Elijah?"

"It's what I said. You listenin?"

"They ain't safe up there. No, it ain't safe." He paced, all the while looking at Elijah's bike lying in the yard. "He kills little kids."

"Please, Uncle Mooks. That was somethin else. That

happened in Vietnam."

He charged for the bike, picked it up, and pointed to the handlebars. "Get on."

His powerful legs pedaled us over exposed roots and jagged rocks. My butt bounced against the steel, and it took every bit of my strength to hang on. For all my life, I'd never seen Uncle Mooks venture off our property, and it surprised me when he took a shortcut I didn't know about.

*

Elijah stood guard over Grover Peek with his trusty stick still pointed at the old man. Samson watched, seated on a large rock.

Uncle Mooks spotted the gun on the ground. "He come after you boys?"

"Yessir, Mr. Mooks, he did." Elijah moved his stick in the direction of the bullet then pointed it to the tree branch. "It hit that up there, then flew back and almost got me right here." He stuck out his foot.

"Sit with your brother." Uncle Mooks said in a severe voice.

He picked up the rifle and turned his full attention to Grover Peek. He got down on his knees, leaned in close to Peek's face, and looked into his watery blue eyes.

"I seen them eyes in my sleep for a long spell." He pointed the gun at Peek's head and raised his voice. "You know, they say time's a peculiar thing."

Peek's eyes fluttered.

Uncle Mooks looked up at me and yelled, "Ain't

that what they say, Jason Lee?"

"I guess." I watched his finger on the trigger, ready to squeeze.

"I know some things 'bout time. Yep, I do. Don't I, Jason Lee?"

I nodded, scared he'd pull the trigger and Peek's brains would fly out. But he kept on talking. "Let's say we was to get you to the hospital so's you'd have a chance of gettin fixed up good as new. Nope, we ain't gonna do that."

"Thought you was gonna help," I said.

"Told you I wouldn't," he grumbled, his eyes still fixed on Grover Peek. "He don't deserve it."

Uncle Mooks got up off his knees but kept the rifle pointed at Peek's head. He looked at Samson and Elijah.

"Let me tell you 'bout this old shit turd layin on the ground. About what I seen him do. He strung up the young'un from that tree over there."

The words came out so fast it wasn't until he nodded toward a chestnut oak halfway up a dusty hill that I understood. The tree had three naked branches poking out from the trunk. I felt like a bucket of cement had just dried on my chest.

"Let's say we was to string you up on that same tree?"

Peek's arm flapped once.

"We ain't gonna do that neither. Too much work. I'd rather stay put and watch you suck your last breath."

Samson and Elijah were still staring at the tree.

"I was a little boy hidin in the shrubs that day," Uncle Mooks said. "Too scared to move. I watched the five a you string a rope round the boy's neck and hoist him." His face twisted and he looked at me. "You know what they did after all the fight went outta him?"

I shook my head.

A blue vein popped out from his forehead. "They beat on him with baseball bats 'til there weren't nothin left to hold him together." Uncle Mooks looked at the tree. "A kid same age as me, no more than twelve."

Grover Peek's face was pure white. If I had to guess, I'd say mine looked the same.

Uncle Mooks kicked the old man in the ribs. "When it was over, you was the one took his hood off. Four white-hooded boogie men and you, celebratin."

He put his boot on Grover Peek's neck and pushed until the old man's throat rattled.

"Stop," I said. "Don't kill him."

"I already told you I ain't gonna do that."

The way things looked, I wasn't so sure.

"We gonna stay and watch for as long as it takes." Uncle Mooks lifted his boot off Peek's neck, walked to the rock, and sat down between Samson and Elijah. The three of them seemed content to witness Grover Peek's life run out, no matter how long it took.

I yelled at them. "I'm gonna help him."

Uncle Mooks yelled back at me. "Help that old shit turd? He kills kids, Jason Lee. Kids no different than you. Like I said before, he don't deserve it."

I had a mind to agree with him, but all I could see was the scar on the side of Uncle Mooks' head, deep as an empty eye socket.

I couldn't stop yelling. "It just ain't right, leavin him here. Wally told me he was bred that way. You weren't."

I looked at Samson and Elijah for backup and got none. They were steadfast as Uncle Mooks. Then a flood of thoughts popped into my head. Things like lynchings and head wounds and wars in jungles where school children are killed. And hate bigger than life, or people.

"Samson, what's goin on?"

He said nothing to me. Not even a grunt. The three of them reminded me of the carved monkeys on our porch ledge. Two blacks, one white. But instead of hands covering eyes, ears, and mouths, they were folded in their laps.

I stomped off. "You're actin just like the old shit turd layin there. You ain't actin no better than him. I'm goin for help. Real help this time."

I ran toward town, thinking back to the day Wally told me my daddy was always, "so almighty sure of what was right and wrong. And strong-willed enough to do the right thing when it went against everyone around him."

Until that minute, my daddy had been a ghost of a man I'd only known from stories and black and white photographs. At that moment he was inside me and I felt driven to do what I thought was right.

When I finally reached the road, my head pounding with a new strength not felt before, a pickup driving past gave me a ride. Like Uncle Mooks always said, fate carries its own clock.

10

I wasn't about to make up with Uncle Mooks or join him on the porch until three weeks of self-induced confinement forced me to reconsider. I missed watching the funeral parades drive past, and studying the squirrels, and recognizing the birds by their calls. I missed the rustle of the outdoors and the sweet smell of evenings, and despite myself, I missed the rasp of Uncle Mooks' voice the most.

The squeak of the screen door startled him.

"What're you doin here?" He stared at me, digging the knife into his newest monkey carving.

"We can't stay mad forever, can we? Thought I'd come out and see if you'd teach me to whittle."

He kept his eyes on me.

"I'm not sorry for what I did," I said.

"Shoulda let him die."

"It's what you think, but I couldn't. Don't you understand? I couldn't."

"Shoulda let him die," he said again.

"They said he had some kind of stroke. Ain't never gonna walk or talk again. Ain't that good enough?"

"He strung up a boy."

"I know."

I took a seat on the swing. "Uncle Mooks, I think

we're havin what you call a conflict."

"Conflicts are for talkin out." His face relaxed.

I didn't really want to talk. Not about Peek or Vietnam or anything else. I wanted to sit still and feel right about my decision to help, no matter who thought it was wrong, and remember how I felt determined to do what was right for me.

As I stared at the monkeys crowded together, lining the rail, I finally said, "You think those monkeys really can't speak no evil? Or see it or hear it?"

"Suppose."

"Or do you think it means they just don't want to see the evil? Or speak it, or hear it?"

"Dunno. I just whittle 'em."

He got up and went inside. I thought he was done with me, but before too long he came back out and stood next to me with something inside the closed fist he stuck out to me.

"Whaddya got?"

He opened his hand. A monkey balanced inside. It looked like the others, except its hands were wrapped around its chest, clutching opposite elbows.

"What is it? A mistake?"

"No. He's the best of 'em. This one don't **do** no harm."

He set the do-no-harm monkey on the porch rail, reached into his bucket of pine scraps, and handed me a chunk of wood and a knife.

"Carvin's easy."

11

1984

That Saturday morning before Easter, the three of us were in the kitchen. It felt childish to be dipping boiled eggs into pots of dye and then hiding them, but I did it anyway, because, small and simple as it was, our annual Easter egg hunt was one of Mama's most prized events of the year.

Uncle Mooks only used the green dye and dabbed it on the shells with a sponge. Mama used every color in her kit, and after her eggs dried she added bows to them with a dab of glue. I marbleized mine.

Mama plucked the last egg out of the pan with a spoon and set it on the wire holder we'd made for drying.

"We'll be in town longer than usual today," she said.

"How come?" Uncle Mooks asked.

"Jason Lee's fifteen and goin in tenth grade next year."

He raised his head. "Why you tellin us what we already know?"

"I'm building up to somethin here." Mama smiled.

"Somethin to do with town?" I said.

"Yes, exactly." She tested the egg in the holder for dryness.

"What?"

"You're sproutin up like a man. Headin toward manhood." Her eyebrows rose to punctuate her sentence. "And I think we should buy you a proper suit."

"What do I need a suit for?"

"Oh, dances."

"Dances?" My voice cracked. "I don't know how to dance. You know that."

"There'll be a time you will."

"We only got two months left of school, and there ain't no dances in summer. Besides, I don't want no suit."

"And you'll need one for funerals, too."

"You're not plannin on dyin, are you?"

"Not anytime soon." Mama laughed. "You two clean up here while I get myself ready to go." She hung her apron on the wall peg and left.

"What's gotten into her?" I asked Uncle Mooks.

"Your clock's headin toward noon."

"I don't even know what that means."

"Means you're gettin older."

*

Mama had put on a fresh coat of lipstick and her cheeks were tinted more pink than usual. Instead of a work dress she wore a black skirt and a blue sweater, the same color as her eyes.

"How come you're so dressed up?"

"No reason, but I'll take that as a compliment." She rubbed a finger across her teeth. "Transcripts are already in the car." She picked up her pocketbook off the dining table. "Fetch the cake, and we'll be on our way."

Puddles from a morning shower filled the potholes in the road. We hit one dead-on. The front wheels bounced against the car frame. Instead of getting upset like usual and checking if the cake had shifted, she turned up the radio and began to sing along. "*Ooh, I'm drivin my life away, lookin for a better way.*" She looked at me. "We're all lookin for a better way. Right, Jason Lee?"

"If you call bein forced to get a suit better."

She smiled. "It won't hurt you."

"Ain't never needed one yet. Why now?"

"I met the owner of the new men's store last week. He said there's a sale goin on and I figure we should take advantage of the timin. Save money."

"Seems a funny way to save money, if you ask me."

"No one's askin you."

"Okay, but..." I shook my head and worked up the nerve to start another conversation about something that had been on my mind for some time.

"Mama, I've been thinkin."

"Thinkin's good."

"I wanna learn about Vietnam."

The words were barely out of my mouth before she shut off the radio. She eased her foot off the gas pedal and steered us to the side of the road by a patch of black-eyed susans. Mama pushed the gearshift into park and leaned against her door to face me.

"Vietnam." Her mouth pulled tight. "That war happened a long time ago, Jason Lee, and after all the cryin and sorrow, I've tried my best to move toward the future and push it out of my mind."

"It's where my daddy died and I don't know nothin about it."

"Hush." She looked out the windshield at the rustling hickories. "It was a crazy time back then. J.L. got his draft papers, but he didn't want to go. He toyed with the idea of desertin to Canada. But, around these parts we were raised that to serve our country in time of war was the right thing to do, even if your heart's not in it."

"Uncle Mooks don't think it was right."

"Can't blame him. Turned out nothin good came of the war."

"Conflict," I said.

"What?"

"Uncle Mooks says it was a conflict. Says they never had the balls to declare it a war."

"He's right. But the name don't matter. The endin does. Mooks wanted to be an engineer when he got back. If he hadn't been wounded I'm sure it's what he'd be today. Not to mention how different our lives would be."

Mama tapped her fingers on the steering wheel. I noticed the fresh coat of pink polish. She took a deep breath and looked at me with a seriousness I'd rarely seen before.

"Mama, it's okay—"

"Jason Lee, you know that Vietnam was the tragedy of my life."

I nodded.

"Turned it inside out and upside down." She pointed to the glove box. "Hand me a tissue," she said, her eyes tearing.

The car swayed when a truck and trailer carrying dairy cattle whizzed past.

"Uncle Mooks said somethin about school kids gettin killed when he was over there. You know about that?"

She shook her head. "He gets confused."

"And one time he said he killed men in a bomb crater."

"It's just his head wound."

"You sure?"

"He's a good man. And, this is the last time you'll repeat anything he says like that."

I looked away.

She said, "I can tell you this. The men who died in the field, like J.L., were looked upon as dyin with honor—same as all the soldiers who died in all wars. Nobody has the nerve to pour scorn on the dead ones. But the men who made it out of the jungle, men like Mooks, came home to angry anti-war crowds who looked down on 'em. Spit on 'em and worse."

"Why?"

She stroked her forehead. "I don't know. Frustration. Anger. The anti-war movement was in full force. It's all so hard to explain."

She looked out the window again, then nodded. "Tell you what, Wally's got a mess a books on the subject—the history, the build-up, the protests. We'll ask him to loan 'em to us. If you're old enough to ask the questions, you're old enough to get the answers. From people a lot smarter than me."

I wanted to yell out and thank the heavens but instead said, "That's a great idea."

I'd finally have the chance to figure the whole Vietnam thing out and why Uncle Mooks had to suffer and my daddy had to die.

"Just promise you won't ever talk about Vietnam around your uncle again. You know it confuses him."

I crossed my heart and held my hand up. "Promise. Never." The fingers on my other hand were crossed.

"Deal," Mama said, looking at her watch. "Much as you want to forget, we got a suit to buy." She stuck the damp tissues in the ashtray and started up the car.

*

The building had been vacant for two years before Parnell Boyle came to town with a few cans of paint, a new sign, and the crazy idea that Hadlee, Mississippi, needed a proper men's store. The sign out front read Boyle's Men's Store, An Emporium of Style.

First off I noticed a glass counter of wrist watches along the wall to the right, and then a rack of men's wallets to my left. We weren't more than five steps inside when a man wearing a plaid sport coat and metal-framed glasses rushed up to us. A cloth measuring tape hung around his neck. He looked at Mama and smiled. "Nice to see you again, Cassie." He offered me his hand. I obliged, and he crunched my fingers.

"I'm Parnell Boyle," he said in an outsider's accent. "How can I be of service." His mustache bounced with each word.

"We're lookin for a suit for my son." Mama patted my shoulder. "This here's Jason Lee."

"A fine-looking boy." He looked at Mama and smiled when he said it.

"The sale you're havin—does that include suits?"

Mr. Boyle stroked his silver tie clip. "It most certainly does. Allow me to show you." He turned. "They're this way." We went toward the back of the store, past the hats and accessories, past the shirts and slacks. My sneakers squeaked across the waxed wood floor.

"Smells like apples in here," I said.

"Cologne. Lacoste. It's their first year with fragrance. Light and fruity."

His hand motioned toward a rack of no more than a dozen suits. He smiled at Mama again. "These are on clearance. You won't find a better value this side of Clarksdale."

"Exactly what we're lookin for," Mama said. "Value."

"What size do you wear, son?"

"Don't know."

"No problem." He reached for the tape. "I'll take your measurements. We'll keep them here on file."

"What for?"

"For next time."

I sucked in my breath at the idea.

Mr. Boyle stretched the tape across my shoulders and down my arms. I jumped when he moved it up the inside of my thigh. When done he shook his head and said, "Your chest measures thirty three. Our smallest sale suits are thirty six."

"That's okay," Mama said. "He's still growin."

Parnell Boyle removed the only black suit from the rack. I had to admit it looked real nice, like the ones detectives wore in the movies. The idea of getting a suit didn't seem so bad right then.

"It's too dark," Mama said.

"That's okay," I said. "I like this one."

She looked at Mr. Boyle and said real sweet-like, "I'd like somethin a little lighter in color so he can wear it all year long."

"But I like this one."

"It sounds like you want something more versatile," Mr. Boyle said back to Mama, as though I wasn't there. He rubbed his chin. "I think this hound's-tooth might be just the ticket." He put the dark one back and held up a tan suit covered with small, slanted checks. "Three buttons with a breast pocket, a hundred percent wool—sturdy *and* versatile. They're all the rage in Cleveland. Very stylish."

"The black one's better," I said.

"Is that where you're from?" Mama asked, like she was impressed to know someone from Cleveland.

"For a time." He smiled. Too much for my liking. "My shop was downtown, within walking distance to Lake Erie."

"Lake Erie?" Mama's voice rose.

"That's right." Mr. Boyle's posture straightened, like walking to Lake Erie was something to be proud of. He shook the hanger. The hound's-tooth suit bobbed. "With proper care this will hold up for years. I sold a lot of these in the Cleveland store." He pulled the jacket off the hanger and held it so I could slip my arms into the sleeves. "Let's take a look." When I turned around to face him he said, "It fits well enough across the shoulders."

"What about the sleeves?" I said, bothered as all get out. "They're hangin past my fingers."

"Don't worry, we'll tailor it to fit like a custom order. Tailoring is my specialty." He brushed his hand across the shoulder.

"Looks good," Mama said. "That's the one. But don't cut nothin off the arms or the legs. Just fold 'em under. I'll let 'em out as he grows."

"It'll fit better if I take the excess off."

"No, please don't do that," she said, firm.

"The dressing room's in the far corner, son." Boyle nodded in that direction. "Put the whole suit on and I'll chalk it."

"What about the black one. Can't I try it?"

"I like this one," Mama said.

The dressing room wasn't more than a closet with a curtain for a door. A folding chair took up most of the space. A mirror hung on the wall. I put the suit on, and when I looked at my reflection my spirits perked up. The pants fit so awful I figured Mama would have to reconsider.

"I don't think this is gonna work," I said, pulling the curtain back.

Mama and Mr. Boyle were nowhere in sight, but I heard her laughing near the front of the store. I shoved the jacket sleeves up to my elbows and held the pants by their gigantic waistband. The excess length on the legs bunched around my shoes and dragged along the floor.

"Mama?"

"Here, Jason Lee. By the hat display."

I hobbled over and stopped cold at the sight of them. They both had sailor hats on their heads.

"What're you doin?"

"Tryin on hats." They both smiled at me. Goofy smiles. "You like it?" Mama said, patting the stupid thing.

That's when it hit me. The make-up and pretty sweater were all for him. I gnawed on the inside of my cheek. "No," I said, then pointed to the pants I had on. "Look at this."

"No need to worry, son. Mr. Boyle can fix that."

"I think I'd better try on the black one," I huffed.

Boyle said, "Like I said before, tailoring is my area

of expertise."

I looked up at the white, dopey, sailor cap on his head. "On what ship, the S. S. Minnow?"

"What's gotten into you?" Mama said and looked at Mr. Boyle. "Parnell, I sincerely apologize. Jason Lee knows better."

He set his hat on the counter. "No offense taken, Cassie. It was funny." But he didn't smile. Mama took her hat off, too.

"I'd like you to keep that one," Boyle said to Mama. "As a token of my esteem."

Esteem? I thought. *Who is this guy?*

"Oh no, Parnell, I can't accept it." *Now he's Parnell?*

"You look so cute in it, I won't take no for an answer."

Boyle reached in his pants pocket and pulled out a piece of chalk. "I've got to tell you, these pants will be tricky, Cassie. They're a thirty-inch waist, and the boy's barely a twenty-four."

"My name's Jason Lee, not the boy."

"Do what you have to, but don't cut nothin off." Mama watched his every move. "He'll grow into them in no time."

*

Relieved to finally be out of there, I headed toward Pinks in the bright, balmy afternoon. Mama journeyed down to the Diversity Coalition. Since Samson was nowhere in sight I went out front to wait for him and saw Reba leaning against the cast iron clock, talking with her friend, Josey. A horn honked from the other side of the street and Josey took off. Reba spotted me and hurried over with her long-legged stride.

"Howdy, Jason Lee."

She was grinning, like she knew something I didn't. She twisted strands of hair between two fingers. It's a funny thing about girls and their hair. Reba's used to be frizzy, but that day it looked like loose, shiny ribbons.

"Howdy," I said back. "You seen Samson?"

"No." She hitched her hands to her hips, like she was prone to do. "I swear, I'll never understand why you and him are friends. You know it ain't natural."

"You're entitled to your own opinion, even if it's wrong."

"It ain't wrong."

"You sure you ain't seen him?"

"I said no. But I did see you leavin the Emporium of Style." She said it in a teasing tone. I felt the blood rise to my cheeks and forehead, and my ears got hot. I glanced at my shoes.

"Had to buy a suit."

"Jason Lee Rainey in a suit? I'd like to see that."

I noticed she'd grown into her big eyebrows. Normally I would have told her to mind her own business, but seeing her there, I couldn't. She looked different. Like a model in a magazine ad for shampoo.

I was spared any further conversation when Noah's truck horn beeped twice. We both looked in that direction to see Noah and Samson pull into one of the parking spaces in front of The Busy Bee. Samson stayed put in the passenger seat and motioned for me to come over.

"Gotta go, Reba. Good seein you." I was anxious to get away and, at the same time, would have liked to linger. Halfway to the truck I looked back. Reba had vanished.

Samson couldn't have smiled any bigger if he tried.

"What're you smilin about?" I said, thinking he'd seen me with Reba, and I was ready to shut him up about her being a bitch.

"Can't make it today."

"What gives?" I said, relieved.

"Gonna practice drivin. With Noah. I take my test next Friday."

"Hey, Noah," I said, wishing I had a brother to someday teach me to drive. "Hope he don't pitch this thing into any ditches."

"Was that Reba?" Samson said.

I turned away. "See you Monday," I yelled, and jogged down to the hardware store.

12

Wally was out front on the bench, his hands folded across his belly. He looked content.

"You're here early." He offered his hand for a shake. A half-a-shake. "How's your day goin?"

"Guess it's fine, if you call bein forced to buy a suit fine."

"A suit?" He pulled sunflower seeds from his pocket.

"You know that man Parnell Boyle? Mama and me went to his new store."

"Crazy idea, that store. I give him nine months, no more." He popped the seeds in his mouth.

"Called her Cassie and winked at her," I said, irked.

He laughed. A couple seeds flew out of his mouth. He patted the empty space on the bench. "Have a seat."

"Don't mind if I do." I sat next to him, crossed my arms, and leaned back. "Winked at her. Like a snake."

"It's none of my business, but I reckon she's due for a wink or two."

"He sounds like a machine gun spittin out words. You heard him talk?"

"Yep." Wally chuckled. "The man sure likes his fancy words. The thing is, about Cassie, maybe you should be glad she's comin out of the shell she crawled herself into."

"He smells like apples."

"What?"

"Apples. He puts perfume on himself that smells like apples."

"What's goin on, son?"

"Nothin, I guess." I looked across the street at the blue and orange Rexall sign and thought they should change it to *Wrecks all*. "Mama said you got some books about Vietnam."

"Lots of 'em."

"Can I borrow 'em? I'll give 'em back."

"Son," Wally said and scratched his head. "I've got one hell of a confession to make."

"To me?"

"On occasion I'm no more than a slow-minded fool of a Southern boy, but right now I'm feelin like I'm two steps behind the town idiot."

"What's wrong, Wally?"

"Before J.L. left for basic trainin he packed all his books in boxes and brought 'em over here. Back then we swapped books like some folks exchange tradin cards. I didn't have enough room on my shelves so I tossed the boxes in the attic and haven't given 'em a thought since."

"His books? Mama didn't say nothing about *his* books."

"She might not have known what he did with 'em. But, I reckon they're your books now."

My resentment of Parnell Boyle vanished fast as

that. The thought of holding, reading, owning books that belonged to my daddy took over.

"Keep an eye on this bench here for me." Wally stood. "I'll go upstairs and get a box for you right now."

While he was gone I noticed the sweet smell of cinnamon buns drifted down from Koman's ovens, and the Rexall sign looked right again.

Wally came back with an old Dr. Pepper carton that had the word BOOKS written on the side panel. He set it on the sidewalk in front of me. "You can get started with these. I'll get the rest to you in due course."

I picked up the box and situated it on my lap. Its weight was solid against my legs and felt like silent wisdom, handed down. I yanked the overlapping top flaps open and reached in to rub my hand across the top book. "Street Without Joy," I read aloud. "The French Debacle in Indochina."

I picked it up and my eyes immediately went to the image on the cover of the book below, a black and white photo of a colored protester in the stranglehold of a helmeted white policeman. It looked like the boy was screaming. The book was titled, *The Movement: Documentary of a Struggle for Equality*.

I closed up the box, my package of gold nuggets, to savor it later, alone.

"Thank you, Wally."

He tossled my hair.

"Mama don't like talkin about nothin that happened back then."

"I know."

"She's so private about everything. Especially those times. But today she talked about it a little."

"That's good." He nodded his head.

"I woulda liked to know more. But didn't want to push."

He pointed to the books. "Maybe those'll help you out."

"How bout you?"

"How bout me, what?"

"Since you and him were best friends, how bout you tell me about it. I mean when he died."

Wally tugged on his earlobe. I figured he'd say no.

"Seein how you put it that way, I guess I could. The thing is I can't help you with anything that went on in Vietnam, only what happened here—after we got word."

"Okay." I wrapped my arms around the box.

"This'll be just between you and me."

"I won't say nothin."

Wally hitched his thumbs under his suspenders. "The place to start is at the beginnin, so that's where we'll start." He took a breath and spit out some shells.

"The bad news came on a Tuesday. I know 'cause it was Election Day. The only time to this day I didn't vote. November fifth, 1967. I was here at the store lookin over my sample ballot. About three in the afternoon, the phone rang. The Army chaplain on the other end didn't mince any words. He called from your house. He said J.L. was dead and Cassie'd asked for me." Wally's legs began to bounce.

"I drove full-speed, but my mind was so numb it's amazin I made it. I could hardly see outta the windshield. When I got there the chaplain and his aide were in full dress uniforms and spit-polished shoes. They met me outside." Wally shook his head. "Lord, how'd you like to be the bearer of bad news for a livin?"

He unhitched his left thumb, put an arm across my shoulder, and gave me a pat.

"The chaplain told me Cassie'd collapsed in the doorway when she saw them get outta their vehicle. They carried her to the couch. She was still there, shakin like a woman possessed, when I showed up."

I held my eyes on the Rexall sign, hoping to keep them from welling up, and took some slow, deep breaths until I calmed down.

Wally's voice brought me back to the story. "When she saw me she said, 'Check on the baby. He's in his crib.'"

"The baby, meanin me?"

"Course."

"I was eight months when he died."

"Yes, I know. And I was a twenty-two-year-old who didn't know nothin about babies." He laughed. "But it didn't take long before I learned how to change diapers, and what it was like to walk around with a child against my chest until he fell back asleep."

"You did that?" I said, feeling self-conscious.

"I was there to do everythin I could. Besides, it's not

as hard as you'd think."

Darla's voice pierced the air. "I need help in the storeroom if you can find the time to haul your backside off the bench." We turned to see her standing in the entrance to the store, lips tight with wrinkles.

"We're talkin. Give me a couple more minutes, will you?"

"Would those be sixty-second minutes?" She turned and went back into the store.

Wally rubbed his hands together. "Sorry. This'll be the short version."

"I reckon."

"That first week was tough. I stayed at your house full-time, knowin it was the only place I was supposed to be. We shared a lot of tears, Cassie and me. Seems we both needed each other to help get through the pain. Not knowin how he died was the hardest. They didn't have the details." Wally wiped at his forehead. "And I'm not so sure knowin woulda made it any easier."

"You ever find out?"

He shook his head. "Then, after the shock and denial and the heartache, when it finally sunk in that he was really gone forever and beyond, the second round of shit news came flyin at us."

"Uncle Mooks, right?"

"Uh-huh. Not even a week'd passed. You, were in the playpen in the kitchen with me and Cassie. I'd finished mixin up a batch of white sausage gravy to put over biscuits when the phone rang. They said Mooks'd been wounded and needed to come home. And he'd need special care." Wally paused. "I thought that second dose of bad news would be too much for her, but I'll be damned if it didn't give her new strength. She saw the phone call as good news. Your uncle was alive."

"Wally," Darla yelled.

"Sorry, Darla needs my help." He stood up with great effort, like his knees had gone bad.

"Thanks," I said. "I won't say nothin to Mama."

"I'll deny it if you do."

*

I bounced the box of books on my lap during the drive home. The radio was off and neither of us said much until I blurted out, "What kind of a name's that? Parnell."

"Not real sure. Suppose it's a family name."

"And Boyle? Sounds like somethin you'd pop."

"Watch your mouth, Jason Lee."

13

"Parnell called today," Mama said while we were doing dishes. "Your suit's ready." She handed me a plate to dry.

"Took him long enough. Thought he's supposed to be a hot-shot tailor. Two weeks to fix a suit?"

She paid no attention to my feeble attempt at an insult. "We'll pick it up Saturday."

"This Saturday?"

"Course, this Saturday."

I stacked the plate in the cupboard. "I was gonna ask if I could ride into town with Samson on Saturday. He passed his driver's test first try, and he's drivin Noah's old truck now."

Along with the keys to the truck came the Saturday errand of collecting the corn for Mr. J's Black Thunder. The truck and the chore were passed down, same as Noah's old shoes and shirts. The first thing Samson did was give the truck a name—Dicey.

"They need you to try it on," Mama said, bringing the conversation back to the suit. "Besides I want to thank Parnell personally for all his help. And for the sailor hat."

"Samson's a real good driver. Please? It'll give you a chance to visit with Miss Therese without me taggin along."

"You're no tag-along and you know it."

I let out a sigh and stomped my foot on the floor—twice. "I'm fifteen years old. I'm headin toward manhood. You said so yourself."

"I guess you got me there."

"Please?"

"Tell you what. You can drive in with Samson, and I'll meet you at the men's store before I go to the Coalition." She pulled the drain plug out of the sink. "Like I said, I want to thank Parnell personally. And you can try on the suit when I get there." She smiled. "Two birds."

*

Two clay jugs chock-full of Mr. J's Black Thunder sat on the seat between us in an okra crate, ready for delivery.

I felt drenched in independence. Dicey backfired farts of smoke that worked their way inside the cab. They smelled of manhood. Wild flowers and weeds spread along the roadside. As if that weren't good enough, a swarm of painted lady butterflies flickered in the distance, working their way north.

When we passed the Grinnin' Catfish, I looked for Mama's car in the parking lot but didn't spot it.

"Wonder if they're ever gonna paint that place another color?" Samson said.

"Think it's orange 'cause catfish are kind of orange."

"Looks like a big glass a Tang."

"Drop me at the new men's store."

"Men's store?" His nose wrinkled.

"Mama bought me a suit." I expected him to tease me about it, but he didn't say anything. "You got one?"

"A suit? Sure. Noah's old one."

"What for?"

"Church and funerals. Ain't no other reason."

"Mama thinks they're for dances." We both laughed.

"You comin in?" I said when we pulled up in front of the store. He revved the engine. "First day on the job. Got to deliver this here hooch."

*

The place still smelled like apples. The only person in the store was a grey-haired lady with thick eyeglasses, hemming a pair of tan pants behind the register.

I cleared my throat. She looked up. "Is Mr. Boyle here?"

"He popped out for a few minutes. Be back shortly."

"Has Mrs. Rainey come by yet?"

"Why, yes." She nodded and smiled. "The two of them went to Koman's for a cup of coffee. You the Rainey boy?"

"Yes, ma'am, Jason Lee. Supposed to meet my mama here to pick up my suit."

She set her work on the counter. "It's in the back. I'll get it."

I walked over to the hat display, where Mama and

Mr. Boyle'd laughed so hard, but saw nothing funny there. I moseyed to the back, next to the clearance rack, and ran my hand over the collar of the nice black suit.

"Here it is." The woman held up a hanger covered with a black zippered bag. *Boyle's Men's Store, an Emporium of Style* was stamped on it in white letters.

She draped the bag over my arm. "I presume you know where the dressing room is."

"You want me to put it on now?"

"It's a good idea," she said. "In case something's wrong."

"I'll wait for—"

"I'm sure they'll be back by the time you're changed. They've been gone quite a while."

"Why'd they go for coffee? She knew I'd be here." The woman walked back toward the register without answering.

The jacket fit fine and the pants felt nice around my waist. When I looked down to check the length, I noticed the lace on my right sneaker had come loose, so sat on the chair to fix it, and landed on something. When I stood to see what it was, nothing was on the chair seat. I reached under the suit jacket, rubbed my hand across the back of the pants, and felt a big, protruding wad.

Mr. Boyle, the man who said tailoring was his area of expertise, the man who walked Mama to the bakery for a cup of coffee, had taken in the back seam of the pants so much there was only room for one pocket. He'd sewn that one stupid pocket smack in the middle of the butt and stuffed the material from the second pocket inside.

I took the extra pocket out, sat back on the chair, and stared at myself in the mirror. Because of Mama's insistence, the extra length on the pant legs had been turned in up past my calves and doubled back again to form cuffs. With my knees bent, the triple thick fabric shot forward, rigid as cardboard from knee to cuff. I pushed the fabric up against my legs, but when I let go, the material sprang forward again.

I'm not sure how long I sat there in my well of doom before I heard Mama's voice.

"Is everything all right, Jason Lee? The lady up front said you've been in there for some time. It must be ninety degrees in that speck of a room."

"No. Nothin's all right."

I stepped out, feeling as low as a person could. "Look." I shook the spare pocket in her face. "Look at the butt on these pants." I turned and pulled up the jacket. "How many pockets do you see? One or two?"

"Don't worry about it," she said, like it was a normal occurrence. "The jacket covers it. No need to act upset. I told Parnell to do what he had to do to make it fit. I'll let it out as you grow."

"No need to act upset? ACT upset? You ever heard of a one-pocket pair of pants on a suit before? Tell him to fix it." She stepped back and smiled at me. "Son, you look so handsome."

*

I sulked on the porch, fuming about my sorry excuse of hound's-tooth, one-pocket, thick-as-a-carpet clown suit. When Mama went to close up her office for the evening, I showed the suit to Uncle Mooks. He said, "You know, Jason Lee, a man don't really need no more than one pocket. Or one pocket watch to put in it." He smiled.

14

Over time Samson's ability for siphoning from Mr. Johnson's still had improved. All the various pickle jars named Judy eventually went from being half-full to overflowing, and the length of time between our drinkin meetins shrunk.

During one such meeting we'd been sitting on our boulder for a couple hours, coated in darkness, the river slapping below us, when Samson handed the jar back to me.

"Kill it," he said. His breath rushed at me.

The last few dribbles missed my mouth and burned my chin.

"Did you know," I slurred. "It's Armed Forces Day?"

"Nope."

Drunker than Cooter Brown, I leaned in to make sure he was paying attention. "You know about my daddy, don't you? You know he was in the armed forces?"

"Course I do."

"And that's what Armed Forces Day is for, right? To honor the men in the armed forces?"

"Yes, I do. I do know that. I know that, yes."

With the full might of Mr. J's Black Thunder in my

gut, I said, "Sometimes I hate him."

"Oh, come on."

"Because I'll never be nothin like him."

The jar slipped from my hand and rolled to the edge of the rock. We both watched it drop to the river.

"Never. No matter what I do. Nothin like him."

"Quit your whining, Jason Lee."

"First of all I don't have none of his courage."

"Courage only means you ain't afraid. What're you afraid of?"

"Mama."

"Your mama?"

"She wants for me to be brave, just like him."

"She tell you that?"

He wasn't getting my point. My voice rose. "No, but it's what everyone wants, and I can't do it. I'll never be as good as him. I wish I'd never heard of him—and he wasn't my kin."

My voice bounced off the night and came back to me with a snap. I held my breath. "I said that out loud, didn't I?"

"Sure did." His words seemed to run together. "But I ain't heard nothin."

"Swear?"

"On spit."

We both dribbled saliva into our hands and shook on it.

"Tell you what I think." He lay back on the rock and put his hands behind his head for a pillow. "The shine's gettin to your brain and you're talkin stupid. He don't hold a candle to you."

"Ha, ha, and double ha."

"Remember the time up there at Peek's place? A couple years back?"

"Never forget it."

"Me neither."

"I got no help from you or anyone."

"Didn't think so then, but you was right goin for help. Me, Elijah, and your crazy uncle, we all woulda let him die."

"Never thought you'd say somethin like that. Especially about the likes of Peek."

"Wonder what makes someone hate that much."

"Wally says his folks beat him."

"No excuse."

The night air was thick, with no stars in sight. We listened to the water slap its way downstream. I said something that wouldn't have come out of my mouth, except for the Thunder. "Saw Reba in town the other day. She looked different than in school."

"Reba the giraffe-bitch?"

"You looked at her lately? She stopped growin. And she's sorta pretty."

"No, I ain't looked at her lately. Why the hell would I want to look at her? Time to talk about somethin else."

"Don't think I feel like talkin anymore. Done too much of that already. Think I'll make my way home."

"Feel like fishin tomorrow?" he said.

"I guess."

15

My head pounded, same as always after a drinkin meetin. Samson called the condition a shineover—the stuff men are made of. I dragged myself downstairs and went straight to the porch so Mama wouldn't catch a whiff of me, the shine oozing from every pore.

Samson came by around noon for a lazy day of fishing at the river. I caught a couple hours of sleep under an oak and even though I slept more than I fished, still managed to hook six big ones—at least a pound each.

When I got home I spotted Uncle Mooks inspecting the wind spinner in the tree close to my bedroom window. A light breeze speckled the ground with the petals of a used-up dogwood.

"Look here, Uncle Mooks. Bluegill." I held out the stick I'd strung them on. He took the catch from me and brought them up to his face for inspection. "They look good."

We walked around back to the picnic table, Uncle Mooks' official cleaning station. His fillet knife and sharpening strap hung from nails at the far end of the table, and a bucket for the carcasses was stashed underneath. He pulled a rag from his pocket.

"How many fish you reckon we've cleaned out

here, Jason Lee?"

"Don't know."

He smoothed the rag on the table. "It's a good time, cleaning fish," he said. "I got time."

"Me, too, Uncle Mooks."

He sliced the bluegill and laid the fillets out on the rag, each one a masterpiece. When he was done, he looked at me and frowned. He pointed the knife toward the house.

"Cassie's actin funny. Somethin's wrong in there."

"What's wrong?"

"Not sure. She's singin to herself."

"Maybe she's happy."

"The table's set fancy."

He wrapped up the fish and handed them to me to take inside.

I dumped the fillets in the kitchen sink. When Mama came in from her bedroom wearing a silky green dress I'd never seen before, and shoes the same color, I said, "What's goin on?"

"Those are huge, Jason Lee." She smiled her approval. "I planned on makin my double-dip chicken fingers, but those'll fry up better. I hope Parnell likes fish."

"Parnell?"

"Mr. Boyle," she said, matter-of-fact. "He's comin over."

"What for?"

"Supper."

"How come?"

"Because I invited him. I told you I wanted to thank him proper."

"Coffee and donuts wasn't proper enough?"

Besides Miss Therese, nobody had been to our house for supper since my daddy's Aunt Violet stopped by on her way to Mobile for a convention. Family members and Miss Therese were one thing, but sharing a meal with the man I cursed under my breath every time I thought about the one-pocket suit that I hoped I'd never have to wear in public, just didn't set well.

Mama handed me the garden basket. "I need you to fetch us some beets. A couple each, while I set the table."

*You gonna **Boyle** em?* I thought.

"And a head of lettuce and some jubilees. Then you can get cleaned up for our company."

Our company?

My resentment powered every step. I stomped to the garden and ripped a head of lettuce from the ground with a hateful tug. "How come we're not havin *boyled* snake in the grass for dinner?" I said to no one. "It would suit *our company* better than chicken or fish." I yanked on the beet stalks like they were no better than weeds.

Why had Mama chosen that man to like? How was it she couldn't see him for what he was, a no-good con artist? And why couldn't she be honest, instead of using the lame excuse of buying a suit, to see him? Not wanting to go back inside, I studied a worm inching its way across one of the beet leaves.

When I finally stormed into the house and dumped the basket on the kitchen counter I huffed, "Does Uncle Mooks know about this?"

Mama stopped whisking the batch of eggs and lemon juice for her homemade mayonnaise and gave me a put-out look. "I don't need no one's permission to invite a friend to supper."

"You shoulda said somethin." I bolted out of the kitchen toward the stairs. The sight of the dining table stopped me in my tracks. Four of Mama's special occasion dishes with green ivy trim were laid out on a lace tablecloth. She'd put a pink cloth napkin folded like a pint-sized fan on each plate.

"You shoulda told someone," I hollered.

*

From my bedroom I heard Boyle's car pull up our drive, and I darted to the window. The setting sun cast an orange backdrop as his dark blue Buick stirred the gravel before stopping out front. He checked himself in the rear view mirror and smoothed his mustache with a small comb. He reached into the back seat to collect a thick bundle of yellow and orange lilies wrapped in the comic section of a newspaper.

I didn't change clothes. Instead, I lay on my bed in a well of loathing and listened to the sounds of laughter downstairs. After a while, Mama called for me.

"I ain't hungry," I yelled back.

She appeared in my doorway so fast she must have flown up the stairs. "Please come down right now," she said, jaw set, hand clutching the doorknob. I looked down at the shirt I'd been wearing all day.

"I ain't dressed yet. And still smell like fishin."

Her face flashed red. "You're bein impolite. Come downstairs right now."

"How 'bout my shirt?"

"Jason Lee, supper's ready now." She left.

*

I sat in my chair staring at the vase in the middle of the table, crammed with lilies. Boyle filled the fourth chair, the one that had always remained empty. He sat there, a dark intruder in a brown suit, and I was quite sure all his pockets were in their proper places.

Uncle Mooks wore his blue and white checked shirt with snap buttons.

I didn't say a word during the meal, but Boyle talked the whole time. He said he'd never tasted a cornbread salad before and went on and on about what a nice touch it was.

Mama beamed. "Thank you Parnell. I like to make it a little different each time. The tomatoes are from the garden, and the dressing's my own special mayonnaise recipe."

He said he remembered back to his own mother's mayonnaise, and blah, blah, blah.

When Mama brought out the battered fillets piled on a mountain of creamed spinach, Boyle said, "My, my, my."

Once we served ourselves and Boyle took his first bite he looked up at Mama and said, "What is this deliciousness?"

"They're bluegill. Jason Lee caught 'em. Just today. Couldn't be any fresher."

I thought, *you'd have to be an idiot not to know the fish we were eating were bluegill*.

He smiled. "It's more the way you've prepared them."

"I cleaned 'em," Uncle Mooks said.

Boyle paid no attention to him.

"What's your special ingredient, Cassie?"

She patted her mouth with the pink napkin. "I soak 'em in beer for a half hour before puttin em in the batter."

"Beer?" He stroked his mustache. "What's the old joke about the one-legged man who works in a brewery?"

"Don't believe I know that one," Mama said.

"He makes the hops."

Boyle, Mama, and Uncle Mooks all laughed like the joke was actually funny.

"Good one, Parnell," Mama said.

"Not as good as this meal. You're a woman of many talents."

"I'm pleased you like it." She straightened her bangs with her fingers.

"Many talents, indeed."

I stared at Boyle's food, willing maggots to swarm the plate. Uncle Mooks studied the pattern of the lace tablecloth. "Jason Lee caught 'em," he said, loud.

"Pardon me?" Mr. Boyle said. The forkful of sliced beets he was bringing up to his mouth stopped halfway.

"And I gutted 'em," Uncle Mooks said.

Boyle glanced back and forth at Uncle Mooks and me. The crack of a smile peeked from under his mustache. "You both did a wonderful job."

A drop of beet juice fell from his fork.

Uncle Mooks cleared his throat. "We did." He seemed satisfied with Boyle's reply.

Mama gathered our plates and excused herself to the kitchen. The dining room went silent. I kept my eyes on the beet stain soaking into the tablecloth. Nothing could put out the fire inside me.

Mama came back carrying a tray with four plates of rhubarb pie topped with vanilla ice cream.

"My goodness, Cassie, that's the best-looking pie I've ever seen."

Mama put the plates in front of us.

Uncle Mooks started eating right away, with bites so big the ice cream oozed out the corners of his mouth.

"May I be excused," I said.

"You never turn down pie, Jason Lee."

"I got a stomachache."

"Suit yourself, young man," she said and looked at Boyle enjoying his dessert. "Just suit yourself."

*

I stared out my bedroom window at the dark night. If Mama and the worst tailor in all of Mississippi, or maybe the whole United States, wanted to make fools of themselves, fine. Let her cook for him. Let her wear his ridiculous sailor hat and laugh at his stupid jokes.

Let him rot in hell wearing his proper suit to the dinner table.

The cry of a hoot owl caused me to look up. Stars splattered across the sky as if they'd been flung there with a giant paintbrush. One star blinked to get my attention.

I'll bet that's you, I thought, and tried to remember how my daddy looked in the old photographs glued onto the pages of our black picture album. One when he was a skinny boy squinting in the sun, holding his mama's hand. Some with his classmates in the official school photos, each kid standing ramrod straight. On one of them he had drawn an arrow pointed down toward his head.

Then there was the picture of him and Mama kissing on their wedding day. He was in a dark suit like the one still hanging on the clearance rack of the Emporium of Style, and Mama had on a puffy dress and a round hat. Wally and Uncle Mooks stood beside them. They all looked young as could be.

But the picture that meant the most to me, because it was the last one ever taken, was the color photo of him in his uniform, standing next to a flag. His blue eyes burned with certainty.

The idea that Parnell Boyle thought he was man enough for Mama gripped my insides and gave them a twist.

16

Not two days after Boyle came to dinner, life around our house took a confusing shift. Mama turned silent, weighed down in sadness. Her manner grew still. She didn't ask for my help with chores, and she stopped tending to them herself. Before long, she took to her bed. I was at a loss to understand what was going on.

At first, it seemed she just needed a rest. After a full week passed, she couldn't gather the strength to dress or work. She didn't set foot in her office, and she unplugged the phone cord from the wall without us realizing.

After a couple days I asked, "What about your work—the transcriptions?"

"That's nothin for you to worry about."

Soon her only reason to leave the bedroom was to use the toilet. The skin under her eyes turned dark, and I couldn't figure how she could sleep all day and still look so tired.

When a lady from the Coalition couldn't reach her by phone she came by the house to drop off the week's cassettes and see if Mama was all right. She wouldn't come out of her room but had me tell the lady she'd caught a flu bug and to give her assignments to someone else.

The phone being dead was one thing, but when we didn't show up at the Grinnin' Catfish two Saturdays straight, Miss Therese rushed over. After Mama gave her the same old flu story, her friend looked at her suspiciously.

"You don't say. Well, I'll be by every day next week to check up on y'all."

Each time she came by, Miss Therese brought a plate of leftovers from the lunch shift and a handful of the pinwheel candies from the bowl by the register.

She said her sickly father had come down from Tippah County to spend his dying days at her place, so she only stayed long enough to peek in on Mama and tell Uncle Mooks and me we were doing a fine job.

Mama's new disposition triggered a curious change in Uncle Mooks' behavior, as if he'd attended a healing meeting and the preacher put a hand to his forehead, and miraculously helped him to be more aware. The special string that weaves through the hearts of twins before they are born began its work. He grew more mindful of the fact it was her turn to be taken care of.

In the evenings he heated up the food Miss Therese brought and carried it into Mama on her favorite yellow tray bordered with delicate sweet pea blossoms. Each time he went back to her room to fetch the tray, she had barely picked at the meal. He left a candy on her nightstand.

Uncle Mooks spent less time on the porch, which meant his messy nature overflowed into the house.

Even though I was in school until three every day, there was no more shutting myself away in the solitude of my room because it was up to me to take care of the real chores. Mama had always made chores look easy, but there was nothing easy about picking up after that messy guy.

The time we ran out of clean clothes I had to wash four loads and hang each and every item on the line. I dropped two of Mama's nightgowns and a whole mess of socks in the clay soil on the way to the line. Yellow clay doesn't shake off. Wiping at it is worse, which meant another washing.

There was the evening I tried my hand at making Mama's Amalgamation cake, thinking it would be just the thing to get her back on her feet so we could all return to life the way it was before.

When I pulled the flour from the shelf it slipped out of my hand and spilled across the linoleum floor. I figured I'd clean it later, until one of the eggs dropped while I carried a handful from the refrigerator. The cleanup took some time, but I finally got back to the cake. For the first time in my life I creamed sugar into a stick of butter and sifted flower with baking soda and salt. It's harder than it looks, with all the ingredients and measurements.

While the cake baked I thought about making the meringue, but I mixed some powered sugar with milk instead. It turned out the cake needed to cool before the frosting went on, so, when I went to spread it with the the knife to get a smooth frosting layer, huge chunks broke off and messed up everything. I closed my fist into a ball and punched the cake clear through to the counter. Uncle Mooks came in and helped me salvage about half of it.

After supper I cut a thin slice for Mama and carried it to her room, fingers crossed it'd be the cure. She turned toward me in bed, sadness all over her. Her arms looked thinner than before. I moved closer. "Look here, Mama. Look what I made you."

"I'm in no mood," she said vacantly. "Take it away."

"You sure?"

She closed her eyes. The sight of her skinny arms stayed like a bookmark inside my head. I gently closed the door on my way out.

Later, Uncle Mooks and I took the rest of the cake to the porch. The song of cicadas filled the distant trees, and we listened to the end of the game. The Braves beat Pittsburgh, 4 to 3. Neither of us finished our cake. I must have confused a couple of the measurements.

The following day Parnell Boyle's Buick came up the drive. I rushed to Mama's bedroom door and gave it the shave-and-a-haircut knock.

"Mr. Boyle's here."

"No, Jason Lee."

"What should I do?"

"Say I got the flu. Now leave me alone."

I went out front and leaned over the porch rail. He stepped out of the car.

"Mama can't see you." I looked him straight in the

eye. "She's sick."

"Yes, and hello to you, too." His shoulders stiffened and he fiddled with the button on his sleeve.

"Give her my best." He got back into his car then rolled down the window. "By the way, your phone's not working."

It was hard to see Parnell Boyle without thinking about that damn suit. As I watched him drive off I had to admit I was getting scared about Mama, and I feared she might be dying. *You need a proper suit for funerals, too.*

I chewed on my fingernails. Uncle Mooks rocked back and forth more than usual. Neither one of us made mention of the problem with Mama.

*

One day while walking home from school I asked Samson if he could keep a secret.

"Course I can. You know I can. This about your daddy again?"

"Somethin's wrong with Mama." I knew she'd have a fit if she found out I said anything.

"Wrong? What kind of wrong?"

"It's hard to explain. She mostly sleeps. Like somethin bit her and sucked all her strength away. She don't seem to have the energy to care about nothin."

"Maybe it's a spell," he said, casual as a breeze.

"A spell? What d'you mean, a spell?

"Oh, brother, you don't know what a spell is?"

"I do, sorta. Heard about 'em. Do they work?"

"Sure do. Seen one with my own eyes. My Aunt

Sophie put one on her no-good neighbor lady for stealin eggs. It caused her to take to her bed, just like your ma."

"A spell did that?"

"Uhuh"

"How'd she do it?"

"Put three rusty nails in a bag with rat bones and some graveyard dirt."

"Rat bones?"

"She collects 'em," he said, matter of fact. "For such occasions."

"Okay, after she put 'em in the bag, then what?"

"She set it on the ground in plain sight of the neighbor lady's house. Then she lit a black candle and dropped it on the bag."

"How big was the bag?"

"Not too big. About the size of a lunch sack."

"How many rat bones does it take?"

"A sack full."

"Did it catch on fire?"

"Course. And after it went up in flames she said the lady's name. Said it over and over, maybe fifty times 'til there wasn't nothin left of the bag but a pile of ash. Then she stomped on the ashes three times to make sure the evil spirits'd all transferred from the bag to the lady. She stomped once more, then went back inside her own house to cook supper for Uncle Silas."

"It worked?"

"Worked good. Wasn't more'n an hour before the lady fell sick."

"An hour?"

"Uh-huh."

"Mama didn't steal no one's eggs. Besides, who'd want to put a spell on her?"

"Don't know."

Samson squinted. "Just remembered somethin important. You can take back a spell if you know how to do it."

"How?"

He shrugged. "I'll ask her."

"Who?"

"My aunt. Who else you think?"

"Does she have any extra rat bones we can use?"

"I'll ask that, too."

*

That next Saturday, Samson came up our drive walking in swift steps, holding a potato sack.

"Got it. Got rat bones, got the dirt, the candle, got it all. We'll do it by the riverbank. Bring your pole as camouflage."

"Thought it had to be in plain sight of the house."

"No, I checked. A spell can happen anywhere and be taken back anywhere, too. My aunt did it out front to make sure the no-good egg-stealin lady saw her."

"Good. I don't want Mama to see us."

When we got to the river Samson said, "We'll do it the same as my Aunt, except to reverse it we gotta say the name backwards. Best I can figure, we say Eissac."

I lit the bag. We chanted Eissac over and over until the fire dwindled to ashes and I stomped on it—one, two, and three—and then again.

*

I felt hopeful, until that day stretched into the next and Mama wasn't any better. By day three my spirits had sunk so low I slipped out back in a flash of panic, out of sight behind our chicken coop, trying to think what might happen if Mama just up and died on us. All I could figure was there'd be people coming around to evaluate me and Uncle Mooks, and my crazy Vietnam vet uncle might not pass their inspection. My head scrambled for answers, but none came. Would Mrs. Johnson take us in? Or Miss Therese? Who would be our mother?

Despite the warm afternoon sun and the calls of the sparrows, my head felt heavier and heavier as I paced behind the coop, scared of what was to become of us.

*

In the evenings I took to reading the books Wally'd given me. One night I came on a story about a fourteen-year-old boy named Emmet Till who was killed and thrown in the Tallahatchie River with a seventy-five pound cotton gin fan tied around his neck. The men who did it used barbed wire for the rope.

They killed him for talking to a white woman in a grocery store. The book said Emmet Till was an ordinary boy, except he had a stutter, and his murder was the spark that helped set the civil rights movement in motion.

It was hard to imagine that the death of a regular boy triggered that part of history, and that my daddy was the kind of man who stood up and fought for things to change.

I went to sleep thinking about Samson and Noah and Elijah and the boy Uncle Mooks saw the old bastard Peek kill.

17

Miss Therese stormed up our porch steps. "Mooks, go get Cassie."

She followed him inside and waited in the living room, her arms folded across her waitress apron. Nothing could be done too soon for Miss Therese.

It didn't take long before they appeared, side-by-side, holding hands. The sash on Mama's blue robe hung loose. Uncle Mooks held his eyes steady on the top of her uncombed hair. She didn't look too happy to see Miss Therese.

"Cassie, you need to get your butt outta bed. It's one-thirty in the afternoon." Her red hair jumped with each word spoken.

"You came out here to say that?" Mama huffed. "During lunch shift?"

Miss Therese looked at Uncle Mooks and me. "Would you two mind. I'd like to have a word with Cassie, alone."

Uncle Mooks let go of Mama's hand and pulled his watch out of his pocket. He rubbed it while he walked out the front door. I pretended to go upstairs but settled on the third step to make sure I didn't miss anything. Miss Therese lowered her voice. "I'm here to take you to Julian."

"Sorry, Therese, I ain't up to goin to Julian. I ain't goin nowhere."

"I'm here to see you get yourself up to it." Miss Therese waited for Mama to respond, but it didn't come. "You and me, we've been through too much together for me to sit still and do nothin while you hide away in your room for weeks on end. I'm hard-pressed to understand what the hell's goin on with you. Look at this place. It's a mess. Don't you think Jason Lee and Mooks could use some help around here? Don't you think they deserve better than this?

"Parnell Boyle came into the cafe and said you refused to see him." The whispering was over. I could hear much better.

"I got the flu."

"Flu Schmu," Miss Therese said, "is any of this about him?"

"Course not."

"Okay, then what?"

"I don't know." Mama paused. "Maybe it is about him, sorta."

My skin jumped. I wanted to run into the living room but didn't.

"Let's sit on down," Miss Therese said. I could tell they moved to the couch.

"Cassie, I don't really know the man, but I know the likes of Parnell Boyle ain't worth gettin yourself sick over."

"I know. You're right. It's just that I'd finally decided to move on. Thought I was ready for a new beau. But my problem's not Parnell. It's a whole lot more than that."

Despite myself I said, "What more?"

"Jason Lee?" Mama said. "Are you listenin in?"

"A little."

"You might as well come out here." She sounded deflated.

When Mama saw me, tears rolled from her eyes.

Miss Therese rubbed her arm. I sat on the chair across from them.

In a low, soft voice Mama said, "I need J.L. here."

Stunned, I blurted out, "J.L.?"

"J.L." Miss Therese nodded. "Well, now we're gettin somewhere. You wanna tell us what this is all about?"

Mama tightened the sash on her robe. "After Parnell left that night, I went to bed and thought about the evenin. That's when it hit me like a sledgehammer."

"What hit you?" I said.

"It hit me how much I've missed J.L. Through all these years I never took the time to mourn him proper. Holdin it all in. Tryin to be strong by not havin feelins."

She sat slumped, as if sitting straight took too much work. "It's like I've only been breathin in halfway since he died. And then that night the emotions smashed into me so hard I haven't been able to think of anythin but wantin J.L. beside me and havin our lives right again. I know it sounds crazy, but lately I think I can hear him."

Miss Therese gave Mama a hug and smoothed her hair. Mama's shoulders shook while she sobbed into

Miss Therese's waitress shirt.

My heart nearly broke watching the hurt pour out. The longer she cried, the more I understood she'd walked around with a broken heart for fifteen long years and never let on.

"Fetch some tissues," Miss Therese said.

I rushed to the bathroom, grabbed a handful of toilet paper and got back in no time. Mama tore off a couple sheets and blew her nose.

"Well, now that we know what set this off, we can work on gettin you back on your feet." Miss Therese smiled. "You know who Henry Tillman is?"

Mama nodded.

"I treat him real good and most often don't charge him for the hushpuppies he has every mornin with his biscuits and ham."

Mama closed her eyes and exhaled. "Is this gonna be a long story, Therese?"

"Sorry. Yesterday Henry and me were talkin about you, and my bein disturbed 'bout this melancholy business draggin on too long."

Mama scowled. "I'm not fond of bein talked about, and you know it."

"Well, lo-and-behold, this mornin he pranced in with his chest puffed up like a proud rooster. Just so happens he has a friend, who called a friend, whose brother's a doctor in Julian. Not a bone doctor. He specializes in people who find themselves slippin toward the dark side. I'm not of a mind to put it like that, but it wouldn't hurt you to talk to the man.

Name's Ratliff, and he knows what he's doin. Been written up in a medical journal."

Mama made a skeptical snort. "I don't need help. Just a little more rest and I'll come around."

I'd never known about melancholy before, but what I heard Mama say about her hearing him, and wanting my dead daddy beside her, sent me to Miss Therese's corner.

"Mama, listen to her. You don't need more rest."

Miss Therese said, "I left my lunch shift to come out here and drive you to Julian."

"Go, Mama. Maybe he can help you."

"Hush, Jason Lee."

Miss Therese stood up. "I'm not one to wait around all day. We'll be goin whether you're dressed or not."

Their eyes linked.

"I don't have an appointment." Mama said, defiant.

"Yes, you do. I made it myself. Come on, I'll help you get dressed. You never know. Maybe Dr. Ratliff's handsome and single."

"That's all I need."

Miss Therese barked orders. "Jason Lee, pour us a thermos of sweet tea for the road. And ask Mooks to locate Cassie's pocketbook. And stop bitin your nails. They're down to the quick and bleedin."

We waited in the living room, me holding the thermos by its handle and Uncle Mooks with the purse strap slung over his arm. When the two of them finally came out from the bedroom, Mama had on a baggy tee shirt and an old pair of jeans she usually wore for chores. She still looked tired, despite the part in her hair and the color on her lips. Uncle Mooks and I watched her trail behind Miss Therese toward the station wagon. She looked like a lone surviving duckling. Miss Therese's hair bounced in the afternoon sun. A glowing halo.

Ray Charles' song "Unchain My Heart" blasted from the car radio. We watched them turn in the direction of Julian. Uncle Mooks clapped, a little slow, to the memory of the music, and sang, "Set me free, oh, set me free, yeah, set me free."

I let out a laugh I didn't know was inside me, an unexpected relief. The wall around my chest relaxed its grip.

"Time's funny," Uncle Mooks said. "She ain't never takin time for herself before. I reckon this is her way of gettin some. Hope she don't take too much more."

18

Instead of marching directly into her bedroom when she got home, Mama dropped her purse on the dining table and sat down in her chair. I joined her.

"Well?" I said.

"Well, didn't think I'd like him, but Dr. Ratliff's a good man."

It was hard to hold back my excitement when she almost smiled. "What'd he say?"

"Nothin much. Nothin for you to worry about."

"But I *am* worried, Mama. Does he know what's wrong? Can he fix you?"

"He said he could, but it'll take time. He wants me back twice a week so I can talk out my troubles with him." Her eyes looked brighter, and even though she still had on her jeans and baggy tee shirt she almost looked pretty compared to earlier.

"He's gonna fix you by talkin?" I didn't care what he did as long as he could make her better.

She opened the clasp on her purse, took out two sheets of paper, and set them on the table. "Dr. Ratliff gave me these prescriptions to fill tomorrow. They're for pills with names longer than my arm. For short he called them Dexies and Bennies."

"But what'd he say's wrong?"

"A buncha mumbo jumbo."

"Come on, Mama."

"It's nothin for you to worry about. All you need to know is that he can help me. He told me so."

"I know you're all private and all, but it seems I got a right to know what he said."

"Son." She closed her eyes. "Right now I'm feelin too tired to have you badgering me." She took another piece of paper from her purse. "And I'm not sure you have any rights until you're grown, but I did write down some of the things he said. I'll let you read it, but listen to me carefully when I say, don't breathe a word."

"I won't."

There were only two lines on the paper. She must have written fast because her scribbles were as bad as his. One line said, "Delayed, incident-related, chronic depression." The other said, "Full-fledged nervous breakdown without help."

I looked up. "Nervous breakdown?"

"Like I said before, the good news is he's sure he can help me."

*

The end of June usually meant three carefree months of bare feet and lazy days, and the beginning of slow, steamy evenings watching fireflies scurry across the yard. Not that summer.

After all that time in bed with the melancholy, it seemed Mama suddenly quit sleeping. She turned restless and took the pills more often than she was supposed to. She quit going to Dr Ratliff's office and began talking up a blue streak, even to herself, and became short-tempered with Uncle Mooks and me for hardly any reason.

The day it started I was drying the lunch dishes.

"Good lord, Jason Lee, make yourself useful." Each word came out with an exclamation mark attached.

"I am, Mama. What more do you want me to do?"

"Well, for starters you can go out to the porch and tell your uncle to turn his damn radio off."

It became hard to tell what would hit her wrong.

One evening Uncle Mooks and I were on the front porch shucking corn for supper when Parnell Boyle's big Buick came up our drive. I hurried inside, irked as all get-out, and yelled, "Mama, you won't believe who just pulled up."

She yelled back from the kitchen, "Liberace?"

"No, wish it was. It's snake-oil Boyle."

She rushed into the living room and tapped her forehead with a fist. "I plumb forgot I invited him."

"You invited him? What'd you do that for?"

"Watch your attitude, young man. Parnell's a good, decent man, and I didn't treat him very nicely. He's entitled to some answers." She paused. "It just slipped my mind a little. No big deal."

"He ain't good and decent. And he's an awful tailor."

Uncle Mooks wiped his hands on his overalls bib and shook Boyle's hand. Boyle spotted me and Mama through the screen. Despite the heat, he wore a dark suit, a brimmed hat, and black shoes. He took his hat off.

Mama smiled and pulled off her apron. "Hello, Parnell."

He looked down at his hat, then raised his head and set his eyes on her. "Cassie."

I could have puked.

She draped the apron over her arm and pushed the screen open. "Come on inside. I'm runnin a little late, but supper's 'bout ready." Without even looking at me she said, "Jason Lee, kindly show Mr. Boyle to the kitchen and set the table, please. I'll be there in a minute."

Since, to me, he wasn't even dining-room company, my brain burned from disbelief that she thought enough of him to invite him to eat in the kitchen.

Boyle sank into the chair at the backside of the table by the dry sink. He placed his hat next to the remains of a pecan pie. I set out the plates and silverware, but didn't talk to him.

Mama came in shortly. "Jason Lee, go see how your uncle's doin and have him shuck a couple more ears."

I plopped on the couch, next to Uncle Mooks. "Mama wants more corn." With a head toss toward the house I added, "He's eatin with us again."

Uncle Mooks carried the corn pot as the two of us walked out to the garden. He pulled back the husks on three ears, checking the kernels for readiness, and twisted them off. He skinned them on the spot.

We went inside. Boyle looked hot, still wearing his

coat, sitting alone at the table. Uncle Mooks filled the corn pot with water and put it on the burner next to the skillet of fried chicken. The two of us sat with Boyle. I got to work chewing on my nails. It felt like an eternity, the three of us sitting there looking at each other, before Mama finally came in wearing a nice clean shirt and smelling of lavender oil.

"Hungry?" She smiled like having this intruder in our kitchen was an everyday occurrence. The three of us nodded. She turned her back to us and tended to some last-minute preparations. When finished she grabbed the bowl of mashed potatoes and a plate of beefsteaks sliced thick as bread, and brought them to the table. Her second trip was the platter of corn slathered in butter.

"I'll help, Mama," I said, anxious to escape the table.

"Stay put," she snapped, picking up the skillet of chicken. The pan shook from her unsteady hand as she carried it toward the table. I reached out to help. "Get out of the way." She joined us at the table. "Take what you want and pass it around."

What happened next made no sense. Mama, the woman who'd have nothing to do with churches or religion announced, "But first I'd like to say a prayer of thanks." She closed her eyes and reached out to Uncle Mooks and me. To my horror, she said, "Complete the circle," which meant I was to hold on to Boyle's hand.

Mama's hand shook as she squeezed my fingers. "Dear Lord," she said out of the blue. "The beginnin of the Good News of Jesus Christ, Son of God."

The pitch of her voice climbed a couple octaves. Then she thanked the Son of God for her bountiful vegetable garden. She thanked him for bringing her pills when she was in need, and she asked him to bless the hearts of those who would hurt her. I yanked my hands from both Boyle's and Mama's grip and coughed like something had gotten stuck in my throat.

"Amen," she said and looked up with a confused expression, as if she wasn't sure what'd happened. We pretended her prayer was perfectly normal and passed the platters. Boyle checked his watch.

"You got some place to be?" Mama said.

"No, quite the contrary." He flashed a smile that looked like he'd been caught at something.

"Say your piece, Parnell. You came here to say somethin, no need to take all night to get started."

"I came because you graciously invited me to join you for supper."

"That's right." Her brow crunched. "But, if you don't mind, I'd prefer you cut the charmin business. Tomatoes, Parnell?" She passed the plate abruptly. The slices shot toward the rim and quaked in her hand.

He took the plate. "Thank you."

Mama excused herself and left for the bathroom.

"She all right?" Boyle asked.

"Yes," I said. "Just went for her pills."

"What kind of pills?"

"Don't know the proper names. She calls them Bennies and Dexies."

Boyle shifted in the chair. Seeing him uncomfortable felt good.

"Don't worry. She'll be right back."

"Sorry," Mama said and slipped into her chair. She made designs with her fork in the mashed potatoes on her plate. "Parnell, about me not returnin your calls, it's only right I explain."

"I'd rather have this conversation alone, just between the two of us." He fiddled with the left side of his mustache.

"Fair enough."

Mama jumped up five or six times during the meal to tend to one thing or another. When we finished she took the supper plates to the sink and put on a pot of coffee. Soon the agreeable rhythm of the percolator on the stove filled the room. She pulled four delicate dessert plates down from the cupboard shelf.

"These were my Mama's," she said and turned toward the table. All four plates dropped to the floor. One shattered and sent bits of china across the linoleum toward our feet.

She clamped her hands on the top of her head. "What have I done? Sorry, sorry, it's nothin. Just a slip. I'll get it."

"It's okay, Mama." I jumped up and rushed for the broom and dustpan.

She took them from me and yelled, "Damn it, Jason Lee, I said I'll do it. Make yourself useful and get another plate."

The little shards clattered against the dust pan as

she swept. When she had finished, she straightened her shirt and smiled at Boyle. "Coffee, Parnell?"

Just like after her prayer, we pretended nothing unusual had happened.

"Yes, please. Black."

She served the pecan pie and joined us back at the table. Then, whatever edge Mama was on, Mr. Boyle pushed her off when he checked his watch for the second time.

"What'd it say?" she said, like he'd committed a crime. She stood up, causing her chair to pitch backward and slam on the floor. "What did your watch say?" All five words bounced out like spit balls. "It's time you get going? It's finally time you get the hell out of here? I don't understand why you're here at all, checkin your wristwatch. You get out of my house and don't come back."

The shocked look on his face made my heart soar, but the truth be told, I was just as shocked. I'd never heard her talk to anyone like that in my life, and I'd never seen her act so, well, crazy. She looked down at the tipped-over chair and her mouth trembled. Her shoulders and head shook. Right then, seeing her that way, I wasn't sure our lives would ever get back to normal.

Boyle rustled himself from his chair and went over to Mama. He drew a handkerchief from his back pocket and offered it to her.

"Thank you, Parnell." She wiped her nose. "I'm sorry I'm such a mess, but I'd still appreciate it if you left."

He reached for his hat, stood tall, and looked down at her. "You're right, it's best I leave."

Mama stayed put, but I followed him into the living room. He made it to the front door, turned around and yelled out, "Jason Lee mentioned you're taking pep pills."

She came through the kitchen door and shot me her look.

"Get out," she yelled at him.

His face flushed, his mouth grew taut, his eyes pinched, and all of snake-oil Boyles politeness vanished. He pointed his hat at her.

"Listen, missy. I've seen what happens to people who take those pills, and I'm here to tell you, your days are short on this earth. You're an addict." He stuck the hat on his head.

She raised her arm and pointed at him. Her hand shook. In a voice I didn't recognize she said, "I believe Dr. Ratliff knows better than you. He's on familiar terms with my condition. And he's a doctor. You're not."

"You're a goner if you don't get help soon."

She continued to point at him. "Well, Mister I-Know-Everything. Like I said, Dr. Ratliff's helpin me. Why can't you hear that? And, he wouldn't do nothin to hurt me. Besides, what do you know about my life?"

"Nothing. But I know what those pills did to my sister." Then he yelled out, "They killed her."

Panic lit into me.

"What the hell's wrong with you?" Mama growled, like his words hadn't fazed her. She wiped her nose again with his handkerchief and shook it at him as if to shoo him away. "I don't need no help."

"They killed her," he said again as he turned and went out the door.

*

I was happy she wouldn't be seeing any more of Boyle, but couldn't get his harsh words out of my head. *You're an addict. They killed her.*

The next day, when she swatted a fly on the kitchen table and beat on it for a good five minutes, I turned desperate, and did the unbelievable. I called him.

*

His Buick pulled up. He'd swapped his suit for tan pants with pressed creases and a plaid shirt. Mama rushed to the screen door, fuming mad, with her mouth set and her hands planted in the pockets of her dress. It looked a couple sizes too big. She pushed open the screen door and charged out to the porch toward Boyle.

"I don't intend to start up anything with you so mind your own business and stop pokin your nose in mine."

He stood at attention and let her have her say, then set his eyes toward her stormy glare. "Rest assured I'm no longer interested in anything to do with you, either, or this absurd family." Boyle gestured around the porch and across the monkey-laden railing and continued, "Completely void of any of the social graces. You can be sure this isn't a social call."

"It's more like a poking-your-nose-where-it-don't-belong call." She looked like she might lose her balance. "There's nothin for you to do here, Parnell, except be in the way and check your watch every five minutes."

Mama turned back to the screen and went inside.

"Come in," I said.

She looked at me in disbelief. "What's goin on?"

"I called him. You ain't right."

He motioned to the chair across from the couch. "May I sit down?"

I nodded.

Mama said, "No. Why can't everyone just mind their own business?"

"Hear him out. You ain't right."

She parked herself on the couch across from him and closed her arms around herself.

I leaned against the doorway to the kitchen where I could stay out of the way but still see and hear them.

"Jason Lee told me you're taking Dexedrine and Benzedrine. Is that right?"

"It's none of your business what pills I take," she said to him, but looked straight at me. "And I'd appreciate it if you'd stop blabbin your mouth all over the county and keep our private business private. Good lord, Jason Lee, I'm your mother." She picked pretend lint off her dress.

"Cassie," Boyle said. "The doctor should have given you one prescription or the other. Dispensing both is reckless."

"Reckless? He's an M.D. You're nothin but a tailor

givin out medical advice. And you're callin him reckless?"

Boyle looked up. "Come in here, boy." I went over but didn't sit. "It's pretty clear she doesn't want to admit she needs help, but it's you who's going to find her dead one day. In her bed, on the kitchen floor, outside, or maybe right here on the couch where she's sitting now."

My stomach pinched. I looked at Mama, imagining it happening. I'd imagined it before, during the melancholy.

Mama's head shook. "What kind of monster are you, sayin such things?"

"I know you don't think much of me. The feeling's mutual, but you need to know what's going to happen, then I'll leave.

"I already told you to do that," she said.

Uncle Mooks had slipped outside into the yard.

I motioned my finger toward the door. "Should I get him?"

Boyle nodded.

When we were all seated he said, "My sister died from ignorance, and since then I've studied this addiction to make sense of what happened to her. These aren't just any pills. It doesn't take a person more than three weeks before the dependency takes hold."

"Thank you very much for comin out here and givin your speech. You can leave now." She crossed her arms again.

"No," I said. "Let him have his say."

"Thank you, boy."

"My name's Jason Lee."

Boyle talked over me. "Cassie, it's important for you to know that these poisons attack the brain."

Mama frowned. "My brain's fine."

"Then the brain tells the body to burn up more energy than it should. Then the body works overtime to obey the brain and uses up everything it can." Boyle's tone was as insistent as a jackhammer. "It affects the nerves, the hormones, and pretty soon the heart works so hard to help, it can't keep up, and you're dead. All I'm saying is it's an addiction, and over time it requires larger and larger doses. Cassie, look around you. Look at your boy. You have to think of him."

It was almost the same thing Miss Therese said to get Mama to go to the doctor and get the pills in the first place. I had to admit that they weren't doing her any good, despite the doctor's best intentions.

"Mr. Boyle," I said.

"You stay out of this," Mama snapped. "You've done enough." She got off the couch and charged into the bathroom.

"Okay," Boyle said leaning forward, looking from Uncle Mooks to me. "There's a clinic in Hattiesburg. He pulled a brochure from his shirt pocket and handed it to me.

I read it out loud for Uncle Mooks. "Delta Community Substance Abuse Services, celebrating 20 years." Below the headline was a picture of a building with a blue awning over the front door. On the inside, another picture showed a nurse with her arm over the shoulder of a patient. They were both smiling.

I scratched my arm, feeling an attack of hives.

Mama came back to the couch. There'd been no toilet flush, which meant she'd gone for more pills. I couldn't let that happen anymore.

"Mr. Boyle brought this here brochure." I reached to give it to her. She flinched like I'd offered her a basket of snakes. Her hands shook and she pointed at the brochure. "That's no place for someone like me." She looked scared as an injured bird.

Boyle started again. "You can't live like this much longer, and the people at Delta Community can help."

"Mama, please," I said, desperate, and surprised as hell to be taking snake-oil Boyle's side. "If they can help you, you gotta give it a try."

She used a fingernail on her right hand to clean under the nails on her left. "I can't."

"You can. I know you can. You have to. You have to go, for me."

Uncle Mooks got up and lumbered over to her. "This ain't right," he said. "You ain't right."

He reached in his pocket and took out his watch. He rubbed the face with his thumb, studying the numbers. "It's time, Cassie." He put the watch in her hands. "Take this with you."

"Melvin, not you, too."

"I can't never get fixed. But you can."

Mama bent her neck back to look into his face. They both tried to smile but couldn't get there. Their chins dimpled and they nodded to each other.

"Me and Jason Lee need you fixed." He placed his hand on her cheek.

She looked over at me. "If it's what you want." Her voice was drained. "I'll look at it. That's all, just a look."

Boyle popped up from the chair. "I'll take her right now before she changes her mind. Jason Lee, bring me the pills she's taking. They're going to need them."

I rushed to the bathroom and put the pill bottles in a little tote bag. I ran to the kitchen and added a banana and the last three pinwheel candies in the drawer.

We all walked Mama to the car. Before Boyle opened the door, her long hug surrounded me with a moment of calm. After we kissed, she said, "Stay strong, like your daddy was."

"You're the strong one, Mama."

"She'll be fine," Boyle said.

Just like the time Miss Therese took her to Julian, Uncle Mooks and I stayed on the porch until they drove out of sight. We sat next to each other, hands on our knees, shoulders touching. I studied the blue veins bulging through his hand and the rough, red patches of hives on mine.

Even with him next to me, the air turned quiet and covered me with emptiness. Hattiesburg was the farthest distance Mama and I'd ever been apart.

"Is she gonna be okay?" I asked. "What's gonna happen?"

"Time'll tell." His head bobbled a slow yes. "Small don't mean weak."

After a while Uncle Mooks pointed to his head wound. "It was bad."

I knew he meant Vietnam and hoped he'd stay relaxed.

"Gooks got me. Whatever you do, don't get in their way."

"I won't."

"Some of us wasn't no better than them. Killin children and all." He looked out toward the road. "But they won't be doin no more of that."

19

Uncle Mooks left the porch for the privacy of his room. I figured he had the right idea and went upstairs to mine, too. When I sat on my bed, all I could think about was Mama and how scared or sad she was, like me. Or, maybe she was still plain old mad.

I decided to write her a note for when she returned later, and reached into my backpack for the spiral notebook and stubby pencil inside. The pencil wrote thick on the page.

Dear Mama. That's how far I got when I realized I'd never written to her before, except on my homemade Mother's Day and birthday cards.

Uncle Mooks and me are getting along, eating proper and brushing our teeth regular. Lame, I thought when I read it. And stupid considering it was a mess of lies, except for the getting along part. I tried again. *Dear Mama, Without you here, the house is too quiet, and it feels like there's no paint on the walls.* No, I thought, that would make her feel worse.

I crushed the paper into a tight ball and tossed it at the wastebasket. It bounced off the rim and landed behind the most recent stack of books Wally'd given me. When I got up to fetch it and try again my arm smacked into the books. They tumbled over and slid across the floor. I wondered if this was the way my life was going be from now on, with everything I tried turning into a big mess. I reached to straighten them up.

Under a book titled, *The Many Faces of the Civil War* was a small notebook about the size of the one I sometimes carried in my back pocket. But this one was handmade. The front and back covers were cut from a marbled composition book and held together with a mess of masking tape. I opened it.

A surge of excitement shot through me when I saw the name *Jason Lee Rainey* hand printed on the inside cover.

> *Sat Mar 6, 1965, 10 pm — Selma. Got off the bus about noon, pumped up like a kid on Christmas morn. Could feel the electricity in the air. Found the George Washington Carver project. All the bldgs look alike. Finally found Spam's place. We hadn't laid eyes on each other since the Moore march. Hardly recognized him. He'd blown up some 45 pounds.*

I held the notes from my daddy's trip to Selma. Sure enough, they were his notes. My first instinct was to run downstairs to show Uncle Mooks, but a streak of possessiveness came over me and I decided I needed to keep it to myself. I settled back on my bed to savor being alone with the most important thing I'd ever held.

I wasn't here more than 20 minutes before we walked to Brown Chapel to take part in a Right-To-Vote protest from the church to the courthouse —2pm. The big one's tomorrow.

I didn't expect to see so many whites here, but today's march was organized by a white Rev. from Birmingham - Ellwanger. A bunch of his followers came with him. The group was small compared to what they expect for tomorrow, but still the biggest march I've been in so far. Being heckled from the sidelines by a bunch of ignorant douchebags was tough, but I controlled my hotheaded tendencies and stayed calm. #1 rule - nonviolence. I'm proud of myself for keeping my eyes straight ahead through all the spitting and name calling.

5 or 6 sheriffs were stationed on the steps of the courthouse. Then the head of the posse, a real asshole, read a telegram from the President of Ellwanger's church, saying he didn't represent them. The asshole spit chaw next to Rev. E's shoe and said, "What do you say to that?" Rev. E stood up to him eye to eye and said, "He's entitled to his opinion." I could tell the head sheriff douchebag didn't want to, but he moved aside. We marched up the steps as a unit, tense but determined. Ellwanger read his statement outlining our aims: To make it easier for Negroes to register to vote, and to stop police brutality and intimidation. That was it. It took no more than 15 minutes, and we headed back.

I stopped reading and said, "douchebag," to try the word out. Then, "douchebag Ratliff" came out of my mouth. "God damn douchebag Ratliff. God damn son-of-a-bitch douchebag quack Ratliff."

The word felt good.

> *That's when the fun started. A whole bunch of douchebag protesters (protesting us protesting) lined up their cars on the south side of the street. When we got close they revved their engines and a god-awful smell blew all over the place. They'd put limburger cheese on their manifolds. Limburger cheese, for christ sake. You'd have to be a double douchebag to put something that smells like vomit, or diarrhea, on your own car.*
>
> *A whole mess of coloreds were on the other side of the street. 100 or so. They didn't do much but watch, but before long they started to clap in rhythm and sing "We Shall Overcome." Then the car douchebags waved a confederate flag and sang "Dixie" even louder. When we got back to the safety of Brown Chapel we shared a good laugh.*
>
> *It was a rough day—but I feel good about what we did. Had thoughts of what the freedom riders went through back in '61. And William Moore. What a man of conviction he was to go it all alone. I vowed to march in his honor tomorrow, the <u>Big One</u>. On to Montgomery! I've got to admit I'm nervous as hell, but can't let on.*

Every pen stroke on the page felt like a gift. Christmas, Easter, my birthday. Fifteen years of them all strung together forming sentences written in blue ink. I studied the rightward slant of his longhand and realized the loops on his y's and g's were so close to mine I could have put them there.

Hearing stories about him was one thing, but holding that small book in my hands gave me a sensation of closeness I'd never known before. Closeness to the real man. And the whole idea of doing right for others, just because it's right, consumed me. I ran my hand over the open page to see if his pen had left grooves in the paper. It hadn't. The smoothness under my fingers made me ache to read on.

> *Bloody Sunday, Mar 7, a day I'll never forget—hopefully, a day no one will ever forget — Written Mar 8, 11am.*
>
> *I want to get as much of this down as I can remember. Yesterday started out calm enough and ended up in a clusterfuck. We met at Brown Chapel in the a.m. A huge crowd, maybe 600 of us, eager to make history. Friends among strangers, brothers in the cause —ignorant as sitting ducks. Around 3 p.m. Lewis and Williams gathered us. First we knelt and prayed, then they led the way for what we thought was to be a five-day march to Montgomery.*
>
> *****Hosea Williams SCLC and John Lewis, SNCC—two true heroes. One day I'm going to work with them.*

Starting out, I had the sense something was off. The streets felt eerie. No police in sight. We marched double file, not much talking going on, just the sound of shoes scuffing. My chest swelled with the meaning of what we were doing.

But when we got to the highest part of the bridge, the marchers in front had stopped. Spam pointed. Beyond the marchers up front was a wall of Alabama troopers in blue helmets waiting. Behind them was a whole mess of douchebags waving confederate flags. Someone might have known, but us peons had no idea Gov. Wallace ordered the march to be stopped. Hell, he probably ordered them to beat us, too.

The troopers charged up the bridge and everything went to hell. The poor saps up front had no choice but turn around and jam against the rest of us. Everything happened like a blur. Just writing about it kicks my adrenalin into high gear, and I'm pissed as hell all over again. I'm sure I'll remember more later, but a little girl ran past, out of nowhere, then the fumes hit me. My nose first, then eyes. I couldn't get air in my lungs. They burned like a motherfucker. All I could hear were screams and people gasping from the tear gas. I ran for the girl and picked her up to get her out of the way, but had to let her go when one of the douchebags, a shit-bastard on horseback, started to beat me with a rubber hose wrapped in barbed wire. He wouldn't let up. The horse reared, its hoof hit my arm, and the man kept right on pounding on me. I crouched to the wet pavement. Wet with blood. Mine. Spam tried to pull me away but got hit, too.

I passed out and woke up in another stinking cell, dried blood all over me. None of the authorities gave a shit. After they released me, three of the marchers put me in the back of their station wagon and got me to Good Samaritan. Waited five hours before getting sewn up—16 stitches on my head and 47 to the shoulder. I'm sorer than I've ever been in my life, and bruised, and proud. Damn proud. BLOODY SUNDAY PROUD!

Spam's ok, but some 50 + were beaten pretty bad, including John Lewis.

****Sheriff Jim Clark. A name to remember. The worst of the worst. The face of evil.

Too engrossed to move, I had to stop reading and took a deep breath. I was exhausted with emotions that ranged from hatred to pride, with a sprinkling of envy. I thought back to the first time Mama told me he'd gotten those stitches across the back of his shoulder. "He did it so you and Samson could be friends," she had said. I remembered how the word "Selma," came out all proud, but back then I was way too young to understand any of what I was reading.

It was a lot to digest. I played it all back in my mind, but instead of thinking about it happening to him, it felt like it had happened to me. I heard the cries and smelled the fear. In my playback I was a man of action, the one battling back, slaying the troopers one by one, and after that, I carried my daddy and John Lewis out of harm's way.

When my reverie ended and I was back in my room in Hadlee, I wrote down the name Sheriff Jim Clark on my own tablet, with four asterisks.

> *Mon, Mar 8, 4 pm — Haven't moved off Spam's couch all day (it's my bed, too). Still in shock about yesterday, playing it over and over in my head. Still sore as hell. Shoulder's still throbbing like a mother, even with a double dose of codeine. Still proud, and still pissed. Nonviolence, my ass.*
>
> *Wanted to tell Cassie about the biggest day of my life so far. Tell her how much I miss her and wish she was here too, but I'll have to walk a couple blocks to a phone booth because Spam doesn't have one. Maybe tomorrow.*
>
> *Mon, Mar 8, 9 pm — Found out Spam's real name is Arnold Jefferson Monroe. How about that for a name – a traitor and two presidents. And I came to understand the reason for his nickname, and the extra 45 pounds. Spam and eggs for breakfast, a deviled Spam sandwich for lunch, then Spamburgers and Southern Comfort for dinner.*
>
> *We ate in front of the TV and watched the lead story on the <u>NATIONAL</u> news. Our story! Right there on TV we watched the whole mess. Heard the screams. Saw the horses stampede, and the*

smoke so thick it looked like footage of a war. My lungs burned again, just watching. Then, lo-and-behold, I saw myself getting clubbed. I'd worried about the little girl, and just about cheered when I saw a man pick her up and run with her. We switched from ABC to NBC to CBS and back again.

Spam and I passed the whiskey between us and celebrated like the march was a success. Then it dawned on me that Cassie probably watched me being clobbered on TV. Signing off to find that pay phone.

P.S.

Cassie saw the news. Wants me to come back NOW, but that ain't going to happen.

I stopped reading to do some figuring. All of this happened only three months before they got married. I propped a pillow against the wall and leaned my head back, overwhelmed by the hugeness of what I'd read. That one little book, about half the size of a paperback, held much more than notes on a march. It taught me something about both of my parents that I would have never known. Even so, I couldn't shake the wave of disappointment that hit me because I never knew him, or any other man like him. The sense of loss engulfed me. I slouched down and sobbed.

My head bobbed and my eyes popped open. Startled that sleep had gotten hold of me, I scooted myself upright again and reached for the journal that slipped down onto the bed next to me.

Tue, Mar 9, 10 pm — *This was another horseshit, bullshit, piece of shit day. I have to get a handle on my feelings, but dammit, I came here to be a part of this.*

News spreads fast as greased lightning in the projects, and we woke up to word that MLK himself asked those who could to stay, to march to Montgomery later today. This morning I wouldn't have left for anything. I felt like fate had laid its hand squarely on my throbbing shoulder.

On top of asking us to stay, he put out a call for more supporters from all over to come to Selma and help out. Believing in what we're all here for, I took a double dose of codeine and went to Sylvan St. to hand out flyers to supporters coming in by busloads. The church was packed. No matter where I went folks were singing hymns or protest songs. The best part—with my sling and the hospital dressings on my head, I was sought after like someone important. The newcomers who'd watched us on TV wanted to hear all about it, and I was interviewed by a newspaper man from the state of Oregon.

The march was to begin at 2:15pm. I couldn't see him up front, but King led the way from the church to the river. I was more nervous than on Sunday, but got my confidence back because of the headcount alone. Lots of people. I'd say triple Sunday's count. When we reached the bridge, the douchebags were on the far side, just like before.

> By King's orders, we stopped at the bridge, then turned around and marched back to the church. I was pissed, to say the least, and caused one hell of a commotion. Some of the marchers around me had to calm me down.
>
> I cooled off later when Spam told me King filed a court order to prohibit the police from stopping us, and the judge needed more time for his ruling. With all the people who'd come to help, King knew he had to make a gesture, even if nothing came of it.
>
> The news people called today's march Turnaround Tuesday. My shoulder's still hurting like hell, but after meeting Abernathy and Young this evening, I'm feeling pumped again, and I'm sure we WILL make it to Montgomery.
>
> Went for a dinner at Walker's Cafe. Spam's friend Eddie owns the place. Funny guy. Talks a lot.
>
> ****Judge Frank Minis Johnson. Right now he's the only man who can make it happen.

The squeal of the screen door brought me back to the reality of my upside-down life in Hadlee. Uncle Mooks had returned to the porch, most likely to wait for Mama to come back from Hattiesburg. I figured it'd be a while, and nothing short of her actually pulling up the drive could budge me from my room, or the soul-stirring trip I was on. Deep in my bones I knew it was the unconquerable spirit of my daddy that brought me the journal that told of everyday people carrying out acts of bravery, and gave me permission to read it.

Wed, Mar 10, 8:30 pm — Stayed on the couch for another day of rest and recoup. We're in a holding pattern while we wait for a decision from Judge Johnson. Some think it'll take as long as a week.

Spam's neighbor came by with the latest news to spread through Selma. Three white men were beaten with a 2 by 4 last night outside Eddie's place—not long after Spam and I left.

Thurs, Mar 11, 9:25 pm — Earlier today I was anxious for something to happen, and sort of feeling out of place. This thing's dragging out. Thought about going home until the plans are more concrete, but then we got word that one of the men who'd been beaten didn't make it—name's Rev. Reeb. When I heard that, I realized it could have been Spam and me if it'd happened earlier. The newspaper said the four douchebags charged in the assault were already free on bond. What a roller-coaster we're on.

Today the leadership dug in their heels and vowed to remain on Sylvan St until we can leave for Montgomery. About 300 of us went down there. All we did was stand on a patch of asphalt by the church. Those close to Reeb were shook to the core.

A folded newspaper clipping was attached with

yellowed scotch tape to the next page of the journal. I pulled at it slowly, a fraction at a time, until it broke free and I unfolded it. The paper had turned soft from age and the ink was worn off along the creases, but you could still see the picture of a group of people standing under tarps and umbrellas, from the *Selma Times-Journal*, Friday, March 12, 1965. The caption under the picture read:

DAMP DEMONSTRATORS — A group of Civil Rights demonstrators sought shelter under makeshift covers of polyethylene as they ended their second night of "vigil" in the street near Brown Chapel on Sylvan Street. The group was informed by Mayor Joe Smitherman at noon today that they would not be permitted to march. The white rope in the foreground marks the boundary line for the demonstrators who have orders to remain behind what they have termed "The Berlin Wall."

Under the clipping was his entry for that day.

Fri, Mar 12, 11 pm — It rained all day. A march to the courthouse was called but the police stopped us at the end of Sylvan. The commissioner tied a rope across the street as a barrier, so we stayed put. I didn't really care. Everyone prayed, sang songs, and talked about Reeb. I finally tossed the worthless umbrella I had and let the rain wash over me.

I studied the picture, the darkness in the sky, the white rope attached to the telephone pole, the trees barren of leaves. But there was no way to make out where my daddy was. I imagined myself there alongside him in the rain, the smell of wet asphalt under my feet, tossing my umbrella.

> *Mon, Mar 15, 8:30 am — On the bus coming back from Hadlee. Decided to go for the weekend. As much as I wanted to stay in Selma, I went to see Cassie, let her see me, and try to patch things over. She was one upset girl. Said if I came back to Selma she wouldn't speak to me again, ever. She's kinda cute when she's that mad, all huffs and pouts. I'll smooth things over with her after we've made it to Montgomery.*
>
> *Mon, Mar 15, 8:45pm — When I got back to the project this morning, the mood around here was sparked with high spirits, which was what I needed. LBJ, the god-damned president of the USofA, finally pledged his support for a peaceful demonstration and said he intended to send a bill to congress. Spam and I stayed home and watched him address Congress. I couldn't believe my ears when he ended his speech by saying, "and we shall overcome."*
>
> *When he was finished with the speech Spam looked at me and said, "We're riding in a boat heading toward change."*

Tues, Mar 16, 8:35 pm — A sit around and wait day. I'm pretty much healed. No more pain in my ribs or arm, but today my shoulder's acting up. It could be infected, but I'm not saying anything to anyone. The whining's over.

Even though Selma's the biggest town I've been to, I feel like I belong here. I could live here.

Wed, Mar 17, 10:30 pm — Today the judge ruled in our favor, finally. The State of Alabama CANNOT BLOCK THE MARCH. Finally, it's time for action. Time to do what we came for. Judge Frank M. Johnson, Jr. made it happen.

We went to dinner to celebrate, and a lady named Viola joined us at our table. I nearly fell over when she said she'd left her five kids and husband home in Detroit to drive here after seeing Bloody Sunday on TV. She drove all by herself. She's not here because of a church, or a political agenda—she's here because she was moved to help. I swear, if she wasn't married and twenty years older than me, I might have proposed right then and there.

Spam and I reminisced about our feeble attempt to finish the Moore march, then after a few more beers, I told both of them about Cassie and how I'm sure she's the one. Spam said she sounds too good to be true, I must have made her up. Viola said I'd better not let her slip away.

Spam's in the other room putting together a

spur of the moment party with some of the other marchers staying in the project.

Thu, Mar 18, 4pm — *Last night's party got pretty wild. We needed to blow off steam, and the consumption of a great deal of malt liquor and Kentucky Gentleman bourbon kept our fear of the unknown at bay. Each one of us was a member of the brotherhood of freedom fighters.*

TODAY? Too hungover to care, but managed to make my way to the clinic to get my stitches checked out. The doc said it looks pretty bad, then gave me a bottle of pills. He said I should curtail any more civil rights antics until the infection quiets down. Who says "curtail and antics"? Dickwads, that's who.

The next page had another clipping from the Selma paper taped to it. I freed that one faster than the first, with less apprehension. Under the clipping, instead of a journal entry, he had written: *There can never be a reversal for what's right. Douchebags can't prevail, nature won't allow it.*

There was no photo on the clipping, just a heading. REVERSE MARCH CANCELLED TODAY. It was circled, with the word douchebags scribbled across in green marking pen.

BIRMINGHAM (AP)—Former Mayor Art Hanes had announced Thursday that he would stage an all white combination march motorcade from

Montgomery to Selma to protest the 50-mile civil rights march by demonstrators. He said then he would go through with it despite the governor's speech to the Alabama Legislature.

Today Hanes said he is cancelling his plans, and would bow to Gov. George Wallace's appeal for citizens to "stay away from the scenes of tension."

Hanes had planned to lead marchers from the state capitol in a show of protest against a civil rights trek being mounted by Dr. Martin Luther King Jr. from Selma to Montgomery.

Hanes, who in 1962 closed all Birmingham city parks rather than integrate them said, "I will not organize or lead a parade on Sunday, even though I have had overwhelming support state-wide for such a move."

Hanes, in a sharp attack on King and civil rights demonstrators, added that "King and his crowd may have overrun us, but they will never overcome us."

In today's statement, Hanes said he announced such plans "for the purpose of pointing out to the federal judiciary the potential danger in such a reckless course (the rights march), for certainly the decent white people have just as much right to demonstrate as do King and his agitators."

"The President and the federal judiciary have stated that demonstrations, marches, chaos and revolution in the streets is the proper way to redress grievances. We have seen over the past many weeks what this action has done to the long suffering, self-restrained citizens of Alabama.

"And we know that such a policy as advocated by the President and federal judiciary is wrong," Hanes said.

I folded up the clipping and stuck it back in its place. Part if me wanted to skip forward a few pages and be dead center in the middle of the march to Montgomery, to grab a piece of the triumph. The other half wanted to go back to the first page and start over, taking pleasure in every word.

> *Fri, Mar 19, 9pm — It's mind-blowing how many more marchers have come to Selma after seeing the violence on TV. The place is a sea of people moving with the tide of change, anxious to do something meaningful, looking as confident and optimistic as I looked on my first day.*

> *Sun, Mar 21, 11:20pm — We got to Brown Chapel at 5am, pumped on caffeine. We stood out front on Sylvan, for what seemed like hours beyond the posted start time. Everyone was singing "We Shall Overcome" and "Ain't Gonna Let Nobody Turn Me 'Round" over and over until MLK finally arrived. The joke is, we were on CPT, colored people time.*
>
> *Helicopters buzzed overhead like loud, giant insects. The air was filled with hope and eagerness and anticipation. I was pumped to the max.*

Finally, we left the church. There had to be at least 5,000 people from all across the USofA. Besides us regular folks there were politicians, people from labor unions, and churches. Spam and I stayed with the people from the project. We walked six abreast toward the bridge. The worthless Alabama Guardsmen didn't do more than watch the douchebags on the sidelines throw their usual insults and threats. We drowned them out with civil-rights songs.

Once it was clear, really, finally clear, that no trouble waited at the bottom of the bridge, we linked arms. I wasn't nervous anymore, just committed to the cause and confident enough to let my soul burn with pride. That's the moment I realized my life had changed. I wasn't a lone rebel butting heads with the douchebags, I was a small part of a large movement. All questions I had about my future were over.

TV crews carrying giant cameras scrambled to get in front of us. We filled the two lanes of Jeff Davis Hwy, heading east for the first eight miles of the march. I felt drunk with self-respect, even after finding out Spam and I wouldn't be able to go the whole way to Montgomery.

It seems you can't have too many court orders, so another one was issued for Lowndes County, limiting the number of marchers to three hundred. Their bullshit reason? SAFETY!! —because the highway narrows to two lanes. It's just an attempt to slow down the momentum. It'll take two days to get through Lowndes.

Bevel picked a team of 300 marchers. They'll spend their nights in fields. I sure would have liked to be a part of it, but accept my fate. Some folks came back to Selma in chartered buses but Spam and I hung around too long, so we had to settle for the back end of a stake truck.

A mountain of disappointment fell on me when I read he wasn't allowed to continue. It seemed to me he'd accepted being left behind too easy. I imagined myself there, going up to Dr. Martin Luther King Jr. himself, looking him in the eye, and saying, "Sir, J.L. Rainey came here to march, and if getting beaten on the bridge, hospitalized, and jailed isn't enough to qualify him to be one of the Lowndes County people, what is?" When my voice boomed, "Answer me," out loud, I brought my hand across my mouth, worrying Uncle Mooks might have heard me.

Mon, Mar 22, 10:40 — Watched the news. First thing this am MLK, Mrs. King, Hosea Williams, Rev. Bevel, Lewis, Young and the rest left the camp to walk in the chilling rain, through swamp and farmland. Spam's right, if anyone deserves to be there, it's them. Besides, the shoulder's killing me.

Tue, Mar 23, 11:55pm — Rain—all day. Sat around and shot the shit with the neighbors, then went down to Sylvan Street. I'm getting antsy,

> and looking forward to tomorrow when we can join in again at the County line. Never thought I'd say this, but with all the new supporters and reporters arriving, I'm getting tired of recounting Bloody Sunday.
>
> This afternoon, it was pointed out to me that I use the word douchebag a lot. Ha, ha, yes I do.

I laughed. "Douchebag," I said. When I turned the page, I was excited to see another newspaper clipping. Another nugget of information he wanted to pass along to me.

The *Selma Times-Journal*, Tuesday, March 23, 1965. LOWNDES SHERIFF VIEWS MARCH, by Rex Thomas

Haynesville, Ala. (AP)—"I feel like any other good citizen. This march is uncalled for. It's a lot of expense for nothing. It's disrupting the people in their homes and on the highway."

This is how Sheriff Frank Ryals of Lowndes County feels about the civil rights march. He says he is doing all he can to get Dr. Martin Luther King Jr. and his civil rights marchers safely through the rural county "without anything happening."

Only one Negro is registered to vote in the county where Negroes outnumber the 3,000 white residents 4 to 1. The Negro acquired that right only a week ago.

The white residents are unyielding in their conservative beliefs, and Ryals is no exception. He agrees with the angry outcries that the march to Montgomery is unlawful, "but the federal courts and federal government make their own laws," he said.

"We have been getting along fine here," the sheriff protested. "And we will continue to unless they come in here with a whole lot of this unlawful stuff and this provocation.

"We don't like our government backing these agitators. I think the people would go along a lot farther if the government would back up the law."

Ryals has been sheriff 10 years. In that decade, he reflected, "we have not had any serious trouble especially racial kind."

The sheriff has little respect for the white demonstrators who come in from other states to join the civil rights movement.

"I'm sure that some of them are good people," he conceded. "But most of them I've seen are beatniks and screwballs and people like that.

"I don't think these professional agitators would be satisfied with anything you gave them."

>*Fri, Mar, 26, Noon* — *On Wednesday, we caught a shuttle to the county line. Can't explain how good it felt to fall in behind the leaders, walking through puddles and doing what's right. On that second to the last leg, I didn't feel any pain in my shoulder and could have walked forever. Toward evening we stopped at Catholic school yard— St. June.*

MLK'd rallied a shitload of celebrities to join us for a "Stars for Freedom" rally. Spam and I climbed up a tree for a birds-eye view of the flatbed they set up as a stage. We watched more people than I'd ever seen in my life mill around for three butt-numbing hours before anything happened. (CPT).

Finally, Tony Perkins jumped up on stage and talked about why we're all here and how we will prevail. I'd never seen a real celebrity before. And then came Belafonte, and Poitier, Peter Paul & Mary, and Tony Bennett—all in the flesh. I found out what being star-struck means and I caught a triple dose. But they're real people, just like us, only famous, all here for the same reason as me, and to encourage us to do what's right, and complete the mission, long beyond this march. Dick Gregory, Nipsey Russell. Sammy Davis Jr. sang the national anthem. What a night! Oh, what a night!

*****Frankie Laine, Nina Simone, Joan Baez, Pete Seeger, Lena Horne, James Baldwin, Mahalia Jackson, Shelley Winters, Odetta, Ina Balin, Gary Merrill, Leonard Bernstein, Billy Eckstein, Alan King, Pernell Roberts, William Marshall, Johnny Mathis.

Woke up Thursday morning to the marshals shouting through bullhorns, "Make way for the originals!" They cordoned us off to allow the "Lowndes 300" to gather, and lead the march. I'd say Spam and I were about eight blocks back from the front. The power of what ordinary people can accomplish, the power I felt from being there will stay with me forever.

When we got into Montgomery proper and marched up Goat Hill, I turned around. It looked like thousands and thousands of people were behind us, marching up Dexter Avenue toward the State Capitol, at last! Thousands more lined the streets to watch us pass.

MLK stood on the steps. I couldn't catch every word, but no one needed to hear perfectly to get the message. HOW LONG WILL IT TAKE? HOW LONG? NOT LONG.

I'll never forget, at the end of his speech he raised his hand and yelled "Glory, hallelujah! Glory, hallelujah! Glory hallelujah, His truth is marching on."

Both history and fate held my hand. The hothead inside me has learned a great lesson from these past 15 days. I'm going home a different man.

We caught a ride back here to Selma right after that, full of satisfaction and gratitude. Stayed up until 4am talking about it all.

Fri, Mar 26, 5 pm — Just found out the best day of my life ended with the worst news I could have heard. Viola Liuzzo was shot last night after driving some marchers back to Selma. She was ambushed by a gang of fucking bastard Klansmen. They shot her in the face at a stoplight while she *waited to cross back over the bridge. I keep thinking about her, the bravest woman I'd ever met, and how she encouraged me to do the right thing with Cassie. Viola will now and forever take her place next to William Moore and Spam Monroe at my table of inspiration.*

Didn't think I'd ever say something like this, but I'm glad I was beaten silly. My scar will be my badge of honor, my Montgomery 47, but I need to get the infection cleared up. Spam and I vowed to someday write a book about the march.

"The greatest march on any capitol there has ever been in the South"

MLK

Another folded newspaper clipping slipped out from the back page of the journal. It had no date on it. I opened it to see a picture of J.L. Rainey, my daddy, standing next to a priest in a crowd of protesters. Like everyone in the picture, he wore an overcoat and a hat. A smudge of newsprint caused his nose to blur, but his whiteness was undeniable. I stared at the picture a good ten minutes, and I read the caption under it so many times it burned into my head. "White man marches alongside Negroes on the certain road to integration."

That day, that fateful day when Mama agreed to get help and J.L. Rainey let me into his life, was both exhilarating and exhausting. I closed my eyes.

20

Uncle Mooks' voice boomed from the front porch and woke me.

"They're here, Jason Lee. They're comin back."

I looked out my window at the pitch-black night. The beginning of a summer storm had kicked the trees into a frenzied motion. The Buick's high beams sliced through the darkness as they inched up the drive, then stopped out front and went dark. The interior light lit up when Boyle opened the car door. Mama was nowhere to be seen.

I took the stairs two at a time and shot through the front room and out the screen door. "Where is she?" I yelled from the porch.

Boyle took his time maneuvering out of the front seat. Once on solid ground, he stood up stiff, his spine hunched. "She's gonna be fine," he said, staring at me.

"Then where is she?"

"They're gonna keep her for thirty days."

"Thirty days? You never said nothin about no thirty days." I looked at Uncle Mooks. "Do something."

Boyle approached the front steps. He stuck his palms out, gesturing for me to calm down.

"You lied to us," I said, unsettled, off balance.

You rat. You no-good douchebag of a rat, Parnell Rat

Boyle. You no-good apple-smelling excuse of a man. My daddy marched from Selma to Montgomery. You can't get the back pockets right on a suit.

"What about us?" I screamed and hit my chest then stretched my arms out toward the highway to make him understand every pebble on our property would suffer from Mama's absence. "What about us?" I said again. "It was bad enough when she took to her bed for weeks on end. We had to fuss over her and do things we weren't cut out for."

I folded my arms and looked straight through his rimmed glasses, into those untrustworthy eyes. "You're a liar. A no-good worm."

Uncle Mooks got to his feet as if nothing was wrong, walked around me, opened the screen and said to Boyle, "Come in."

Boyle settled in the armchair across from us on the couch.

"Today was a hard one." His hands settled limp in his lap.

My chest heaved. "Did someone take your mama away for thirty days?"

"Listen boy, don't give me that crap. I took her for help. It's out of my hands."

"Was she still cryin?"

"Some," he admitted, surprising me. Boyle looked like he'd had a real hard day, but who hadn't?

Uncle Mooks took my hand and squeezed it. "Give her time."

Boyle said, "They've provided her with the

essentials, some toiletry items and the standard gown and slippers."

I couldn't do much more than huff at him.

"She'll need to have some of her own things. Clothes, mementos, anything that will help make her comfortable. I'm going back to Delta Community on Thursday. If you'll pack a suitcase for her I'll take it with me."

I couldn't get past the idea of thirty days. What was that in minutes? Thirty days times twenty-four hours times sixty, plus a couple more hundred minutes to drive her back from Hattiesburg. It took me time to figure it out. Forty-three-plus thousand minutes. A lot could happen in that amount of time.

Small amounts of time, Uncle Mooks had said. But right then, with a night storm slapping the tree limbs against the windows, it felt like a big shadowy hole might swallow the house without her there.

After Boyle left, Uncle Mooks plopped himself back down on the couch and hummed the Polly Wolly Doodle song, but it sounded more like he moaned it. I paced past the doorway into Mama's room, around the dining table to the kitchen door, back to the doorway, and around the table again. On the fourth trip back past Mama's doorway, I stopped and noticed her olivewood hairbrush resting on the dresser across the room. Her mama's handed-down hairbrush.

When Uncle Mooks had hummed his way through the song a good number of times, he shuffled into his bedroom and closed the door. I found myself struggling with something I hadn't experienced before. The burden of loyalty.

Even though my heart slid to the floor when that con-man came back without her, it soared at the thought of getting back to the journal. Since there was nothing I could do for Mama right then I ran upstairs to compare J.L. Rainey's handwriting to mine again, read his every word again, and fill myself with the spirit of him.

*

For the next two days I walked around with his journal in my pocket, feeling its pulse with each step, exhilarated to be the keeper of its new life, and barely able to think of anything else—not even Mama all by herself in Hattiesburg, or Uncle Mooks alone on the porch.

Come Wednesday evening I realized I'd plumb forgot to pack a suitcase for her, and I crossed the threshold into her room, the only one in our house where I didn't feel I belonged.

She kept her blue molded Samsonite suitcase on the shelf in the closet. I pulled it down and placed it on her flowered bedspread. Feeling at odds with myself about intruding into her privacy, I ran my finger across the rough-textured plastic before clicking open the two silver latches.

Deciding what to put inside came next, what she might want, or like. The olivewood brush caught my eye. I picked it up and smelled the hair entwined in the bristles. Every night Mama stood at the dresser in front of the mirror with her head cocked to the side as she pulled the brush through her hair.

I looked into that same mirror, noticing my rumpled shirt and then realized, with great surprise, that my reflection was cut off at the forehead. It'd been some time since I'd thought to glimpse at myself, and I leaned in for a better look. Thin brown hairs sprouted from my upper lip. A turn of my head exposed the shadow of a sideburn in front of my ear. I wondered how long it'd take them to fill in. My eyebrows had also darkened.

Mama's mirror was the only eye witness to my march toward manhood. The more I studied myself, the stronger the thoughts of J.L. marching from Selma swirled in my head. If he was nineteen when he went there, he must have been seventeen when he got arrested for the Moore march in Alabama—just two years older than me. And what was I doing? Whining like a little girl because Mama might be gone a month.

I tossed the brush inside the case, then picked up her fuzzy house slippers with the thin rubber bottoms and put them inside, too.

The mirror beckoned me for another look, to double-check the hairs on my lip and to verify I'd grown taller than the mirror itself. While doing so I slid open Mama's top dresser drawer by its crystal knobs.

Her unmentionables, all various shades of beige and white, were folded and neatly laid out. I'd seen them all before, hanging on the clothesline, but being up close took some time to get used to. I glanced at her underpants, folded and stacked like slick pancakes, and scooped them up between my forearms to avoid hand contact. I walked to the case and released them.

The brassiere section was less threatening. I saw them more like foreign objects to be studied and I picked one up to examine the soft, small padded mounds that were hardly mounds at all. One had a safety pin securing a frayed strap in place. After my brief inspection I set two in the suitcase.

Her socks, each folded into its mate, didn't look any different than the ones in my drawer. I reached for a couple pair and smashed my fingers into a box under them—a wooden box no bigger than my fist, with a white and black marbled top.

I hadn't intended to pry or snoop or anything close, but curiosity's a sneaky emotion, so I shook the thing. Whatever was inside clanked, but the top of the box wouldn't open. I spotted a very small keyhole on the front side and quickly shoved the rest of the socks to the side, and uncovered a little key attached to a tassel. A half twist and the top opened.

Inside was a coin fastened to a yellow ribbon with red and green stripes. By then I should have been numb to surprises and my life spinning out of control, but a flash of heat ran through me when I pulled out the medal with a dragon behind a grove of bamboo trees above the words REPUBLIC OF VIETNAM SERVICE. On the backside was a torch above the words, UNITED STATES OF AMERICA.

I stared at it, the bamboo, the dragon and the ring

holding the ribbon, before laying it on the dresser, and reached back into the unknown.

I came across a piece of paper folded around something close to the same size as the medal. I pulled it out and opened it. Inside I found a charred strip of metal. There were letters pressed into it. I ran my thumb over it and soon realized they spelled out J.L.'s name. My name, too. It was his dog tag.

No one ever told me how he died, so over the years I'd worked up the notion he'd been shot. I played my version of what happened in my head like a newsreel. *The bullets come rapid fire from a blind spot in the jungle and hit his chest lightning fast—a constant stream. The soldier, the one playing my daddy, convulses in the spastic bullet dance they do in war movies. And then he's down.* End of newsreel, and I'd get back to whatever I was doing before.

The notion that he'd been burned to death hit like an ambush. I closed my eyes, willing the image to fade, and tried to hold back the sting of tears. Minutes went by before I opened them again, and picked up the paper off the floor to re-wrap the tag. Mama'd written something on the inside. In her soft handwriting of sadness it read,

Recipe for a Hero

Hometown boy
Civil rights activist
Newlywed
Soon-to-be father

Vietnam Conflict

Mix first four ingredients into Vietnam Conflict. Heat with napalm to 1,200° and stir gently with charred dog tag. Dish up with American flag and a young, grieving widow holding her infant son.

Serves: A small town of 3,000.

With trembling hands I put everything back in the box, slammed the lid closed, dropped it on the dresser, and sat down next to the suitcase until my heart slowed. Then I forced myself to finish packing for her, racing across the room from closet to bed with no more room for feelings. And no more grief about Mama being gone.

Her drawers were no longer sacred. I rummaged through them and bunched her clothes into the suitcase like they didn't matter. Soon her hair rollers were in there along with the envelope of bobby pins to anchor them at night. Her *Better Homes and Gardens* magazine from the nightstand. Her reading glasses. Two clicks of the latches and the job was done. While taking the suitcase to the front room I stopped at the mirror for another look. My eyes had changed. They were harder, or older, and less trusting.

The box and key went upstairs with me. Fatigue settled in as I remembered Mama's extra-long goodbye hug before she got into Boyle's car, and the sight of

J.L.'s dog tag, charred as a briquette. Sleep smothered me until the nightmare attacked.

There were no submarines or dead children that night. First I fell into a deep hole and landed on my back, pinned under a tractor. I wiggled myself out but couldn't walk, and when I looked down, my feet were gone. I didn't yell out, but woke with a start on top of the bed, still in my clothes.

I'd slept through the roosters' crows and the cries of the jays. The box and key were next to me. *Why had she picked that box to put his things in, and why had she kept it all a secret from me? Why hadn't she told me how he died? How many more boxes of secrets were there?*

I got up and glanced out my window only to see snake-oil Boyle's Buick parked out front. I hurried downstairs with the box still in my hand, to find Boyle in the living room with Mama's suitcase in his hand, heading for the front door.

"Hey, Boyle?"

He stopped and turned around.

"Can I go?"

"Sorry, kid. Take care of your uncle. He looks like he needs it." Boyle glanced toward Uncle Mooks, who was scowling at me.

"The grits is burned." He pointed toward the kitchen.

I looked at the clock on the side table, coming on ten o'clock.

"I got a right to sleep in," I said, defensive.

"The grits is burned!" He shook his head and

moved toward the kitchen, hunched so far forward his head barely showed above his shoulders.

Douchebag Boyle slipped out the front door.

My thoughts were stuck on J.L.'s journal and the box in my hand, but I decided it would be best to head for the stove and set things right with Uncle Mooks. He sat bent over the table with his hands cradling his forehead.

"Sorry," I mumbled and got to work making his breakfast. I sprinkled a handful of marshmallows on the top, and when I set the bowl in front of him, he stayed at the table to eat with me instead of taking it to the front porch, as usual. He plucked the marshmallows out of his bowl with his oversized fingers.

He noticed the box I'd left on the sink counter. "Where'd you find that?"

"It's Mama's.

"No it aint, it was my mama's."

21

I asked for an emergency drinkin meetin on Sunday, when church got out. In true Samson style he showed up in Dicey around three p.m., with a half jar of shine and a tin of chew. We drove straight to Mosquito River and hiked up to our boulder, our sanctuary for two, surrounded by the blues of the sky and water, and the greens of the treetops entwined across our horizon.

My whole week's worth of worries and discoveries bubbled inside me, ready to blow. If I told any of it to Uncle Mooks there was too much of a chance he'd go bonkers on me. I'd taken the dog tag out of its Recipe for a Hero wrapping, and brought it along. And, of course, the journal.

I stalled some, talking about things that didn't matter, like the chance of rain and the water current.

"If you got somethin on your chest, Jason Lee, might as well get it off."

"You ain't gonna believe what happened."

"You want me to guess?"

"I think my daddy's tryin to reach me from the beyond."

"Oh, Lord," he said under his breath. "You mean from the grave?"

"Yeah, but I'm not sure he even has a grave." I talked fast. First I told him all that happened with Mama. About the pills and Boyle taking her to Hattiesburg.

Samson twisted the lid off the jar. Instead of taking the first swig he handed it to me. "Here, sounds like you need her more than me."

A prism of sunlight bounced off the jar and flickered against our stone perch.

"What're you sayin, your daddy don't have no grave?"

"It's what I think I'm sayin. But before I tell you 'bout that—" I dug the journal out of my backpack and handed it to him. "Found this right after Mama left. Put down by his own hand."

"What is it?"

"Open it and you'll see."

"Looks old." He rubbed his thumb along the masking tape to secure it down. Then he opened the journal, leaned it against his knees, and read the first entry. He shook his head. "Well, I'll be a monkey's mama. He was really there. This proves it."

He read straight through every page, not stopping once. I listened to a family of magpies scold each other in the distance, and went over in my head what I'd memorized from the journal, and drank from the shine jar. I couldn't decide whether we'd gotten a bad batch or if it just tastes better at night.

He finished reading.

"Man, Jason Lee, this is something."

"Like I said, I think he's tryin to reach me."

"Because?"

"Because not more than two days after I found the book, I found this." I handed the dog tag to him.

"It's burned."

I nodded. "Read it."

He held it close to his eyes.

RAINEY, JASON LEE

RA56772363

O NEG

NO PREF

"What is it?"

"His dog tag."

"Oh, man," Samson said. "Oh, man, oh, Lord, oh no." He gave it back to me. "I need a swig."

"And another thing," I said. "I just learned about O negative blood in a magazine article. That can't be a coincidence. He musta arranged it."

"What blood?"

"O neg. Third row, there under his ID number. They call the people who have it, universal donors, bein other people's bloods don't reject it."

"He had it?"

"Says so here."

"Why's it burnt?"

"I figure he died in a fire or an explosion, and he wants me to know 'cause ain't no one else gonna tell me. Especially Mama."

"Don't seem right after what he did here in this book. I can't believe he was there, marchin with Martin

Luther King Jr. himself." He tapped the journal, then opened it again and read the first entry out loud.

"Saturday, March sixth, nineteen sixty-five, ten p.m." He boomed, the way a radio announcer would broadcast it, and threw his fist in the air. "Selma. Got off the bus about noon, pumped up like a kid on Christmas morn." Samson brought his fist down and got more serious. "Could feel the electricity in the air. Found the George Washington Carver project. All the buildings look alike." He smiled at me. "Damn, Jason Lee. I mean DAMN."

When finished with the first entry he handed the book to me.

"Bloody Sunday," I read. "March seventh, a day I'll never forget—hopefully, a day no one will ever forget—Written March eighth, eleven a.m. I want to get as much of this down as I can remember. Yesterday started out calm enough and ended up in a clusterfuck. We met at Brown Chapel in the a.m. A huge crowd, maybe 600 of us, eager to make history. Friends among strangers, brothers in the 'cause—ignorant as sitting ducks."

We passed the small-but-mighty journal back and forth, taking turns until Samson read the last sentence before handing it back to me. "The greatest march on any capitol there has ever been in the South."

I said, "Do you think Dicey could make it to Selma?"

22

Miss Therese took forever to get out of her station wagon, and walked up to our house slow as an old lady. She didn't have any plates of food or jars of canned preserves, or pickles, either.

"Have a seat, Miss Therese," I said because she appeared so weary. Her red hair had no shine, and I noticed her updo sagged along with her disposition. She helped herself to the couch.

"You okay?"

"I got a sea of troubles facing me." She patted her hair like she knew I'd noticed.

"You look tired. You're not catchin the melancholy, are you, Miss Therese?"

She managed a small chuckle. "No, it ain't that. And maybe troubles ain't the right word. It's more like a shit-load of rotten bad timin." Her voice wobbled. "You know my mean ole bastard of a pa's been one step from the grave for awhile?"

"I remember you sayin somethin like that."

She shook her head, looking downright put out.

"Well, he finally up and did it."

"What? Died?"

She nodded. "Took him weeks to get to it, but he chose the night before last to pass." She leapt up from the couch and rubbed her neck. "I gotta take his body back to Tippah County later today. Then there's the chore of plannin the burial, not to mention goin through his things and figurin out how to sell his house." Miss Therese paced no more than two steps each way, about the length of our coffee table.

"You need help?"

"Thanks, no, and that ain't my point. Because of this up-and-dyin whenever it suited *him*, I plumb forgot to keep track of y'all. I stopped by work this mornin to let 'em know about my pa, and before I got a word out I heard about Parnell takin Cassie to Hattiesburg."

"I hate that Boyle, but turns out Dr. Ratliff's pills were the cause of her troubles."

She sighed. "It's all my fault."

I didn't say anything, because she was right.

"I came over here fast as I could. Hattiesburg. Good Lord, it's a two-hour drive. Jason Lee, tell me you know I'd take you there myself under normal circumstances."

"I know." I couldn't help but notice, without makeup her face looked ordinary.

"It's just that this pile a shit bad timin got dumped in my lap and I don't know how long I'll be gone. It means I can't watch after the two of you."

"We don't need no babysitter."

"Course you don't. But it's my fault she's gone." She did it again—sighed. "I was plain-old stupid to listen to Henry Tillman. And if that ain't bad enough, I insisted she go to a quack. Hell, I drove her there." She took a breath. "We've always been there for each other, ever since we met. Wouldn't you know, at the very moment we could both use each other's help, we're on our own. I promise, if it weren't for my damn pa—" She laughed even though nothing seemed very funny. "I'll call often as I can to check on you."

She ripped a sheet from her order pad and wrote down a number on the back. "Here's where I'll be up in Tippah. If you need anythin, call collect." Her handwriting looked like a delicate thread had broken off its spool and spilled onto the paper.

*

Living without Mama got easier with each day, and soon I wasn't angry at her anymore. After the first week had passed I wanted to talk to her something awful. I dialed up Delta Community. In my deepest voice I said, "May I speak to Mrs. Cassie Rainey?" The lady put me on hold for a good ten minutes of tinny music. "Delta Community Services," she said again.

"Mrs. Cassie Rainey, please."

"Sir, Mrs. Rainey's restricted from calls right now. She'll most likely have phone privileges after next week's evaluation."

I sulked for a good while, then remembered an old, unused postcard I'd seen in the catch-all drawer. The background showed two paddleboats, the Delta Queen and the Mississippi Queen. Big red letters across the middle said *Hello from the Mississippi River Parkway*.

I wrote in the small section on the backside and told her it'd been seven days since she left. "I know you're working real hard to get better, and Uncle Mooks and me are working real hard, too."

That's all that fit. I didn't mention anything about the box, or the many secrets she'd kept from me, or how I was starting to feel like a man.

I stuck my thumb in a jar of beet juice and pressed hard where the signature would be, then signed J.L. inside the smudge—just J.L.

Every other night Uncle Mooks and I ate a supper that Mama would've made. We picked vegetables from the garden and thawed meat from the deep freeze. On our nights off from real cooking we ate ketchup over spaghetti noodles, and bowls of popcorn, and Twinkies.

Some of the nights, to pass the time, we made phone quarters before turning in.

Miss Therese called twice. We didn't have much to tell her except we were getting along fine. She had a lot on her mind up in Tippah. It came through in her voice.

I transferred the box of secrets to my own dresser drawer, under my socks. Each night before going to bed, I took it out, opened it, and thought about the soldier in my imaginary newsreel being burned, but it was always the same. *The bullet dance, then he's down.*

By the time Uncle Mooks and I made it through two whole weeks alone, the heat of July was on us. Flies buzzed the screen doors, ready to bombard the house at the first opportunity, and the mosquitoes continued to feed on my ankles. Aside from Uncle Mooks constantly looking for his pocket watch, not recalling he had given it to Mama, we settled into a rhythm and routine.

He filled the hummingbird feeders, watered the

garden, and gave special care to the Queen Anne's lace. I picked up the house as best I could, fed the chickens, and collected the eggs. I joined him on the porch most evenings around six to watch the wind spinners twirl in the summer breezes.

"Why don't they make a real sound?" I once asked him.

"It upsets the cardinals. Ain't no need to upset 'em. Besides, the birds sound better." He gave out a cardinal's whistle that sounded so true I couldn't help but look toward the closest cypress for the songbird.

Some evenings I'd wander across the road with a pocketful of pecans to toss to the squirrels. The brown dirt boiled with commotion as they bobbed and scrambled to get to them. I tried to understand what it was that made the fierce ones unable to see the others needed to eat too, and how the young ones learned to stay clear but still get by. Then I wondered how many secrets their mamas kept from them.

But I had secrets of my own. Of course, I couldn't say a thing to Uncle Mooks about the journal or the dog tag, so during the third week I left Uncle Mooks alone to fend for himself and spent all my time with Samson.

We drove from one fishing hole to another, but we read from the journal more than we fished. The weight of what'd been achieved during those days in the 1960's—the sit-ins and boycotts, the brutality and disruption in the name of freedom and equality—took root and grew inside us. We held a first-hand account of what everyday people could accomplish, and drew inspiration from it.

Our daydreams of the future took a significant turn. One day Samson said, "Changed my mind about bein a fireman."

"Me, too. I'm gonna do somethin that matters, like J.L. did. But I don't know what."

"I do," he said with confidence. "I'm gonna be a lawyer. A lawyer for the NAACP."

"That's a great idea." I perked up. "You'll be real good at lawyerin. You got a knack."

"I got more than a knack. I got a fire."

"Wally told me J.L. wanted to be a lawyer."

"Or I'll work for Jessie Jackson," he said, not even listening to me.

"Think he'll run for President again?"

"Got over three million votes this time. I'll bet even J.L.'d be surprised how well he did. He's bound to get more votes next time."

"He'd probably be more proud than surprised. It's part of what he went to Selma for."

Being in constant possession of the journal made me itch to leave Hadlee. I longed for places bigger than the little flea turd on the map where I was born. Places that mattered. First stop, Selma. I knew Samson felt the same, and it was just a matter of time before we could start the lives we'd come to believe were possible.

By Friday of that week, we'd all but memorized every entry in the journal and finally tucked it safely in the glove box. Our big ideas took a vacation, and we spent the afternoon catching fish and swatting flies.

Samson pulled out a bag of Taylor's Pride, worked his fingers into the pouch and pulled out a pinch the size of a quarter. He rolled it into a ball, placed it under his lower lip, and handed the pouch to me. I wasn't too fond of the taste of chew but took some just the same. My mouth juiced right away. I swallowed by mistake, causing a dizzy spell.

Along with the chew we managed to drink a fair amount of shine. Despite ourselves and the summer heat and the afternoon thunderstorms, we caught enough fish for supper.

Around six o'clock I was hit with a pang of guilt about neglecting Uncle Mooks. "If we leave now," I said, holding up my string of bluegill, "I can get my uncle to help clean these babies. And yours, too." Samson raised his eyebrows and nodded like he thought I'd turned into a genius before his eyes.

23

We were heading home when Dicey's right front tire blew a flat. She shuddered and skidded and twirled, causing her backside to lead the way before Samson managed to get us front forward again, and on the right side of the road. When he pulled the truck to the shoulder I let go of the handle I'd grabbed on to for dear life, and looked over at him. He was grinning like we'd just gotten off the Tilt-A-Whirl at the County Fair.

"Look there, Jason Lee," he said, reaching down to the floorboard. Lil' Buddy hit me in the ankle. Musta been stuck under the seat." Samson pulled up an old pistol that looked like it should have been holstered to a cowboy's hip. "My pa traded Thunder for it."

"Lil' Buddy?"

"You gotta better name?"

I laughed. "No."

He set it on the seat between us. "Haven't seen Buddy in a blue moon. Didn't even know it was still around."

I reached over and touched it. "What's it for?"

"Mostly for turkeys and rabbits. Come on, let's change that tire."

Samson crawled underneath Dicey's truck bed where the spare and jack were attached. "Come down here and give me a hand. I need help gettin this bolt loose," he yelled.

I wormed my way next to him and held the spanner while he smacked it with a rock to break it loose.

Samson was banging on the tire iron so hard we didn't know a truck pulled in behind us until we tasted the grit on our teeth from the dust it churned up.

Both truck doors slammed and two sets of hard-soled boots hit the dirt, walking in our direction.

"Well now, we ain't seen your sorry asses in a coon's age."

There was no mistaking the voice. Samson scurried from under the truck, holding on to the tire iron. I went out the opposite side. When I got to my feet I saw the miserable faces of Eugene and Culver Chubb. A cigarette hung from one of their mouths, his eyes squinting from the smoke. The other one had bruises turned greenish yellow under both eyes.

Remembering the gun on the seat, I backed my way to Dicey's cab and opened the door.

"Hey you nigger-lovin pussy," the one said, letting the cigarette drop from of his mouth. He stomped it out with his boot. "Where you goin?"

With wily swiftness the other Chubb grabbed the tire iron from Samson's grip. Samson lunged to get it back, and fast as a bad thought both Chubbs were swinging at him.

I seized the gun and ran around the front of the truck where the three of them were coming to blows. I held Lil' Buddy in both hands and pointed it at them, about chest height. My right finger awkwardly searched for the trigger.

"Look here, douchebags," I said.

When the two brothers saw the gun they froze and Samson got out of the way. So wrought up at that point, my voice barreled out like a locomotive. "We're gonna settle this misunderstandin of you pullin up behind us when no one asked you to, this conflict, I'd like to call it, in a nonviolent manner."

The one with bruises gave me a toothy grin and snickered. I looked into both of their weather-beaten faces.

"This thing's got bullets, right Samson?"

"It's full," he said without hesitation.

I waved the gun back and forth the way Grover Peek had done to us a couple years earlier. The Chubb with the tire iron dropped it and put his hands in the air.

"Whoa, pal."

"Pal? Is that what we are?" I took a breath to try and calm my nerves. "Which one are you?"

"Easy," he said.

"What's your name?"

"Culver."

I felt I was in the driver's seat, but had no idea how to drive, and I didn't know what to say next. The best I came up with was, "Listen here Culver. We been reading a book, Samson and me." But the more I talked, the words tumbled out without much thought. "Don't suppose you know how to do that, read a book, but this particular book I'm talkin about was written by a real good man who didn't take shit from the likes of you. It's about achievin civil rights in a nonviolent manner. You know what nonviolent means?"

Culver looked at me glassy-eyed. "Take it easy."

"It's the practice of achievin goals without using violence. The good news is it means nobody gets hurt."

I could feel my expression change to determination. "I'll put it in terms you might understand. Since you did pull up behind us where you had no business bein, it means this nigger-lovin pussy'd be much obliged if you'd pick up that tool, and he'd be grateful if you both got your sorry asses to work changin the tire on his friend's truck."

I was so scared my brain almost stopped, and I didn't know how the things I'd just said could have possibly come out of my mouth. All I figured was I was channeling J.L. at his best, and that felt chest-splitting good.

But, after all the time I'd spent over the years wondering how it'd feel to hold a gun, I had my answer. The thought of shooting a bullet into someone or something, no matter how low they were on the ladder of evolution, be it a Chubb or a boar, made my throat tighten and I wanted to rid myself of the whole idea. I handed the gun to Samson. He pointed it at the Chubbs and said, "It'd be smart to follow his orders."

Their sneers were gone. Culver picked up the tire iron, and after a long, awkward silence, they began. Eugene jumped on the lug wrench and grunted the lug nuts loose. Culver jacked up Dicey, and together they switched out the shredded tire for the spare one—without a drop of violence. It barely took five minutes.

Samson held the gun on them through the whole ordeal, until they pulled out and drove away. "Damn, Jason Lee. Remind me not to get on your bad side."

"Wasn't me. It was your pa's Thunder. Not sure how smart it was 'cause they might circle back any minute. But what else could we do?"

He shrugged. "Pretty sure there ain't no bullets."

On the drive home I rested my head on the back of the seat and took in the feeling of finally standing up to those two hateful bastards.

When we pulled up the drive Samson said, "Look. What's that?"

"What?"

He pointed over the steering wheel toward the house.

Uncle Mooks was face down on the lawn in front of the azaleas, thrashing like a demon had entered his body. Both his hands were cupped above his left eyebrow. Dicey came to a screeching stop. Samson and I jumped out. Uncle Mooks' deep, uneven wails echoed through the property.

"Uncle Mooks, God, oh, God, Uncle Mooks, what happened?" I slid down on my knees and grabbed him by his arms. His low-pitched, ghostly sound continued. I pulled his hands from his face. His fingers trembled and he clawed at the grass. "Uncle Mooks, I'm here." I shook him. He quieted down when he realized I was with him, and then he flopped back, flat and colorless, gasping.

I heard my blood pounding, echoing through my ears. My first thought was the Chubbs got to him. "What happened?"

He strained to sit up but fell back onto his elbows. Samson got behind him and pushed him upright. He crossed his legs Indian style and then studied the ground like he was searching for something in the grass. "The hurts gone."

"Did someone do this to you?" I asked.

He nodded. "Gooks." Spittle stretched from his mouth down his chin. "Time's a thief," he said. "Don't let it rob you." His gaze left the grass for the road. He half smiled.

"What happened?"

"It moved."

"What moved?"

He mumbled. "Just a matter of time. Time's a friend, or it ain't."

"You ain't makin sense. What moved?"

"Shrapnel."

"Shrapnel?"

"In my head," he said and glanced up at me.

Except for the spittle, he looked like himself again.

"I need help gettin up. I was doin somethin."

Samson and I each took an arm and, on the count of three, got him to his feet. He brushed the dirt off his overalls, wobbled toward the porch, and stopped in front of the steps.

"Hold up, Mr. Mooks." Samson took him by the arm and helped him climb the stairs. Once seated on the couch, Uncle Mooks picked up the pine monkey he'd been working on.

"We gotta go see a doctor," I said.

"I ain't leavin,'" he said, commencing to whittle.

It was the first time I'd heard anything about shrapnel. How many more family secrets were there?

After Samson left, I studied Uncle Mooks, searching for signs of shrapnel on the move. On top of a bellyful of remorse, my head overflowed with thoughts of him dying right in front of me. It was my responsibility to look after him, but with all that had happened since Mama left I'd lost track of almost everything.

Uncle Mooks didn't seem to give a hoot about my apologies and had no understanding of my pleas for forgiveness. I finally gave up saying I'm sorry and just said, "I promise I won't leave again until Mama comes home."

"Time," he said. "You can't get more or make more." He smiled.

"I mean it. I won't leave."

*

I got up early, thinking my hellish thoughts about what would have happened if Uncle Mooks actually up and died right there in the yard. That thought accelerated into similar thoughts that I had when Mama went through the melancholy. What if the authorities caught wind of her being admitted to Delta

Community? They'd come out to our place and haul me off. And sure as the sun comes up at dawn, they'd take Uncle Mooks to the loony bin. How could I ever explain to Mama that Samson and I were chewing tobacco and drinking shine and standing up for ourselves against the Chubbs, instead of looking after Uncle Mooks?

After breakfast, I read in my room until about eleven, then went into the kitchen to mix hot water into a bowl of lime gelatin. Uncle Mooks called out, "Funeral parade."

"Comin."

I set the gelatin on the refrigerator shelf and grabbed the plate of leftover fish fillets with okra bits still stuck to them, then poured us each a glass of sweet tea.

The parade was short—the hearse, six cars and a beige Ford pick-up. They all appeared to quiver through the vapors of the midday heat.

Before we started our customary speculations on who the "lucky stiff" leading the parade might be, the beige truck turned onto our property. The chassis swayed side to side over the dusty drive. I stopped wondering who was in the hearse and concentrated on who might be in the Ford truck.

24

Uncle Mooks seemed as surprised as me when we finally figured out it was Wally behind the wheel. I wondered if Darla knew of his whereabouts.

Wally jumped out of the cab and grabbed a canvas bag from the truck bed. "Got stuck behind the Perdue funeral."

Uncle Mooks gulped his tea. "Perdue?"

Wally nodded toward the road. "Lawrence."

"Hear that, Jason Lee? Lawrence Perdue's the lucky stiff."

Wally trudged up the porch steps and set the bag on the floor in front of me. "These are some of mine. Thought you'd like 'em."

"Books?" I picked up the bag and loosened the drawstring.

"Yep." Wally made his way to the porch swing. It groaned its protest.

"Cassie ain't here," Uncle Mooks said. He reached for his pocket watch.

"I know she ain't here," Wally said with a snip in his voice. "I been fishin up at Enid Lake for the past two weeks. Got home last night. And this mornin that outsider Boyle came by the store. He told everyone within shoutin distance how he saved Cassie from the brink of death when no one else paid her any attention." Wally's face turned red as his hair. "I had a mind to punch him right then and there." He paused to calm down. "Sure do wish I'd been here to help. Turns out my timin was worse than the fishin."

My stomach flipped. Wally's news was my worst fear—not about the bad fishing, but about Boyle running his mouth off in public. How long would it take the authorities to catch wind, and toss both Uncle Mooks and me in our separate hells?

"What's that no-good, festerin Boyle doing talkin about her for?" I said. "Talkin about anyone?"

"Not sure," Wally said, and then he smiled. "The good news is, he's got some big troubles of his own. Words out the bank's fixin to foreclose on his shop. Guess he forgot to make his payments."

"Douchebag," I said.

"I told you before, a men's store in Hadlee's a harebrained idea."

Wally looked at Uncle Mooks, leaned forward, and clasped his hands together. "Been a dog's age since I laid eyes on you. Why don't you come to town sometime, we'll have a go at a game of checkers."

"I like it here." Uncle Mooks took a bite of fish. "Want one?" He dangled the fried bluegill in Wally's direction.

"Looks good, but I'm tryin to cut back." He laughed and pointed to his truck. "I brought some supplies—nothin much—but there's a sack of rice and some cans a baked beans in the back. And there's a dozen round steaks and a carton of Mounds in the cooler. Why don't you take 'em to the kitchen, son?"

"Mounds?" I said, almost tasting them. "My favorites. Thanks, Wally."

He looked at Uncle Mooks again. "A dirty dog's age. Seein your face brings back memories." He looked at me. "We were both in your folks weddin, Mooks and me. Did you know that?"

"I seen pictures."

"I'll tell you all about it when you're done puttin away them supplies."

I took my time with the food—long enough to rip open a Mounds and eat both of the sweet coconut-filled pieces.

"Thanks again, Wally," I said when I got back outside.

"Least I can do."

Wally fiddled with the band on his ring finger. "Like I was sayin to Mooks here, I shoulda done more for Cassie over the years."

"There's still time," Uncle Mooks said. "Time works for you and against you."

"Tell me about it," I said.

"About what?" they both said together. Uncle Mooks licked his thumb and stuck it in the air. "Jinks."

"The weddin. Mama's never told me about it. Keeps things like that to herself."

"Probably because lookin back to the good times is sometimes too painful," Wally said.

"But I dreamt about it once," I said. "At least I think

it was about the weddin."

I told Uncle Mooks and Wally how in my dream Mama wore a crown on her head, the kind queens wear, with diamond-covered points all the way around it. And a dress made of thousands of puffy cotton balls. She cradled stalks of white gladiolas in her arms and rocked them tenderly, like they were a baby. I watched all this from a window with no glass in it, but she caught me staring and sent me off to find my daddy. In the dream she said, 'He's missin in action, Jason Lee. Go find him.'"

I shrugged, feeling self-conscious. "That's all I remember."

"The real story's better." Wally cleared his throat and adjusted himself on the swing.

"Mooks, remember J.L. and Cassie's weddin day?"

"Uh-huh," he answered and grabbed another fillet.

"The four of us left before the break of day and drove to Pontotoc in J.L.'s Chevy."

"Bel Air," Uncle Mooks added.

"Cassie planned for them to be the first couple married in the courthouse that day. It was June fifth, 1965. She thought the date was a lucky one."

"Why?"

"Six-five, six-five."

"I get it," I said, but I'd never made the connection before.

"J.L. was drivin. Mooks and me were in the back seat with a cooler of beer wedged between us. You remember, Mooks?"

"Uh-huh." His face softened.

"Cassie got the wild notion to get hitched in Pontotoc because she'd read that the walkway goin up to the courthouse was lined with heaven trees and they'd still be in bloom in early June. Just the idea of a tree called heaven felt right to her and she wouldn't settle on a weddin anywhere else. You know your mama."

I wasn't so sure of that.

"We was four young kids dressed in our finest, makin our way toward the future." Wally waved his half-a-hand in the air. I'd seen it so often it looked natural. "Just like Cassie said, the heaven trees lined the walkway. We marched up the steps and waited for the doors to open. Cassie was flush with nerves, her face as pink as a wild rose, and she kept tuggin on her gloves like they might fall off."

I remembered seeing the gloves in the grainy snapshots.

"Oo-ee, she was decked out pretty as a model in a magazine, wearin high heels and all. Remember, Mooks?"

"Uh-huh." Uncle Mooks looked out toward the yard. "Real pretty—looked like *my* ma."

"A lot like her, only your ma woulda never worn a hat like that. You remember when she told us it was called a pillbox hat, we poked fun at her?"

Uncle Mooks nodded but looked lost in thought.

"Remember how she turned to us real stern and said, 'You can make fun, but I'm wearin it to honor

Mrs. Kennedy.' That shut us up lightnin fast." Wally chuckled and pumped the swing with his legs. "She was somethin else back then. Had the spirit of a warrior."

"Want a beer?" Uncle Mooks said to Wally.

"Thought you'd never ask."

Uncle Mooks went off to the kitchen.

"Sorry I was away when this all happened," he said to me. "How's she doin?"

"Don't know. Ain't seen her." I considered confiding to him that she was gone for a reason—so J.L. could reach out to me, to tell me things. But even in my head it sounded lame. Besides, Uncle Mooks would be back in no time.

He did come back, with two Falstaff's in one hand and a third in the other. "How 'bout you, Jason Lee?"

"What?"

"Beer?"

"Sure." My voice rose.

With the heat of the day coming on strong, that first sip tasted just right. Wally pulled a handful of sunflower seeds from his pocket and shook some in the palm of my hand, then in Uncle Mooks'.

"Were they the first to get married?" I asked.

"Yesiree. They handed over the results from the blood tests and filled out some paperwork. Then the four of us squeezed onto a bench more suited for three people, and waited."

"My daddy had O-negative blood," I said. A part of me wanted to be asked how I knew that particular bit of information, a part of me thought I should have kept quiet about it.

"Didn't know that." Wally said, like it wasn't important. "Once the judge's assistant called their names, those two were hitched faster than it takes a fat man to eat a cheeseburger."

He caught me in the middle of a swallow, and a stream of beer blew out of my nose. That set off a laugh session with the three of us and a burst of relief inside me. Three men, drinking beer and telling stories. It felt almost normal.

Wally leaned back into the swing. "Not to change the subject, but how is it you haven't seen your mama?"

"Miss Therese woulda taken me, but she's tied up with her pa's funeral and all."

"I'm sure she's wantin to see you somethin awful." His soft, heartfelt tone put a sting in my throat.

"I know," I choked.

"Let's all get in the truck," Wally said. "We'll go right now."

I jumped off the couch. The screen door slammed behind me. I shot upstairs to the bathroom three steps at a time, wiped my armpits with a washcloth and ran some water over the plastic comb to slick down my hair. A fresh shirt, and I was back outside in a flash, only to remember my promise to Uncle Mooks.

"I can't leave him here alone," I said, frozen with disappointment.

"He's comin with us," Wally said.

Uncle Mooks shook his head like a kid being forced

to eat something he didn't want.

"He never leaves. You know that, don't you?"

"Guess I do, but let's talk this through."

Everything inside me ached to hop in Wally's truck and speed like hell to Hattiesburg. I told Wally about the shrapnel moving and my promise not to leave Uncle Mooks' side.

He cleared his throat. "Well, that puts a wrinkle in the plan. Melvin?" he said. "How 'bout you make an exception this one time?"

"I got work to do." He lifted his whittling knife.

"Whittlin can wait."

"No it can't. Times a tickin."

"The thing is, Wally," I said, "I made a promise."

"You gonna hold him to that promise?" Wally asked Uncle Mooks.

"Nope. Take him. She needs him."

"I can't go," I said.

"He's right, Jason Lee." Wally talked to me for the better part of a half hour about Mama needing to see me and how it would do more good if I went than if I stayed. The last thing he said was, "We won't be gone more than five hours. It'll be my full responsibility if somethin happens to Mooks."

I knew if anything happened it would be my fault entirely, but the chance to go see Mama, and do what I could to help her won over.

While getting in the truck I looked at the grass where Uncle Mooks had fallen the day before. For a split second I heard his hideous wails again.

"Stay put on the porch." I pointed to him. "Don't do nothin else but sit there."

He gave me a nod and waved.

*

The cab rocked like the struts had been replaced by a giant Slinky toy. Wally's air conditioner quit on him some time earlier that year, and he didn't believe the luxury of cool air was worth the price tag to repair it.

"It's about two hours away, right?" I yelled over the road noise and the sharp-pitched whistle rushing through the cab.

He shouted. "Bout two hours, yep." I barely heard him.

We yelled back and forth, both straining to hear.

"What's the town like?"

"Hattiesburg?"

"Yeah."

"Like most towns."

I put my sneakers against the glove box and looked at the magnolias, our guardians of the roadside. They were barren of flowers, and the summer heat had turned the underside of the leaves dark.

With the hot air coming at me in drifts I yelled, "They know we're comin?" He shook his head no, keeping his eyes on the road.

I hollered on, thinking we should be talking. "After the weddin, did you and Uncle Mooks go on their honeymoon with 'em?"

"Nope," he yelled back.

I wanted to hear more about my folks back then,

when there was a "them," and I wouldn't have minded asking Wally why he married Darla, but there was something else I wanted to know more.

"You know that last box of J.L.'s books you gave me?"

"What?"

"The box of books?"

"Yep."

In spite of the heat I rolled up my window. "J.L's journal was in it."

Wally rolled his window up, too. "You say journal?"

"Little one." I formed a rectangle with my hands. "This big, or so. About his time in Selma."

"I'll be. He never told me about keepin one."

"Wrote in it every day he was there."

He shook his head. "Just like him to keep all the details."

"Showed it to Samson," I said. "We been readin it a lot, and I can't help but wonder what it was made him so different from all the other folks around here."

"You don't know?"

"Nope."

"Thought you knew."

"Turns out I don't know nothin." I breathed in the closed-up air mixed with gas fumes.

"Coulda sworn I told you."

"What? Told me what?"

"About after his pa died."

"Nope," I said again.

"J.L.'s folks didn't have much more than two sticks to rub together, but his pa, your granddaddy, got by as a field worker pickin crops with the coloreds, until the cancer killed him when J.L. was about five or six.

"I never knew his folks," I said. "Never knew Mama's folks neither."

"For a good three years J.L. and his ma lived with a family of pickers, out in an area used to be called Chicken Gristle Valley."

"Chicken Gristle?"

"Most all the places out there are torn down now. Things weren't easy back then and it was a simple case of the poor feedin the poorer—damned if I can remember that family's name. Coloreds, black as coal. The whole bunch of 'em were crammed in their splintered, one-room place. J.L. loved that family like they were his own."

"I never heard any of this before."

"J.L. always had a short fuse, even as a kid, and when he saw people he considered his own kin treated no better than dirt, it lit a fire inside him that was still burnin when he died."

"You sure you can't remember their name?"

"No. They moved up north a few years after J.L. and his ma left. Their kindness stayed with him and shaped his way of thinkin. He was always sayin, 'It's not about skin color or what people say, it's what they do.'"

It must have been 120 degrees in the cab by then. Despite myself I said, "Thanks, Wally, can we talk more about it, later?"

We both rolled down our windows and welcomed the wind and the road noise.

*

I recognized the building from the picture on the brochure, blue awning and all.

Inside, the smell of molasses cookies filled the reception area. I looked around for the lady who had answered the phone when I called but only saw a girl in a pink-striped apron. She looked to be my age or younger.

When we asked, she said, "Mrs. Rainey's in room 410A, past the nurses' station, to your right. Visitin hours are over in an hour." She handed Wally a brochure from a wire basket on the desk, the same one Boyle had pulled from his shirt pocket. She offered me a cookie.

Wally put his hand on my shoulder as we made our way through the green corridor toward the nurses' station. A man in a loose grey bathrobe shuffled down the center of the hall toward us, concentrating only on the movement of his feet. Wally and I broke apart to let him pass.

"Mama might not recognize us."

"Don't get ahead a yourself, Jason Lee. That ain't gonna happen."

Three Delta Community workers behind the chest-high nurses' station were discussing a woman they didn't seem to like much, named Ofelia. Five hallways shot out from the station like wheel spokes, with a number at the entrance, from one to five. We didn't stop or interrupt them but just went toward hall number four on our own. I walked behind Wally, my nerves on high alert.

A woman with tired, sad eyes was parked in a wheelchair in the hallway leading to Mama's room. She strained to see us as we passed, like she was looking through cobwebs. A different smell came from each room: spoiled meat, dried urine, mildew, loneliness.

We finally reached number 410. Mama rocked in a white wicker chair, her back to us, looking through the window at the cloudless sky. I spotted my postcard taped on the window's lower right corner.

"Mama?" I choked the word out.

She turned her head slowly, like she couldn't trust what she'd heard.

"Jason Lee?" she said and popped up from the chair. She rushed toward me, wearing the blue sweater I'd packed and the dress she wore when she left home. Uncle Mooks' watch hung on her neck from a yellow plastic lanyard. Her trembling hug wrapped around me, and my knees almost buckled from the relief. Mama loosened her grip, leaned back, and looked up at me.

"You okay, Mama?"

While reaching her hands to my face, she nodded.

I nodded back.

"Sit here, Jason Lee." She patted the twin bed and we sat down side-by-side. Her hand wrapped around mine in a firm, strong grip. "Look at you." The surprise in her voice was clear. "You're a grown man," she said with a self-conscious laugh. She reached toward my face again and touched the hair above my lip and then my brows.

Her eyes teared

"My boy's a man." She hadn't noticed any of this before leaving home. I allowed myself the notion she was back to herself. The worry creases between her brows had eased, and her face seemed soft again, like it was before she got the pills. She cradled her hand around Uncle Mooks' pocket watch.

"How is he?"

"Fine, Mama. Just fine." I hoped she'd never have occasion to find out about the shrapnel incident.

I looked over at Wally standing in the doorway, big as the door itself. Mama's eyes followed.

"Wally?" She ran her fingers through her bangs. "What're you doin here?"

"I only heard this mornin you was out here by yourself, Cassie." He rocked on his feet. "Thought it right to bring Jason Lee for a visit. Hope you don't mind."

"Mind?"

"And I needed to see for myself that all's right with you." His words began to tumble out faster than I'd ever heard him talk before. "I should a done more for you over the years. There's no excuse except lack of courage. Darla can be strong-headed about some things. It was easiest to meet her terms."

"All's right, Wally. I hope you comin all the way

out here don't cause too much trouble." She looked so full of thanks, I needed to turn away. "You brought me the best gift of all."

She kissed me on the ear and squeezed me for a time before letting go.

"I phoned here." I wanted her to know I'd tried. "But they told me you was restricted from calls."

"Don't know how I got myself in such a mess," she said. "This place ain't exactly a picnic." She made a snort-laugh and shook her head. "I had a rough spell at first. But got through it."

"You look good, Cassie. Real good." Wally came by the bed, sat on the other side of her, and placed his good hand over hers.

"I *am* good, Wally. I'd say better than most of the folks here. You seen the people here?"

"Some."

"You recognize any of 'em?"

"Recognize 'em?"

"They look like anyone you know?"

"No. Only seen three."

"You seen enough. They're all the same, broken as used-up egg shells. I don't belong here anymore." She stood and walked over to the door, then turned back toward us and held on to Uncle Mooks' pocket watch again. "I'm better than anyone in this place and I belong at home. I gotta get out of here, Wally."

"You look real good to me, Cassie," Wally said.

"I swear I can get better at home."

"You might be jumpin the gun here. What do the

doctors say?"

"Doctors? It's on account a them I got myself in this mess. Besides, there ain't no real doctors in this place." She looked into the hall to make sure no one could hear. "Just assistant this and assistant that. I've only seen one bona fide nurse this whole time. Or, at least, one that acted professional enough to be a nurse."

"What're you sayin, Cassie?"

"You need a translator? Take me home."

I held my breath, my heart soaring at the idea.

Wally pushed his chin forward. "You serious?"

"Serious as a funeral."

"Speakin of that, Lawrence Perdue was buried today."

"Don't try to change the subject. Will you help me?"

"You know I'd do anything. But I'm pretty sure you have to be officially discharged."

"Bull-pucky," Mama said.

Wally and I traded looks. "Course I'm not familiar with the procedures," he said. "But didn't Parnell Boyle admit you?"

I stood up, hot at the mention of his name. "Boyle don't matter. His word's no good."

"When he dropped off my things he said he'd come back, but never did," Mama said. "Jason Lee's right. He don't matter."

Mama walked back toward the two of us on the bed. "I've come a long way and I'm to the point I can recognize my old self. The pills are out of my system, and that's the most important part. There ain't nothin more this place can do for me but babysit. I figure I can get that at home."

Wally shrugged. "You get permission, we'll walk out the front door and drive home."

"I'll tell you what I learned from Laverne." Mama's voice held steady. "I sit with her at breakfast. It's her third time in this place. She says they keep people here longer than they need to in order to collect the insurance or government money, whichever program you're on."

"Third time?" I said, shocked at the thought.

"Laverne told me they can collect for thirty days without any extra paperwork to the insurance companies. Thirty days. It's their magic number. Routine, slam-bam payouts. It don't matter if you're ready before then or not. They'll keep you for the money."

I was busting out of my skin over the idea of Mama coming home with us, riding up front next to Wally, and me in the back with the hot wind blowing away all the sorrows the summer had thrown at us.

"They can't keep me against my will, and I'd say my will has had its fill of Delta Community Substance Abuse Services as of right now."

"Who do we talk to?" Wally said.

"About what?"

"Permission."

"You're not listenin to me, Wally. I don't need no one's permission."

"You got to sign somethin. I'd bet my dog on it."

"What'd happen if I don't—and we all know you don't have a dog.

"Nothin, I guess."

"And didn't you just say you should've done more for me?"

Mama was back to her old trick of trapping people with their own words.

"I don't know. If anything happens, I'd be responsible."

He spoke those same words to me not more than three hours earlier, about Uncle Mooks.

"What are they gonna do to you or me?" Mama said. Her arms went out with the question. "Look at me, Wally. I give you my word, I'm gonna get better. That's what'll happen to me. And nothin'll happen to you, not squat."

He saw something in her face that hit him in the right place. His eyes crinkled. "What do you want to do?"

"I want to leave. I'd prefer to slip out quiet, without anyone takin notice. I'm not of a mind to sit in an office for hours or days while someone fetches someone else who takes their sweet time to work up the papers and give me grief about Parnell Boyle havin his signature stuck in my business. Besides, I'm not signin no papers. And I'm not gonna sit through a lecture on the benefits of stayin. The two of you are here now, so now's the time. Let's do it quiet. We'll pretend you're just visitin and everything's normal."

"Then, let's strategize," Wally said. "The suitcase

has to stay. Carryin it through the halls'll look suspicious."

"There's a yellow bag from a place called the Clothes Encounters Boutique in the closet," Mama said. "We can use that instead."

I held the bag open by its loop handles while Mama stuffed clothes from the drawers into it. I handed the bulging sack to Wally and he carried it down the hall, out the front door, across the parking lot to his truck, and dumped the contents on the passenger side floorboard.

Mama pulled a tube of lipstick from her purse, looked into the square mirror attached to the inside of her closet door and colored her mouth. Before Wally got back from the first run, she'd brushed her hair back and attached it in a knot with hair pins.

"You look right nice," I said, thinking it was the first time I'd seen her hair up in some time.

Wally had stuffed the Clothes Encounter bag under the bib of his overalls before coming back for another load.

"How come you did that?" Mama said.

"In case someone's payin attention."

"No need to worry about that."

For the second run we filled the bag with her bathroom items, and for the third trip, clothes from the closet.

"That ought to do it," Wally said.

"Wait." Mama took her nightgown out of the bag. She laid it across the bed. "Let 'em think I'm still around." Then she placed two silver barrettes on the dresser. "They check on us every evenin between five and six. They'll think I'm still in the rec room."

When he got back from the last run, Wally put the bag and the Samsonite suitcase in the closet and closed the door. "Ready to go?"

The plan was to stroll around like we were taking a tour of the place. "We should start by goin up to the recreation room," Mama said. "Elevator's straight ahead."

When we stepped inside, Wally asked, "What number?"

"Three."

Mama tapped her shoe against the gray linoleum floor and studied the ceiling. We inched upstairs slow as molasses in January. The doors finally slid open. A pale woman with springy gray hair trying to escape from a knit cap stood in front of us.

"Laverne." Mama's voice rose. "This here's my son Jason Lee." She nudged me into the hallway. The woman offered her thin, bruised hand for a shake. Mama and Wally stepped out behind me.

Laverne raised her eyebrows at Mama. "What're you up to?"

"This here's Wally. Brought my son to see me."

Laverne fixed her eyes on Wally. "Nice to meet you," she said with a nod.

"Pleasure's mine," Wally said, fidgety as all get out. "Cassie, where's that rec room you want us to see?"

"Down there." Mama pointed in the direction of a

three-legged easel next to an open door. A paper sign pinned to the easel said, *Bingo Today at 4:00 P.M.*

"Nice talkin with you, Laverne. Sorry, I gotta go."

We walked toward the easel. To maintain our strategy of taking a tour, Mama said, "We use this room for watchin TV."

Three men slouched on a drooping couch, their necks cradled against the back cushions, their eyes fixed on the television bolted to the far wall. A preacher pranced back and forth across the screen, waving his arms above his head. The sound was off.

"And this area's for doin crafts and puzzles." She pointed toward a group of tables scarred with cigarette burns. "Let's sit down like we're havin a visit."

Laverne dashed through the door and parked herself in the chair directly across from Mama. "You goin?"

I held my breath, wondering how she knew what we were up to.

"Goin where?" Mama said.

Laverne said, loud as a freight train. "You are, aren't you? I see it on your face."

"Shush," Mama said.

"I know that look." Laverne laughed louder than she had talked.

"I'd like you to hush up, please," Mama said with tight lips.

"Why should I?"

"Because if you do, I got somethin for you."

"For me? What?"

"A pair of barrettes. I set 'em on top of my dresser, just for you."

"They're real nice," I said, anxious for her to get out of our way.

"Is this a payoff, a bribe, hush money?"

"And there's a nightgown, too. On the bed. Might want to claim them promptly." Mama gave Laverne her best smile.

Laverne stood, brought her hand up to close an imaginary zipper across her mouth, and locked it with a twist. Then she returned to the elevator to get down to room 410 and collect her bounty.

I glanced over at the men on the couch. They hadn't budged from their television program.

Mama checked the time on Uncle Mooks' pocket watch. "Tour's over. We'd better get movin before Laverne ruins everything. Let's take the stairwell down the hall."

We managed to fly down the two flights to the landing on the first floor without twisting an ankle or falling. Wally peered through the thin rectangular window on the door that opened into the reception area, and then he pushed on the handle. The door didn't budge. He pushed harder. The shrill of an alarm rang through the stairwell and shook every fiber of my bones.

"So much for not makin a scene," Mama said. "How do we get outta here?"

"I think we'll be okay." Wally rapped his knuckles against the window.

The girl in the striped apron opened the door. "I don't believe you're supposed to be in there."

"Much obliged," Wally said.

The alarm continued. The three of us ran like we'd just held up the joint. Mama and Wally hopped into the cab of our getaway truck. I climbed in the back and held on when we peeled out of the parking lot, tires squealing, back end pitching. When we got to the highway the truck settled down. I turned around and looked through the window. Mama and Wally were laughing like teenagers.

*

We pulled into our drive. I stood up and held onto the cab to see Uncle Mooks on the porch listening to a ball game. A reflection of the setting sun glowed on the windows behind him.

"We got her," I yelled. "Wahoo! She's back."

He slapped his thigh and jumped to his feet.

First thing Mama did after Uncle Mooks set her down was to take the lanyard off her neck and hand his pocket watch back to him.

"You were with me every day," she said. "The watch helped me get through."

He cupped her face and kissed her on the mouth. Then he kissed the watch.

"You boys visit while I go inside and mix up a batch of my lip-smacking pimento cheese spread."

That moment felt like time rewound itself and her stay in Delta Community had never happened.

She brought out a platter of sandwiches and a

pitcher of lemonade mixed from one of the cans in the freezer. We took turns giving Uncle Mooks a detailed account of our great escape.

"Tell me again," he said when we were done. His face beamed.

"We set off the alarm," I said. "Then the girl opened the door and the alarm kept ringin. We headed for the truck fast as three jack rabbits." I jumped off the swing for drama. "And Wally sped outta Dodge City."

We talked into the evening. Wally told stories about him and my daddy back in their heyday. My favorite was about the time they trapped a mess of crawfish for a backyard boil and filled the bathtub with water to keep the critters alive until cooking time.

"They tasted great," Wally said. "There wasn't a tail left to pinch or a head left to suck by the end of the party." Wally shook his head and paused, enjoying the memory. "It wasn't 'til the next day we found out Wesley Garrett had taken a piss in the tub of crawfish instead of the john."

25

Mama stomped and pouted, and tried most every other form of protest to get Wally to go home that evening.

"I'm responsible for you bein here and I'm not leavin until I know you're a hundred percent, however long it takes."

"I'm fine now, I promise. Besides, I know Darla'd skin you alive for stayin. Come to think of it, she might start with me."

"Darla doesn't have nothin to say about this." His voice turned stern. "Like I said before, I shoulda done more. I'm not leavin 'til I'm comfortable you're okay. It's my number one priority towards makin amends, and I owe J.L."

They went on like that until Mama looked at the wall clock and said she'd be retiring to her bedroom because, "After the day I've had, I need some rest."

Wally slept in the front room, slumped on the chair. The man could snore. He stayed for five days, stubborn with his self-proclaimed responsibility for Mama's return to health. He made sure she ate everything on her plate and saw to it she settled down for a nap after lunch.

His being there crowded the house in the evenings,

but each morning after breakfast he filled a mason jar with sweet tea and went outside to tend to whatever needed repair. He started by patching the rotted wood under the porch eaves, then moved on to the garage. I asked if I could help, and he made good use of me.

The first thing we did together was fell a dead cypress. Wally taught me to limb the tree from the base of the trunk, and how to avoid the kickbacks. He taught first by example, then passed the tools my way, talking me through the task. His bad hand didn't affect any of our work.

We cleared underbrush, replaced shingles on the roof of the office headquarters, and mended the fence. We managed to empty an entire 16-ounce can of WD-40 while cleaning tools, lubricating hinges, and removing rust from just about everything.

"I'm thinkin to start a WD-40 fan club one day," he said, serious as could be.

"Can I join?"

"How do you like the sound of vice president?"

Each day's lesson introduced me to a new feeling of achievement. I became a man of action, and it filled me with a sense of worth.

The afternoon we were setting fence posts I asked, "Why'd you give me the book about the Klan?"

"Which one?"

"*The Light of Liberty*. The one about their beginnins."

He stood back and leaned on the handle of the post-hole digger. "You're on the outskirts of manhood, ready to walk in. It's best you have some views of your own when you get there. Readin about all sides'll help."

"I never heard nothin good about the Klan before. The book made 'em out to be regular folks, no different than the crowd at the Grinnin' Catfish. Did you read it?"

He nodded. "There's two more books there. They tell a different story. Learn all you can before forming any opinions to take with you."

"Take where?"

"Into manhood."

I smiled, hopeful it was near.

"There's no denyin the Klan put their stamp on the South. Some around here still see things the same as their kin did for generations back. But it's changin. Slow."

"Grover Peek, he's one of 'em."

"Among others." He frowned. "What I'm tryin to get at is, don't accept what I say or what your mama says or anyone else. It's up to you to think your own thoughts and see things your own way. It's what J.L. always did."

Wally handed me the digger. "Let's get back to work."

*

The next morning while waiting for Mama to serve up her pan-fried ham steaks simmering in butter, the phone rang. I heard Miss Therese's voice yell with surprise because Mama answered. They both talked loud, like they didn't trust the phone lines to carry their words. It felt good to see her in her phone position, back against the wall, receiver cocked under her chin, face in a smile. After a while they settled down and I only heard Mama's side of the conversation.

"Wally and Jason Lee busted me out," she said with a laugh. "I know. That's right, no permission or nothin. It's a long story. I'll tell you when I see you." She listened for a time. "I know. Good Lord, that's right. No. No. Everything's fine here. No, not a hundred percent. No. Well, yes. It'll take time. I couldn't be more proud. He's growin up to be his daddy's son."

Uncle Mooks kept a cautious eye on her. "It'll take time," he said.

Wally got up from the table to whisk the eggs Mama'd put in the mixing bowl. I popped the bread in the toaster. Mama kept on talkin, so we ate without her.

I knew Wally couldn't stay forever. He never let on while he was with us, but the day he took me to Hattiesburg, Darla caused a fuss that would be better described as a tantrum. Word was, when he had told her he was coming out to our place, Darla took a crowbar to the paint aisle and knocked all the cans onto the floor.

On our fifth day of work, while securing the overhang on the chicken coop, Birdette Foster drove his truck up the drive, around the house, and parked it next to us. I'd seen him plenty at the hardware store, but he'd never come out to our place before. He rolled down the window.

"You might wanna get back to town," he said to Wally. "Darla ran off yesterday and left the store wide open. It's none of my business, but I thought you should know."

Wally set the hammer down and walked over to Bird's truck.

"Appreciate it."

"That ain't all."

"I don't suppose." Wally took off his glasses and wiped the lenses on his shirtsleeve.

"She flipped her lid again, worst than last week with the crowbar."

"What'd she do this time?"

"First she knocked over the barrel of sunflower seeds."

"Course," Wally said.

"Sent the whole mess of 'em flyin out the door, down the steps, and onto the sidewalk. Wasn't more than ten minutes before a pack of pigeons swooped in and claimed the seeds as theirs." Birdette put his hand up to shield his eyes from the sun. "Next thing she did was fill her trunk with every can of WD-40 in the store and every box of sheetrock screws. Said she was headed home to Lake Superior. Said 'good riddance to bad places' and drove off."

"I reckon there's somethin else," Wally said, like he already knew.

"Yep. It appears she scattered the screws on the highway, at the bend by the water tower. There's been a run on flat tires."

"Darla's never been happy here. Didn't want me to be neither." Wally shook Bird's hand. "Much obliged.

Sounds like I got a lot of tires to fix."

When we finished working on the chicken coop, he patted me on the back a few times. "I'm proud to be your friend, Jason Lee. You're a good worker."

"You gotta go, don't you?"

"Much as I'd like to stay, it seems I'd best go back and tend to the store. Cassie's getting along fine, and I'll be checkin in on you more often than your Mama'd like." He lowered his face and eyed me over his glasses. "Make sure she stays stable."

"Stable?"

"Stable. Eatin right, not gettin too anxious about things, sleepin through the night. Let me know if she does anything unusual, even the smallest thing."

"What're you gonna do?"

"What I'm gonna do is order a couple more cases of WD-40." He glanced at his watch. "But right now I got somethin to do before I go."

When Wally told Mama he wanted to cook up his famous country-fried steak for us, she complained. "You'll make a big mess and I'll have to clean up. I'll be the only one cookin in my kitchen."

"Ain't no one makes 'em better," he said. "Let me do this. I've been lookin forward to it. It's been my plan all week."

"Me and Uncle Mooks cooked when you were gone," I said. "And the other mornin Wally scrambled up the eggs. I made toast."

"I promise," Wally said, "on our friendship. I'll clean up my mess."

Mama fiddled with a button on her dress. "You don't know where anything is."

Wally won the argument and Mama retreated to the tub for a bubble bath.

He asked Uncle Mooks to collect half-dozen turnips from the garden, and he had me mix a bowl of brownie batter. Then he set three beers on the table and told us to sit there while he cooked.

It was all I could do to keep from laughing when he put on Mama's pink flowered apron with the red heart pocket. First thing he did was crank open two cans of black-eyed peas.

"Mama only makes black-eyed peas on New Year's Day."

"She put greens with 'em?"

"Uh-huh."

"You know why?"

"No."

"The peas are for good luck. Some people add a penny to the pot for extra good luck." He wiped his hands on the apron, picked up a turnip and twisted off the leaves. "The greens stand for prosperity 'cause they're the color of money."

"Me and Jason Lee make money," Uncle Mooks said, a little too loud for my liking. "Outta old magazines. Wanna see?" He stood up, reached into his pocket, and pulled out a phone quarter.

"Put that back." I lowered my voice. "I told you, never let Mama see 'em."

"She ain't here."

I reached to snatch it. His hand jerked and the quarter flew over the table onto the floor by Wally's feet. He picked it up and said, "One of these jammed my gumball machine. Cost me twenty bucks to get it fixed." He stuck the fake quarter in his pocket. "I reckon someone owes me."

Damn that Samson, I thought.

That night I had the best country-fried steak of my life, and I ate more black-eyed peas than I ever care to have again, just for luck.

Knowing Wally needed to leave made me think about life and how lopsided it could be. And how most of the things that you think are good eventually fade away. Like hunting boar, or the idea of good luck for a year, or even the smell of brownies cooling on the counter. And then I thought about how the bad eventually fades away, too, like a wife who leaves you, or the pain of losing a husband who's killed.

After Wally left, Mama said, "He's a good man. There was a time—" She began to clean the refrigerator door and didn't finish her sentence.

Later that night when I flopped on my bed, I started my usual thinking about traveling to other places like J.L. had wanted to. The sound of Mama's footsteps on the stairs brought me back from my daydream. She pushed the door open and leaned her shoulder against the frame.

"Something's missin from my dresser drawer. You know anything about it?"

A heartbeat's a funny thing, the way it speeds up at

times of uncertainty. I sat on the edge of the bed. "I reckon you mean the box?"

"You know anything about the word *private*?"

I concentrated on the lines between the floor planks. "I wasn't snoopin, just packin your bag for Boyle."

"Where is it?"

"The box?"

"I believe that's what we're talkin about."

"My top drawer."

She came in the room and sat next to me. "You looked inside?"

I nodded. "Why's it burned? I thought he was shot. Ambushed or somethin." *The bullet dance, then he's down.*

"I never said he was shot. I never said anything."

"That's for sure. How come?"

"It was too awful."

"I got a right to know the truth, Mama. And you got no right to keep it from me."

She wrapped her arm around my waist. Her next sentence began with a sigh. "You ever hear about somethin called Napalm?"

"Sure. It's in the books. Read about it—and Agent Orange."

"Your daddy was killed by Napalm."

It came out simple as if she'd said he was killed by a bullet or a grenade. "Napalm's like a fireball they drop from a fighter plane that wipes out everything in its path. So, there was nothin left of him but a pile of ashes that caught the wind and blew away." She released her arm from my waist and used it to hug herself.

I should have known, I thought. I read it in her recipe for a hero. It was in the directions. *Heat with napalm to 1,200°.* It was right there.

"Sometime later," she was saying, "another soldier, a friend of his named Corporal James Davis, found that dog tag in the burn area. When he got back to the States he came down here and hand-carried it to me. He said he was supposed to turn it into the Army but just couldn't bring himself to do it, and brought it to me instead. We're not supposed to have it. They say it's the Army's property."

I was about to ask why, when she said, "The terrible thing, the really terrible thing is, it was a mistake. A bad mistake. Our own soldiers dropped the Napalm on him. They call it friendly fire when that happens."

"But he was fightin, wasn't he? You can't die a hero unless you're fightin someone, can you?"

"He wasn't fightin at the time of the mistake." She got off the bed and turned to face me. "You're the first person I've told any of this. I kept the truth to myself and buried it along with him in the box you found."

"He got a medal," I said. "It's in the box."

"It's the Vietnam Service Medal. Everyone who went there got one."

"Not 'cause he fought?"

"No."

"You didn't even tell Uncle Mooks or Wally?"

"No, son. I was too full of sorrow to talk about it. Some people had changed their tune about him and I got comfortable bein the widow of Hadlee's only Vietnam war hero."

"What else didn't you tell anyone?"

"Corporal Davis said he found it in a jungle near a town I can spell, but don't have the foggiest idea how to pronounce. It's spelled X-a-u-n, then L-o-c."

I tried to sound it out.

"The truth is," she said, "I figured the more I knew the worse I would feel, and I had a little boy who didn't deserve that."

I remembered how Wally said she'd collapsed in the doorway when she saw the two servicemen get out of their car, and they had to carry her inside. Then he said she was shaking like a woman possessed.

"Sorry I took it outta your room. I'll get it."

"I suppose it's as safe in your drawer as in mine." She couldn't have said anything better to me—but then she did. "Let's look at it another way, Jason Lee. You, his son, unburied him."

"Mama?"

"Yes."

"Do you know my blood type?

"It's O negative."

I could almost feel it pump through me and thought about how it could help others in the future.

"I'd like to be called J.L. from now on."

26

I stayed close to home to keep an eye on Mama. Almost three weeks had passed and she seemed to be doing fine.

Because I hadn't seen Samson since the shrapnel incident, I asked if I could ride with him on his Saturday deliveries before going into town, and then go fishing in the afternoon. Mama said, fine.

When Dicey rattled up our drive, I leapt off the porch, eager to get going.

"You boys be careful," Mama yelled from the front door. I tossed my fishing gear in the truck bed.

"Don't worry, Mrs. Rainey," Samson yelled over Dicey's engine noise.

I opened the passenger door and hopped in. The smell of shine seeped from every inch of the cab. I rolled down my window. "What happened in here?"

"Spillage accident."

"Let's hightail it before she gets a whiff." I leaned out the window with a big grin, waving goodbye while Samson turned the truck around.

After several miles, Samson said, "Look there." The familiar, broken-down shack I'd ridden past so many times was nowhere to be seen. Kudzu vines had smothered it from sight and were working their way up the trunks of some red cedars close by.

"Scourge," I said.

"What?"

"Mama says kudzu's the scourge of the South, the way it shows no regard for anything other than itself."

"Scourge, huh? There's some folks that act like that too."

"Yeah, kudzu and douchebags."

"My pa says eatin kudzu cures a hangover."

"Eatin it?"

"We'll have to try it next time we're sufferin from a shinover."

"Your pa sure sees things different from Mama."

Not far beyond the shack, a bearded man sat by the side of the road on an old leather bag, with his thumb hitched skyward. I'd seen drifters all my life, and each time we'd pass them I thought we should help them out. Mama'd have nothing to do with them.

"Let's give him a lift," I said to Samson.

"What?"

"Help him out."

"The next guy can. I gotta get to the Otis place."

The guy stood up and jerked his thumb back and forth as we went past.

"Come on, he needs a ride."

Dicey shook when we slowed to the shoulder, well past the man. He grabbed his bag then rushed to meet up with us. The hiker leaned in my window. A smell close to burnt rope and alfalfa came off his checkered shirt. Thin spikes of hair hung down his wide forehead, well past his eyes, and his forearm had what looked to be a homemade tattoo that said, *Gone To Pot*.

"Goin to see kin," he said.

Samson hollered past me, "We're headed to Hadlee but gotta make a stop first."

The hiker grinned, showing a set of chaw-stained teeth. "That'll do."

Through the side mirror I watched him fling his scarred duffle in the truck bed and hop in. He tapped on the rear window and gave a thumbs-up, then settled against the hay bale next to the cab.

"You ever seen him before?" I said.

"Nope."

"Me neither. How old you think he is?"

"Can't tell. He's had it hard. It's in his eyes."

"Looks kind of like a Chubb."

"No he don't. Your still on alert 'cause of the Lil' Buddy incident." Samson laughed. "Still remember how you told 'em the way things are."

Foot-high itch grass lined the skinny road to Mr. Otis' place. After taking a curve, the truck shimmied across a creek bridge made of twisted pine planks.

"I never knew about this place," I said. "Other people live out here, too?"

"Not too many. Used to be called Chicken Gristle."

"Chicken Gristle Valley? J.L. lived here."

"Doubt it," he said. "Old man Otis keeps to hisself. Don't mix or socialize. Got no need since his wife passed."

A small house wrapped with tarpaper sat in a

clearing. Vines heavy with honeysuckle climbed the south wall toward the roof. A wash pot teetered on the porch rail, next to a pair of clay jugs. Further along the property, the old barn looked as dark and tired as the old man in front of it. He wore no shirt under his overalls, and his scrawny arms were wrinkled as a dried tobacco leaf. In no particular hurry, he pushed a wheel barrel holding two cloth sacks.

Samson stopped the truck by the porch. He grabbed the neck handles of the jugs sitting between us and got out.

"Mr. Otis?"

"That you, Noah?" The man's eyes narrowed to a squint.

"No sir, Mr. Otis, it's Samson. Remember me? I been doin the collectin instead of Noah."

He nodded slow. "Reckon I do."

"And I'll be comin from now on. And droppin off the Thunder every week."

His old man's stare watched Samson's every move while he hauled the full jugs to the porch steps and swapped them out with two empties. He hurried over to the old man and tossed the empties on the corn sacks in the wheel barrow.

"Let me push that, Mr. Otis."

"Much obliged."

Mr. Otis looked our way, studying the truck.

"Son," I heard him say. "What you doin with a white boy?"

"We friends."

"You sure?"

"Yes, sir."

When the drifter jumped to his feet to lend a hand with the corn sacks, Mr. Otis stopped dead still. Worry spread over his face. He pointed at the drifter. "That's two whites you got there, Noah." He stepped back.

"I'm Samson, Mr. Otis. We're givin this one a ride to town."

"Just bummin a ride," the drifter said.

Mr. Otis coughed into his fist, then stared at Samson. "Then you'd best be goin."

Samson shook his hand. "I'll be back next week."

"Come by yourself. Be careful, now."

A few miles from the Otis place the drifter slapped the roof of the cab. I twisted to look through the rear window. He was standing, his duffle strap hitched on his shoulder. Samson slowed to a stop, but the man had already jumped.

"Where you goin?" Samson yelled. No answer came. The man walked toward the direction we'd been, his left shoulder weighted down from the load in his bag. "Suit yourself."

"Let's skip town today and head straight to the river," I said.

"I'm for that. Hope they're bitin."

Samson parked Dicey close to his favorite fishing spot, where the current twisted at the bend and confused the fish for a split second, causing them to bite at anything. Fishing being his specialty, Samson had a natural talent for spotting them, especially bluegills, and plucking them out of the water

"Go ahead. I'll get the gear," he said heading for the truck bed.

I walked toward the water.

"Come back, Jason Lee," he shouted. "Look at this."

I ran back. Samson held up a knife.

"That's a Bowie," I said, stunned. "Same as the one Jim Bowie had at the Alamo."

"Saw a flash under the hay bale. Must be the drifters. Musta slipped under there when he got up." Samson smiled.

The foot-long blade was close to two inches wide. An upper guard bent forward at an angle and curved toward the point. Sawteeth had been machined on the backside of the blade.

"See this?" I pointed to the two letter C's scratched into the steel. The sun bounced off it like a warning signal.

"Could mean Chubb."

He shook his head. "Could mean anything. Chubby Checkers. Calvin Coolidge. Cassius Clay."

"He's Muhammad Ali, now."

"I know. Could be his old knife."

Samson clenched it by the leather grip while we made our way toward our fishing spot. About halfway there he said, "I reckon this is mine now."

"You ain't gonna give it back?"

"Sometimes I wonder if your brain works. Give it back? To a drifter I ain't never gonna see the likes of again?"

Before setting up our poles we took a seat on the riverbank. Samson handed the Bowie to me. Its weight pressed across my palm, willing me to curl my hand around it, the same as any red-blooded frontiersman would.

"Let me see it again," Samson said. I wasn't ready to give it up but passed it back anyway. He studied it like it held answers to questions not yet asked, then he tossed it from one hand to the other before lifting it above his shoulder. He flung it across the river toward an old oak stump. The Bowie stuck, stone still.

"I'll fetch it." I took off my shoes and shoved the socks inside. The water cooled my legs as I crossed the lazy-moving river. When I was halfway across and waist-deep in water, a deer fly bit my ear. I swatted after the fact. It circled back for another strike. I swung wild, lost my balance, and went down for a full soaking.

Samson's laugh bounced through the air. "You sound like a donkey," I yelled, but I had to laugh, too.

The knife was stuck solid in the stump and gave me a battle. Conquering its resistance filled me with a sense of power. I held the blade high while trudging back to the other side, and thought, *this piece of steel suits me better than Lil' Buddy, or any gun.*

"Your weapon has returned from the war," I said and handed it to Samson the way you would a sword.

He studied the blade and tested the jagged teeth along the soft of his thumb. "I'm gonna call it The Shark."

"You gotta name everything?"

He smiled and sang, "Oh the shark's got pretty teeth, dear, and he shows 'em pearly white." He rubbed the knife again. "Let's play stretch."

"Soon as I get my shoes back on."

We headed for the clearing behind the river, our usual playing field.

"You first." Samson handed me The Shark. Then he paced off the area between us, calling out each step to twenty. He turned, stood still as a cut-out figure, and nodded for me to start the game we had played so many times before—but with simple kitchen knives.

I aimed to the outside of his right sneaker and stalled. "I never really asked before, but how come you only wear green shoes? Since the day I met you, you been wearin green shoes."

"They more than green shoes. They green converse high-tops with brown laces. My trademark."

I threw the knife. It fell short and slid down the incline. He snickered, picked it up and squinted toward me. He flung it straight into the ground, six inches from my left shoe.

"Sweet," he said. "Glad you talked me into givin him a lift."

I moved my foot to meet the steel and pulled the knife from the ground.

"This here's your reward." I gave a toss that felt like pure energy, the way the knife left my hand and raced through space. The blade entered the dirt like a missile—eight inches from him.

"We'll celebrate," he said. "I got some extra Thunder." Then he stretched out his foot to meet the blade.

"Tonight?" I said.

He came back with another good hit—about twelve inches away.

"Yea, tonight."

I reached for the blade and snapped it hard with another surge of excitement. He jumped and dropped to the ground in a crouch.

"My foot, my foot," he screamed, clasping his sneaker. "My foot." He heaved and twisted like a rabid dog.

I ran to him. "What happened? Let me see."

I pulled on his shoulder. He rolled over and let go with a belly full of donkey laughs. I punched his shoulder. "I'll get you for this."

"Almost did." He laughed some more.

"I'm done with this game. You can stay here and laugh all day, but I'm gonna get me some fish."

While waiting for a bite I watched the leaves float past, working their way downstream toward Hadlee and beyond, free as the drifters who come through.

27

The day had started with a head full of freedom and the strength of a Bowie knife. It promised to get better with a drinkin meetin.

The knapsack slapped against my back with a rhythm that moved me through the moonless night. The chirp of crickets looking for mates filled my ears, and I felt better than I had all summer.

The sound of a smooth-running engine hummed in the distance. It wasn't long before headlight's bounced on the road in front of me. A shock of light burst from a side-mounted spotlight and lit the surroundings like daylight. The black and white cruiser stopped. Sheriff Videlle's deep, no-nonsense voice came from the driver's side.

"Where you headed, Jason Lee?"

"Not sure." I put a hand to my forehead to shield my eyes.

"Stay right there." It sounded like a dog's bark. The car door opened. He stepped out. The dim interior light shined on Deputy Willard, sitting shotgun.

Sheriff Luther Videlle was an ex-Marine and an ex-alcoholic who was still as fit as he'd been on active duty. Early each morning before sunup, he ran the county roads, the only man around our parts to do such a thing. He stood in front of me tall as a stretched-out shadow in the night.

"I ain't doin nothin wrong," I said. "Just goin to the river." Then, stupidly, I guess due to nerves, I walked around him to continue on my way.

Sheriff Videlle grabbed my shoulder and whipped me around.

"What?" I yelped.

"Stay put. I'll tell you when you can move on."

I squeezed the straps on my knapsack. "Yes, sir."

"That's better. Now, it just so happens we were on our way out to your place. I understand you paid the old nigger Clarence Otis a visit today."

"Mr. Otis? Yeah, with Samson. We picked up corn from him."

A grunt came from Deputy Willard when he got out of the car. With each step he took toward us, the fabric on his pant legs rubbed together, sounding like the scrape of sandpaper. He stood next to the sheriff, blocking the glare of the spotlight. "I'd say you did more than pick up corn."

It didn't make sense, why they talked to me like that.

"I stayed in the truck," I said. "Samson picked up the corn. For his pa." With those words, I realized I could be setting Mr. Johnson up for big trouble.

"Funny," Deputy Willard said. "The nigger boy said the same thing. You work on your alibi together?"

Sheriff Videlle shot him a look. "I'll take it from here." He stepped toward me, leaving little space between us.

"What alibi? What boy? What's goin on?" I said.

"Sir," Sheriff Videlle said. "You mean what's goin on—sir."

"Yes, sir."

He stood straighter than before and hitched his thumbs in his belt. "You leaving town?"

"No, sir. Just headin to the river."

"On your own?"

"Uh-huh."

"With a pack?"

"Uh-huh."

"Your mama know where you are?"

"No, sir." My forehead tightened. "Is this about Mr. Johnson?"

"No. It's about what happened at the Otis place. I believe you know more than you're saying, Jason Lee."

"No, sir, sheriff. I swear, I don't know nothin."

Deputy Willard stepped forward again. "Take the pack off and give it here."

I worked it off my shoulders and handed it over. Deputy Willard took it to the rear of the car, popped the trunk, and threw it in.

"What're you—"

"Tell you what," Sheriff Videlle said. "Your friend's sitting in a cell at the station."

"What friend?"

"Who do you think?" Willard said.

Sheriff Videlle said, "How about you, me, and the deputy here take a little ride to town?"

"Samson's in jail? Jail?"

"Not officially. Just holding him 'til we set things straight. Now, turn around."

Before it all sank in, Sheriff Videlle gripped my arms above the elbows, then pulled them back. In no time it felt like he'd fastened handcuffs around my wrists, but it was his fingers tightening around them. He steered me toward the car. Deputy Willard opened the back door on the driver's side.

"Watch your head," Sheriff Videlle said, then he heaved me into the backseat. I landed on my shoulder. The sudden, searing pain caused me to gasp for breath, and the sour smell of the seat washed over me. I stayed put. The cruiser moved out. Dirt and loose leaves whirled under the tires.

I got myself upright. A honeycombed grill separated me from the two of them. "You arrestin me?"

Deputy Willard twisted sideways to look at me, chewing a wad of gum. "The nigger boy says you picked up a hiker."

I froze, except for my heartbeat.

"Shut your trap, deputy." Sheriff Videlle pointed his thin index finger at him. "Take a break and shut your trap." His eyes fixed on me through the rear-view mirror. "We're not arresting you. Just want to talk."

"About the knife?"

"Just what I thought. You *do* know something." His eyes pierced me from the mirror. "This is the first we've heard about a knife. Why don't you tell us about it."

"It dropped under the hay bale and we figured it to

be his."

"His?"

"The hitchhiker. A Bowie knife. After we found it, when we went to go fishin."

A surge of static from the radio cut me off. Fractured words erupted from the car speakers. I couldn't make them out.

"Sonuvabitch," Deputy Willard said.

"Holy fuck." Sheriff Videlle picked up the mouthpiece.

"10-4, we're on our way."

The voice from the radio came through better—almost clear. "What's your ETA?"

"We'll make it in ten minutes, come hell or high water."

"Copy that."

"What's goin on?" I said, every cell in my body on high alert.

"Sit back, kid."

The car lurched. The siren shrilled. We raced through the Mississippi night toward town.

The cruiser bounced when we turned into the alley behind the jail and screeched to a stop by the back door. Large spotlights mounted to the corners by the roof of the beige building beamed down. Both men ran inside, leaving me alone, scared, and clueless. My shoulder still ached.

I wondered what my Mama was going to do when she found out I was being held prisoner in the back of a police car. Locked in like a no-good criminal, with the car's rear doors stripped of handles and knobs.

Soon lights moved down the alley. A white panel truck pulled into the space next to the cruiser. The driver jumped out and ran into the building.

"Hey," I yelled, too late. Then I screamed, "Bastard," and slammed my fist against the window. I kept banging on the glass even though the man was already inside the building.

Pretty soon I gave up and slumped back, brought my feet up and hugged my legs. My eyes fixed on the words stenciled on the panel truck's door. Dunlap County Coroner. County Coroner. I read it over and over.

Deputy Willard came out of the jail and opened the car door. He dropped one shoulder and leaned in. "Jason Lee, we got a problem inside." His voice was low. "I need you to come with me." He reached in to offer to help me exit the back seat. His armpits smelled like onions. "Now, when we get inside there, I'm gonna put you in a cell. For your own protection. You hear me? For your own protection."

I walked stiff as a robot. The gravel crunched under my shoes. "With Samson?"

He took hold of my arm. "Don't do nothin stupid."

He maneuvered me into the first cell directly beyond the back door. A stained cot, no more than five feet long and two feet wide, hung from hinges attached to the bricks wall. Attached to the middle of the side wall was a rusted sink next to a toilet with brown water in it and no seat. I looked around and began to shake.

Deputy Willard slammed the cell shut, rushed toward the front portion of the building and slipped through a door, out of sight. I wrapped my hands around the iron bars and pressed my head against them. Across the room, separated by a desk and workspace, was another cell. An empty cell. They'd said they were holding Samson until things were straightened out.

"Samson?" I yelled. "Samson?"

I looked toward the door to the front but couldn't see much through the sliver of an opening, maybe four inches wide.

"What's goin on? Ain't I entitled to a phone call?" I yelled, too afraid to allow the thoughts I feared to surface. "I need to call my mama," I said with a shaky voice. "She don't know where I am." I might as well have been a speck of dust. "Where's Samson Johnson? I want to talk to him. Did you let him go?" My voice had turned into a thin whine.

I sat on the cot trying to calm down, but my lungs could only hold small breaths. I rubbed my shoulder, wondering if it was dislocated. And I stared at the paint chips on the floor that had dropped from the plaster ceiling.

The back door I'd come through with Deputy Willard busted open so fast it smacked against the wall. A man in a blue jumpsuit with silver reflective strips stepped inside to hold it open. He grabbed the front of a gurney and maneuvered it through the door. Another man pushed from behind. They rushed past me and opened the door to the front room, and I could finally see inside.

The gurney stopped next to a man lying on the floor. A halo of blood circled his head. My eyes darted to the marking on his arm. *Gone To Pot.*

Sheriff Videlle shot me a look overflowing with misery. I'd seen enough to be certain the drifter was dead. It wasn't long before they had him on the gurney, and then they rolled him past my cell and out the back door. A bloody sheet covered his body. A heat rushed through me and my chest felt like it was tightening.

"I need to call my mama," I said again to no one, holding back tears. "Where's Samson? I wanna talk to Samson."

The same two men in the jumpsuits came back with their gurney. Again they went to the front room. They turned right, past the door, and moved out of my sight. Sheriff Videlle, Deputy Willard, and the men pushing the gurney were all there, but I only heard low mumbled voices and scuffing sounds, until Deputy Willard said, "What a mess. What a fuckin' mess."

The gurney banged into the doorframe on its way back through. As it glided past me, Samson's green high-top sneakers with brown laces poked out from the sheet covering his body.

The world went silent. I hurled the remains of my supper through the cell bars. *Give it back? To a drifter I ain't never gonna see the likes of again?*

My knees buckled. I hung onto the bars until I couldn't hold on anymore, and I slipped to the floor.

*

Sheriff Videlle woke me. He helped me from the floor to the cot. "I called your mother." He covered my shoulders with a blanket and sat next to me, close enough that I could feel his deep breaths. "She didn't know you were gone."

I rubbed at the barf stuck to the side of my face. "What time is it?"

"Ten-thirty." His voice cracked.

"Was she mad?"

"Surprised. I didn't tell her about any of this. I just said I'd bring you home."

Sheriff Videlle leaned forward, shoulders hunched. His hatless forehead glowed with sweat. His eyebrows pinched. It took some time before he said, "Come on, son, we'd best be going."

I rode up front with him. The only sounds came from me—groans and a heavy, whining breath. The memory of Samson's motionless sneakers burned on the lids of my closed eyes.

"Son."

Sheriff Videlle's voice startled me. I opened one eye, then the other, and looked his way. The reflection from the dash lights darkened his eye sockets and caused the tip of his chin to glow. He rolled down his window. The warm night air smelled putrid.

"When I was about your age, one of my brothers was shot in the back."

I looked away, out my window. Several shades of night blurred past. Why was he talking to me about his brother? What did it have to do with Samson? Why was Samson there, and what was the drifter doing there? Why wasn't anyone on duty? Whose fault was all this?

"Gunned down over a pet dog that wandered into the wrong neighborhood," he said.

I wanted to tell him to shut up.

"We were raised with Italian pride. Where I grew up, neighborhoods were built on pride and hatred. We hated the Micks. You ever see the movie, *West Side Story*, about the Sharks and Jets?"

"Yes," I said, even though I hadn't.

"It was sort of like that."

We drove past Cobb's Creek School. The night fog rolled through the deserted playground. It looked haunted and heartbroken, like it knew one of its children was dead.

"After my brother was shot," Sheriff Videlle said, "my dad settled the score by killing the guy who did it, and then their people came after him."

I didn't care about Sheriff Videlle or his brother or his dad. But what he said sent my mind racing with thoughts about hatred. How strong it could be, like the way I hated Boyle and Uncle Mooks hated Peek. All the hatred J.L. had seen, and how it'd shaped the Chubb boys. I thought back to the time we ran into them on Wilders Grove Road and what might have happened if the crows hadn't run us all off. And how nothing good ever came from hate.

A doe flashed past the headlights. My chest heaved against the seat belt as Sheriff Videlle slammed on the brakes and swerved to miss her. I wished we'd hit the damn thing, crashed into a tree, and burst into flames.

"You know what they call a flock of crows?" I said.

"Afraid I do."

"A murder."

We didn't talk again until we reached the drive up to my house.

"Son, I haven't sorted out everything that happened tonight, but I will."

He drove slow as an old lady up to our place. Uncle Mooks' huge silhouette paced on the porch, backlit from the house lights. He bounced down the stairs when he saw the cruiser, arms flapping. He looked like a bird too large to leave the ground. Mama was close behind.

By the time Sheriff Videlle turned off the engine they were next to the car.

"What's goin on, Luther?" Mama yelled through his open window. "What're you doin with my boy?" Uncle Mooks came around my side and opened the door.

"Samson's dead," I said.

"What?" Mama said. "What did you say? Oh, my God. Are you okay, Jason Lee? Are you hurt?" She ran around to my side of the car. "Get out of the way," she said to Uncle Mooks. "Let me see him."

I reached for her hand. "I'm fine, Mama."

She leaned in and felt my face. I let her help me out of the car. Sheriff Videlle got out too, stiff like his bones ached. We all walked toward the house.

I didn't care to go inside, so I sat on the porch

swing. Uncle Mooks sat down next to me. "I saw Samson's shoes," I said, staring out into the night. "His dead shoes."

Uncle Mooks put his arm around me and pulled my face into his chest. A wail made its way up from the depths of my lungs and bounced off the cypresses throughout our property, then shot its way back through me. The more Uncle Mooks rocked on the swing, the louder it got.

28

The Johnsons held the settin-up the following Wednesday. While we drove to their house, Mama explained the practice to me as best she could.

"Some folks call it a wake, some a vigil. Around here the coloreds call it a settin-up. Samson'll most likely be laid-out on a table or a bed for a couple days so family and friends can come together and say their goodbyes."

Parked cars and trucks with license plates that hailed from Arkansas and Louisiana and east to Florida were jammed into the front yard. Even more lined the road. We passed the Johnson's place, parked on a side road, and walked in.

The familiar glass bottles hung from their cedar tree in the front yard. "A bottle tree's for protection," Samson had once told me. "They ward off evil."

Mr. Johnson's collection of old hubcaps trimmed the wood siding on the front of the house.

There were so many people inside it seemed the walls could have burst open any minute, and the place smelled like deep fried everything. Mama handed me the fresh rhubarb pie she'd made and asked if I'd take it to the kitchen. I worked through the crowd, bumping against people as downhearted as me, carrying vacant expressions on their dark faces. Some stared at me like they thought I'd walked into the wrong house.

Food for the grieving covered every surface of the kitchen. Cast-iron pots of chitlins and hog maws boiled on the stove. The counter, usually tidy and scrubbed clean by Mrs. Johnson, was packed with mounds of fried chicken and catfish piled on platters. Dozens of wooden spoons were wedged in crusted casseroles of macaroni and cheese, sweet potatoes smothered in marshmallows, and large bowls of every kind of gumbo you could imagine.

Two women came in carrying bowls covered with foil. The older one had a long, stretched-out face and arms skinny as chicken bones. She set her bowl next to a pot of red beans, peeled back the foil, and pulled out one of her red Kool-Aid pickles. The other one did the same with her pickled watermelon rind.

"What you doin here boy? You sure you're in the right place?" she said.

I wanted to tell her I knew Samson better than she did and that we were blood brothers, but instead I just said, "Yes, ma'am."

"Yours goes there, fool." She nodded toward a long table against the far wall, crammed with desserts. I set Mama's pie next to a glass dish of Samson's favorite peanut butter cream fudge squares. For an instant, I could see him eating one, biting off all four corners first, the way he always did.

I knew I'd have to look at his dead body before too long, and that brought on the memory of seeing his shoes on the gurney. The thought sucked the air from me and set off a dizzy spell, the kind you get from twirling too fast. By the time my head cleared, the two ladies had me blocked in against the dessert table.

"Hallelujah!" The skinny one hollered, throwing her hands in the air. "In the name of Jesus, Samson's a comin home. Comin home where there ain't no pain." Long beaded earrings hung from her earlobes and swung in circles as she raised her hands high. The smell of Mr. Johnson's Black Thunder seeped from her breath.

"Excuse me," I said.

"He's headin for the sweet light of Jesus." The other lady threw her hands up, too, and screeched even louder, "Where there ain't no darkness."

They grabbed each other's hands and began to sway back and forth. "Let's pray to the light." They carried on like I was invisible, like they didn't even notice me anymore, a white face in a sea of black.

Right then the kitchen filled with people pushing their way toward the food, anxious to load their plates. My head was spinning, and instead of working my way past the two ladies I got down on my knees like a five-year old idiot child and crawled under the table. I sat there Indian-style, hunched over because my head kept hitting the underside of the table.

"You see that?" someone said. "The white boy?"

Flushed in humiliation I watched the ladies' skirts sway back and forth with each "Hallelujah," and the other folk's shoes march across the floor. One lady's ankles were swollen, and her thick feet oozed out of a pair of shoes that must have been borrowed from someone with feet half her size. Before long, a pair of boots I recognized came toward the table. They were Noah's brown ones with paint splatters.

"That white boy's under there," the skinny lady said. "Just sittin there for no good reason."

"What?" Noah said and crouched down to look at me. His bloodshot eyes had no expression. "What the hell, Jason Lee?"

I moved over and tapped the floor, signaling for him to join me.

"Get yourself outta there. What're you doin, anyway?"

"Got dizzy. Couldn't breathe and my knees gave out. Felt like I didn't belong and needed to get outta the way." The bulky seam and the one pocket on the back of my pants pressed against my tailbone, and I knew sitting under the table was a crazy mistake. I worked my way out, excusing myself as folks stepped out of the way with raised eyebrows.

"Where is he?" I said.

"My folks room."

"Why's he there?"

"Pa figured the livin room'd be too crowded."

"Sure is."

"Think I'm ready to see him now."

Noah led the way through the crowd to his parent's room. A pine wedge propped the door open. There, on the bed, Samson lay on top of a quilt fashioned with large blue stars stitched on red and white squares, except for one, lone, purple star down by his right foot. A lit candle was on the nightstand. I squeezed my eyes shut, wishing I were blind and never had to see again.

"What's that smell?" I said, my eyes still closed.

"Embalmin. Pa's friend did us a favor. Learned embalmin when he worked in Gulfport."

"That's nice." I didn't know what else to say.

I finally opened my eyes and then we stepped inside the small room. I was forced to stand so close to the bed my knees brushed against the quilt. The threat of vomit hit the back of my throat when I saw someone had set two slugs on his eyes. My guess, probably the uncle who made electrical boxes.

The first dead body you see is supposed to be an old person, not your best friend in a stiff black suit you've never seen him in before and a stupid yellow bow tie. Samson's face looked waxy, or, greasy. His arms were crossed over his chest as if he was taking a moment to warm himself before jumping up and shouting, "Gotcha, Jason Lee. Good one, huh?" I thought of Saturday, how he pretended I'd hit his foot with the knife. I couldn't help but notice he had on brown shoes.

"Why are those on his feet?"

"Mama," Noah said.

"It ain't right."

"I know."

"They were his trademark."

"She couldn't bring herself to it."

"Why are those on his eyes?" I said, fixated by the

eerie silver disks.

"Keeps 'em closed."

"It don't look right."

"I know," he said again.

"What'd happen if I took 'em off?" Noah shrugged, the same way Samson always had. I inched a couple steps forward to get closer to Samson's face, held my breath, and fast as I could, snatched the disturbing circles off his eyes. It was the least I could do. His eyes stayed shut. The slugs felt cold as ice cubes in my hand. I dropped them in my pants pocket.

I needed to do one more thing for Samson. I took hold of his right hand and pressed my index finger against his to remind him, in good times or bad, we'd always stay blood brothers— an amalgamation of two. As I left the room, I remembered all the Pepsis we'd bought using slugs just like the ones in my pocket.

I went out to the front yard and saw Dicey parked out on the road. *Let's give him a lift, help him out.* I walked toward the truck, lost in the darkest shade of sadness, and didn't hear Elijah come from behind me. He yanked on my arm.

"You was there, Jason Lee." His eyes accused me. I stared at him, wordless as a mute. "You was there."

"What're you talkin about?"

"You was with Samson when he died."

"No, I wasn't," I said, unable to stop shaking my head back and forth. I reached in my pocket and felt the slugs. "No, I wasn't," I said louder.

"Yes you was, when it happened at the sheriff's."

"No. It happened before I got there, and I couldn't see nothin."

"We got a right to know." Elijah's voice turned angry.

"I told him," I said, my voice in a full yell, my head still shaking no. "I told him not to pick up the hiker." The lie came out of my mouth so strong it almost seemed right. "And I told him not to keep the knife."

"The one that killed him?"

"Ain't none of this my fault. I told him not to do it. That's all."

"I gotta know," Elijah said again. "You was his friend. You was supposed to watch over him. It's what friends do."

"I *am* his friend." I wiped my nose, wanting to run, get away—die and be with Samson. "Leave me alone."

I looked past him toward the house just as Mama burst out the front door, headed toward us with a pace that sent her pocketbook bouncing against her hip. When she reached us she said, "It's time we go." She put her hand on my shoulder and steered me to the car.

Elijah yelled, "We ain't done talkin, Jason Lee."

Mama held me tighter.

*

We drove home in a ball of silence. I finally asked her what'd happened.

"Nothin."

"It's for sure you were mad when you come out of the Johnsons'."

"You mean stormed out in a rage?"

"Uh-huh."

"I can't talk about it now. I have to calm down first. What with all that's happened I'm havin trouble copin."

We didn't go far before she exhaled and brought her hand up to her forehead. "There was a man in the house. A relative of the Johnsons', from Boonville. He'd been drinkin quite a bit, so I shouldn't take it to heart. He had a chip on his shoulder and started mouthin off 'bout marchin in Selma with J.L."

"He marched with J.L.? Which one was he? Did you catch his name?" I was thinking it could, just maybe, be Spam.

Barely three weeks had passed since Mama'd come home from Delta Community, and I didn't want to bring up something that might interrupt her recovery or cause a relapse. Samson and Wally were the only ones I told about finding the journal. Besides, she'd kept so many secrets from me I figured I was entitled to that one.

"His name's not the point, Jason Lee. The point is I feel like such a fool."

"Why, Mama?"

"That man, that horrible drunk man said J.L. had no business bein in Selma. Said the whites were only there for themselves—to get their white faces on the front page of the newspapers."

She might as well have thrown a brick at my head. "What you sayin?" I slumped a little further in my seat.

Mama clutched the steering wheel. "And I didn't

say nothin, just stormed out. J.L.'d be ashamed of me. I'm ashamed of me. Too polite to stand up for him. Too weak to cause trouble. Sometimes it gets the best of me."

"You got that wrong, Mama. He'd be proud."

When we got home she took to her room. I was scared to death she'd caught another case of melancholy. And also scared that one day I'd have to tell the truth about it being my idea to pick up the devil drifter.

*

Three days later we went back to the Johnsons' for the funeral services. We had thunderstorms every day after the settin-up, and Mrs. Johnson held strong to her belief that rain on a funeral day meant the heavens weren't ready to receive the deceased.

The warm air coming through the car windows smelled of moist asphalt. The services had started by the time we pulled in behind the cars and trucks, each with a strip of purple cloth tied to its antenna. Mama wrapped her hand around my elbow as we walked up the soggy drive toward a large plastic tarp extending out from the front of the Johnsons' house.

Since the coloreds' old church burned down after being hit by lightning, the Reverend Lamar Tippett held services wherever the Lord sent him. His voice sprang from under the tarp.

"We give thanks for this day, oh Lord."

A chorus of "Amens" came back to him.

The mourners formed a half circle facing the

reverend. A sea of dark hats bounced as the people spoke back to the reverend. We stayed behind the crowd. My head felt empty from lack of sleep since the settin-up, and my face felt pinched from too many days of sadness.

Reverend Tippet jumped onto a tree stump. He clutched a worn Bible in his right hand. Samson lay next to him in an open box made of knotted planks. It balanced on saw horses draped with a purple velvet cloth. The reverend's receding hairline shined dark as a polished eggplant. The whites of his eyes were more yellow than white, and projected fury, while his voice delivered authority.

"It's a sad day," his voice boomed. He raised his Bible. "And it's a day for rejoicing."

There were more "Amens!"

Mrs. Johnson began to moan, "Samson. My son, my son."

Reverend Tippett smiled up to heaven. His teeth were white as pearl buttons. "God has reviewed and judged this young boy worthy. God has granted him entry into the celestial city." Beads of sweat ran down his sizeable forehead.

"Preach on," a man shouted. A chorus of others followed. "Preach on."

I felt like a spectator at a performance I didn't understand or belong at.

The reverend leapt off the tree stump and pranced around the casket, with his hands in the air. The congregation shouted, "Hallelujah," and stomped their feet on the damp ground.

"Like the shroud feeling its way home," Reverend Tippett said, with his palms open to the sky and eyes closed. "Ashes to ashes, dust to dust."

I glanced over at the Johnsons. Mrs. Johnson looked like she could fall over at any time. Mr. Johnson and Noah stood on either side of her and Elijah fanned her with a pleated-up newspaper. He waved it with all his might, as if each stroke would force strength back into her.

"There ain't no dirt roads or two-room shacks in heaven," the reverend said on his way back to the tree stump. "And no storms or sufferin or hatred," he said louder. "Hallelujah, in the name of Jesus Christ our Lord," he screamed. "Young Samson's light will shine the brightest of all."

I looked back at the Johnsons just as Mrs. Johnson fell to the wet ground. Noah and his father tried to catch her but she went down too fast. My mind exploded, thinking she dropped dead at Samson's funeral.

"Lord, help us," the chicken-armed lady screamed. "It's Odetta."

Reverend Tippett threw his Bible on the stump and hurried to Mrs. Johnson's aid. Samson's service had been cut short.

They carried Mrs. Johnson into the house.

"Let's stay out here," I said to Mama, thinking about the man who had upset her at the settin-up.

She looked at the clouds in the distance. "It's best

we go in."

We stood together with our backs against the living room wall, to the left of a framed pencil sketch of President John F. Kennedy. The dim light helped us fade from view.

Mrs. Johnsons' two sisters hovered over her, each fluttering a church fan with a picture of the Last Supper on it. Other people watched, gathered in clumps and holding paper plates filled with ribs and dirty rice and cornbread.

This went on for some time until Mr. Johnson took matters into his own hands. He placed a small glass vial under his wife's nose. The sting of the smelling salts caused her to sit upright and cough a ball of phlegm into her hanky.

She studied the green discharge for a while, then looked up and glanced around the room. "I believe it's time to take Samson to his sleepin place."

We walked toward the cars in a hush. The rain clouds moved closer. A woman wearing a hat fashioned from peacock feathers handed Mama a purple ribbon to tie on our antenna.

The cars fell in line behind the black pick-up truck carrying Samson's burial box wrapped in the velvet cloth. We followed, taking last place in the procession.

As many times as I'd watched funeral parades roll past our house, cars at a crawl, lights on, antenna flags flapping, it was my first time riding in one. I couldn't take my eyes off our house when we passed. Uncle Mooks was on the porch, watching like always.

"Do you think he knows which one's us?" I asked Mama.

"Course he knows."

I gave him a wave he didn't seem to see, then shut my eyes and wished he was with us.

The cars traveled slow in the damp midday heat, straight past the Odom Hill Cemetery. We continued up Country Road 38 another two miles, then turned down a road that ended at a rundown graveyard. A wooden plank nailed across the top of two tall posts had the name Old Trinity scorched into the face.

We parked out front by the sign and walked in. Mr. Johnson, Noah, Elijah, and three of Samson's uncles led the way, carrying the box on their shoulders. The six of them wore dark suits. They sang in low, hushed tones, like they'd practiced all their lives for this moment. *My sin is forgiven and my soul set free, and I heard from heaven today.*

Mrs. Johnson and the reverend swayed in rhythm behind the pallbearers. We passed plots that were little more than depressions and walked by gravestones barely visible under heavy brush and weeds. We kept walking until we came to the hole in the ground with a mound of dirt beside it. Reverend Tippett placed himself at the head of the grave space.

"The Lord gave, and the Lord hath taken away. Blessed be the name of the Lord." He flipped through the Bible pages to his next passage. The clouds rolled closer. The coarse wool of my one-pocket suit gnawed on my legs and itched worse than poison oak. Despite the sweat dripping down my back, I wasn't about to take off my jacket.

"Let not your heart be troubled." The reverend didn't need to look at the words on the page. His yellow eyes surveyed the congregation. "In my Father's house are many mansions."

The pallbearers shuffled to the hole, all six faces filled with heartache. As the sermon continued, they held the casket steady, three on each side.

Before we left the house that morning, Mama had told me about how it's a custom to bury the dead with their head facing east, so they don't have to turn around in their grave to see Gabriel when he blows his trumpet on Resurrection Day, and how the coloreds put coins around the gravesite as a token for admittance to the spirit world. When she told me that, I wondered how it was she knew so much about the subject she avoided the most—religion.

I lost track of the reverend's preaching until he lifted his finger straight out. It seemed to be pointed in the direction of my heart.

"Greater love hath no man than this, that a man lay down his life for his friends."

My knees wobbled against the wool pant legs. I looked into the reverend's eyes. Out of nowhere came my voice. "Samson was gonna be a lawyer for the NAACP." Every black face turned to watch me. "Or work for Jessie Jackson." Mama yanked on my coat sleeve.

With a slam, the reverend closed his Bible and his

voice yelled out the final words, "For many are called but few are chosen."

"Amen," I said with the others and held on to Mama's hand as they lowered Samson into the ground, his head facing east.

The storm clouds glided overhead and sun rays streamed through the gaps. Mr. Johnson, Noah, and Elijah picked up shovels. The crackle of rock and earth hit the box. I reached into my coat pocket and took out the quarter I'd polished up the night before. As we left, I dropped it on the freshly turned mound of Mississippi dirt.

Walking back to the car, through the musky graveyard, it hit me. Not only did I lose Samson, but my childhood had come to its end.

29

My feet moved possum-slow on the walk to school that first day back. Tenth grade was supposed to be the best year yet, one to get serious about the future Samson and I dreamt about, but how could it be?

The stench of fresh paint filled my nose as I opened the classroom door. The old beige walls had been painted over with a coat of flat grey, the color of misery itself. Miss Dodd stood at the head of the class, her black hair pinned back so tight it pulled her eyes into slants.

"I want to welcome y'all," she was saying, but then she stopped and looked at me in the doorway. She glanced at her watch. "Jason Lee, you're late."

Everyone turned in their seats, all eyes on me. I checked the clock above the chalkboard. *Three minutes.*

"Take your seat, young man."

I looked toward Samson's old desk to find Elijah sitting there, the first I'd seen of him since the funeral. His eyes and nose and lanky body were so similar to Samson's, I had to press my fingernails into my palms to help calm myself before taking the seat next to him. He turned away and stroked the grain on the wood surface.

"As I was saying," Miss Dodd cleared her throat. "I

want to welcome y'all back from your summer vacation."

The word vacation wrapped around my brain so tight I couldn't do much more than stare straight ahead. Welcome back from your summer of nightmares would have been more like it. Her mouth moved, but my mind wandered so far away I didn't hear anything until Elijah shot out of his seat.

"Yes, ma'am?" His voice stammered.

"My condolences about your brother. May God give you comfort."

Elijah looked at the floor. "Thank you, ma'am."

He knew as well as I did that she didn't mean a word of it. Miss Dodd had been our teacher the year before. She was an old-fashioned Southern woman who didn't hide how she felt about desegregation in schools having been wrongly forced on a proud society steeped in tradition. At every opportunity she stopped Samson and me from studying or working on projects together.

Before Elijah's butt landed back in its seat she said, "I spent time in New York City this summer." She took the occasion to turn her visit into a history lesson, one we'd already learned in the fourth grade. "I'm sure y'all know it's the largest populated city in this United States. Three times more people live there than live in all of the state of Mississippi."

New York City—bought for twenty-four dollars worth of glass beads, its natural harbor critical to America's growth, twelve million immigrants entered through the halls of Ellis Island blah, blah, blah.

I raised my hand.

She stopped abruptly.

"Yes?"

"I was wonderin when we're gonna study the Civil Rights Movement."

Miss Dodd squinted and pointed at me. Blood-red polish covered her fingernail.

"That interruption was uncalled for. I'll see you after class."

"It's important." I held my eyes steady. "The movement."

She looked at her watch, just like when I came in. "After class, Jason Lee."

"I'd like to be called J.L. from now on," I said, and looked around the room to see that everyone heard me. A few of the kids nodded, but they did it slowly, like the act itself might cause Miss Dodd's foul mood to turn toward them.

"Class," she said. "Can anyone name the five boroughs that make up the city of New York?"

I wondered if I'd ever be able to study or learn anything again. The recess bell shook me out of my daze.

Outside, I stood by a dogwood next to the road, its leaves scorched from the summer's heat. I looked back toward the schoolhouse and saw Elijah on the stoop, slumped over like his bones were missing.

I turned away and spotted Reba in the lower grades' area, parked on one of the wooden seats hanging from the little kids swing set. Her legs were stretched out and crossed at the ankles. When she noticed me watching her, she pulled herself out of the swing and walked toward me, past some younger boys playing kickball. Her pleated skirt swayed.

She took my hand and placed a folded piece of paper in my palm. My first instinct was to pull back, but I didn't. She smelled like honeysuckle, and I noticed a blue powder coating on her eyelids. I realized we were finally the same height.

"I'm sorry, Jason Lee. I mean J.L. I came over to tell you how bad I feel and to say I was wrong about you and Samson bein friends. After I heard about that awful, awful killin, I couldn't think 'bout nothin but you and Samson, friends forever, no matter what anyone else thought."

"Nice of you to say somethin."

Reba twirled a few strands of her hair around a finger. "I thought about it more than I've thought about anything else in my life. The very idea of bein friends with a colored, no matter what anyone else thinks." She looked around the play yard. "The two of you laughin and goofin around, just like you were brothers."

"We were. Blood brothers." I turned my hand over to show her my index finger, where the small scar could still be seen. "His blood's in me."

She twirled her hair tighter. "My folks don't think that's right. None of their friends do either."

"They can think what they want, but they can't think for me."

An out-of-bounds ball skipped toward us. Reba

leaned down to pick it up. She tossed it back with a put-out expression, brushed her hands on her skirt, and said, "They're set in their ways, my folks. But I finally figured out that I don't have to believe somethin just 'cause they do."

"That's right, 'cause you're you." I wasn't sure what else to say so I said nothing, and turned all my attention to the color on her eyelids. What finally came out surprised her as much as it did me. "You look real pretty today, Reba Lynn."

She brought her hands up to her mouth the way the contestants who win beauty pageants do. "Thank you," she said into them. Then she put one hand over her heart. "To tell the real truth, I was a little jealous of you two 'cause you didn't give me the time of day."

Again, I couldn't come up with what to say. Luckily, the recess bell rang. As we walked back toward the classroom together, Reba said, "I just wanted to say again how sorry I am."

"Me, too."

"Can you tell me what happened?"

"Sheriff Videlle said he'd sort it all out, but we ain't heard a word from him. Not sure we ever will."

"You don't need to read that note I gave you. I wrote it just in case I didn't have the nerve to say those things in person."

I slipped the paper in my pocket.

She smiled. "And you're right. Learnin about civil rights is important."

With a pumped-up sense of pride I said, "Did you

know my daddy marched in Selma?"

"Really?" Her voice rose. She seemed unsure and curious all in one.

I nodded. "Yes, really. And he wrote about it. Someday I'll show you his journal."

"I thought he died in Vietnam."

"He did that, too."

I spent the rest of the day with scattered thoughts about friends and feelings and idiot teachers and how it is everyone seems so different than me.

30

Mama and I were having coffee at the Grinnin' Catfish when I heard the unmistakable sound of Sheriff Videlle's steel boot-taps hit the wooden floor. I turned around and watched him claim a spot at the corner table. It was the first we'd seen of him in over two months, the last time being the night of the killings.

"What's he doin here?" I said.

"I suppose he's here for a bite to eat."

"He's a dick."

"Jason Lee. Watch your mouth."

I stood up. "I need to talk to him." I headed for his table.

"Jason Lee," Mama called out to me.

I stood across from him with my hands shoved in my front pockets. "You got somethin to say to me?"

He took his hat off and set it on the table.

"Good morning." His mouth smiled, but his eyes didn't. "You here for a social visit?"

"You said you'd sort out what happened and haven't shown your face since. The way I see it, you owe me some answers."

In no time Mama was standing behind me. "Don't mind him," she said. "He's been outta sorts, and I can't really blame him."

Sheriff Videlle lifted his leg and put his boot on the chair opposite his, shoving it out from under the table. "Have a sit down, son." He looked at Mama. "Might as well join us, Cassie."

Mama went back to retrieve our coffee cups. When we settled in at the sheriff's table she said, "Thought we'd hear from you by now, Luther."

"I'm a busy man."

"Have you figured out what happened?"

Sheriff Videlle nodded. "Pieced it together best I could."

"Care to share any of that with us?" I said, ready to explode.

Miss Therese came to the table holding two fresh cups of coffee and she set them down.

"This belongs on the rack next to the door," she said real sweet, picking up the sheriff's hat. She carried it over to the hat tree. Then she came back and plopped herself down into the empty chair across from Mama. "Y'all don't mind, do you?"

"Course not," Mama said.

"Cream?" Miss Therese handed Sheriff Videlle the small pitcher on the table.

I watched him pour the cream, burning for answers. With answers I could talk to Elijah again, tell him everything. And maybe it would help slow down the nightmares I'd been having. I let out a sigh and leaned forward, elbows on the table.

Sheriff Videlle cleared his throat. "Now, bear in mind there are one or two pieces missing from the puzzle."

Puzzle? I thought, taking offense at the word. "You make it sound like a game."

"But one of the things I'm good at," he said, like he hadn't heard me, "is filling in the blanks." He took a packet of sugar from the bowl. "A skill I honed while assigned to Marine intelligence." He tore open the pack and sprinkled the granules into his cup. "You see, no matter how little you have to go on, if you gather the evidence in the right manner, you can work the case." He set his eyes on me and I blinked. "Marines don't play games."

Miss Therese scooped up the empty sugar packet and stashed it in the pocket of her apron along with the left-behind napkins and toothpicks she'd collected from her other tables.

"When were you planning to tell us?" I said.

Sheriff Videlle took a huge breath. "But first I want to say that rumors, like the ones about the Johnson boy's killing, have a way of sprouting-up, then spreading fast. Rest assured, they didn't play a part in my investigation—or official statement."

"Johnson boy?" I said in a tight, angry voice. That's not what you called him the night you threw me into the back of your car." I looked around the cafe. All eyes were fixed on our table. "And threw him in jail and let him get killed. You kept callin him the nigger boy that night, remember?"

"Jason Lee?" Mama tapped a finger on the table.

"His words, Mama."

"If you remember right, those were Deputy Willard's words," he said.

I bristled. "Nothin would have happened if you believed Samson, and me. Then it sunk in, what he'd said. "What rumors?"

Sheriff Videlle reached for another packet of sugar.

Mama dropped her voice, "I heard the rumors."

"What you talkin about?" I said, not understanding how she knew any of this.

"Therese told me about 'em."

I frowned at Miss Therese.

"Tongues were waggin here at the cafe about Samson causin this all on himself. Bein too big for his britches. Not knowin his place. Jason Lee, you know I tell Cassie everything."

"Samson never did nothin to cause nothin." I looked at Mama. "How come you didn't tell me about what you heard?"

"Because I knew none of it was true and figured you were goin through enough."

"Sorry I brought it up," Sheriff Videlle broke in. "We'll go straight to the things I do know." He took his first sip of coffee and set the cup back on the table. He looked at me again.

"Number one, your hitchhiker was one of the Chubb clan."

Feeling instantly sick, I wiped my sweating palms on my pant legs. My brain pounded.

"A Chubb?" Mama said. "How's that?"

"A cousin. Hails from Kentucky. His proper name's

Cody Chubb, but he's known mostly as Moody."

Sheriff Videlle had called him *my* hiker. Did he know it was me who insisted we pick him up? The hiker said he was headed to see kin. I should have shot Eugene and Culver after they changed the tire.

"According to my sources," Sheriff Videlle was saying, "he had a history of small-time trouble all his life, and his temperament was true to his nickname."

I stuck the spoon in my cup and stirred, just to give my eyes someplace other than Sheriff Videlle's face to look, scared he'd be able to "fill in the blanks" and figure out I was the one responsible for Samson being killed.

"He's got a two-bit shyster lawyer for an uncle, named Booney Benders," the sheriff went on. "Sounds like Booney spent a good deal of his time in front of the authorities getting his nephew out of trouble. I called a buddy in Kentucky and asked him to find out what he could about those two. Turns out Cody Chubb was on trial for murder a few years back and Booney persuaded the jury that the evidence necessary to convict was lacking. The best I can figure, Cody's been drifting from place to place ever since.

"The day the two of you picked him up he was headed to the Chubb place on his way back from Louisiana." Sheriff Videlle took his second sip of coffee. I thought back to the hiker sitting on the road. Samson said the next guy could help him.

"Turns out old man Otis lent a hand with filling in the puzzle about what took place that day—as best he could."

I couldn't hold my tongue. "Now he's 'old man Otis,' and you're talkin real nice about him?" I raised my voice in a fit of frustration. "That night you called him 'the old nigger Otis.' Now he's your good buddy?"

"Enough," Mama snapped.

"I ain't lyin." I lifted my palms up to the sky like an innocent. "It's what he called him."

Sheriff Videlle went right on like nothing I said mattered.

"At first Otis was so far gone he couldn't think straight, but a dose of Videlle persistence paid off."

I knew what a dose of Videlle persistence meant. He was a harsh man and I figured he must have been especially rough on Mr. Otis.

Sheriff Videlle's eyes locked onto mine, again. "It so happens that after Cody jumped off the back of the truck, he made his way back to the Otis place to get his hands on the shine you left there."

"Is that right?" Mama said. "Samson's errand was deliverin shine?"

The conversation wasn't going the way I'd thought it would and I shrugged. My lip began to quiver.

Sheriff Videlle cleared his throat. "Of course these aren't old man Otis' exact words, but I've been in this business long enough that I can figure out the gist of most any conversation.

"By the time Cody got back there, Otis had already polished off half a jug. The way he tells it he was stretched out on the porch taking a sun bath, happy as a tick on a bloodhound and half asleep. Then he heard footsteps against the gravel. He looked up and saw the man."

"Mr. Otis don't trust whites." I said.

"Jason Lee, stop interruptin," Mama said. "Mind your manners."

"Much obliged, Cassie." Sheriff Videlle continued. "Otis said Cody Chubb strutted toward him, looking cocky as a jaybird. His shotgun was by the front door, but it'd been dry of buckshot for years. He yelled, telling him he had no business being on his land. Otis said Cody laughed at him like a hyena."

I thought back to the brittle old man pushing the sacks of corn in a wheelbarrow, worried about Samson being with two white boys.

"How 'bout a refill?" someone called out to Miss Therese from a window table.

"Be with you in a minute," she yelled back. "Can't you see I'm talkin with Hadlee's finest?"

Sheriff Videlle gave her a nod and a smile.

"Okay, keep goin." Miss Therese said fast, as if it would hurry things along.

"Otis was on the porch shouting at the man to get off his property. Cody hollered back, 'Just need a drink, old man,' then he proceeded to walk toward the porch. About half way, he reached for his knife, but the sheath was empty. I'd say he was most likely going to use it on Otis and take what he came for."

"How do you know that?" I said.

"The process of deduction. Working backwards.

Old-fashioned detective work. It's what I do."

The sheriff continued, like he'd actually been there, when it seemed more like he was making it up in his head, on the spot. "Then, much as I can figure from what Otis said, Cody charged the steps and grabbed him by the front of his shirt. 'Listen here, nigger,' he shouted. 'I ain't got time for this shit,' and he punched on Otis until he dropped him to the floorboards. Otis didn't dare move, but he watched Cody drink from his full jug of moonshine.

"This is where things took a turn. Cody said, 'I'll bet my left nut your black bastard of a delivery boy has my blade.'"

"Mr. Otis said that?"

"Son," Sheriff Videlle's tone sounded disgusted with me, "do you want me to tell you what happened, or do you want to keep interrupting?"

I didn't answer.

"Instead of leaving, Cody Chubb ran across the yard. He howled like a dog and smashed the hooch jug against the corner, splashing shine across the rotten timbers. 'Gotta get back what's mine,' he yelled and fired up his Zippo. He tossed it in the dry grass next to the barn."

I hadn't heard anything about the fire. *Old man Otis keeps to himself,* Samson said. *Got nothin left since his wife passed.*

Miss Therese got up. "I'll be right back. If I don't get a movin someone might burn *this* place down."

There was a long, uneasy moment after she left. I

took a sip of coffee. It had turned room temperature and bitter.

"Is he okay?" I said. "Mr. Otis?"

"Had it rough. Lost his mind for a spell." Sheriff Videlle sounded like he didn't give a shit. "The barn burned to the ground, but the fire didn't spread to the shack. He's settled back there now."

A flush came over Mama's cheeks. "Knew about that, too."

I looked at Miss Therese across the way. She'd wiped a table clean and placed four catfish placemats on it. I couldn't figure why both she and Mama treated me like I didn't have the right to know things.

Sheriff Videlle looked around. "Should I wait for Therese?"

"No," Mama said. "Keep on goin, Luther."

"A man named J.T. Lord, a do-gooder Baptist savior type who drives through these parts on his way to the Promised Land, found Otis alongside the road curled up like a wounded deer, covered in soot from all the smoke. He picked him up and brought him into the station."

Sheriff Videlle was turning out to be a long-winded blowhard. I just wanted him to get to the part that was most important—Samson.

"The old man was half out of his mind from the ordeal, and talking gibberish." Sheriff Videlle shook his head. "Even though his body was in the chair across from my desk, his mind was long gone."

His was the only voice talking in all of the Grinnin'

Catfish, and knowing he had a full audience, he cranked up the volume.

"He said something like, 'I warned dat boy. Dat Johnson boy.'" His imitation of Mr. Otis was pretty close. "'Ain't no good to mix. No mixin. I tol' him, be careful, be careful with dem white boys.' And then the old man's face turned grey as ash and his arms were stretched out like he was the holy cross itself, fingers shaking."

He looked around at his audience, popped up from the chair, and raised his arms in the same way he said Mr. Otis had.

"He yelled, 'Da devil's white. There weren't no eyewitnesses, and no record. Just like my Jessie. My son, Jessie. Gettin away with murder.'"

"Luther, please," Mama said. "You're causin a scene." Sheriff Videlle put his arms down but remained standing.

"I think, when his barn collapsed, the strain sent his mind back to the day he pulled his son's flesh off the tree."

I popped out of my chair and yelled, "Stop." I looked at Mama. "What tree?"

"Son." She reached my way. "Please sit down." She glanced around the room. My eyelids fluttered, my stomach was queasy, but I didn't sit down.

"The oak on Peek's place? Was it Mr. Otis' boy Uncle Mooks saw 'em lynch?"

Mama closed her eyes and nodded.

I felt off balance. "How come I never know nothin?"

"Please sit down, both of you." She looked over to Sheriff Videlle. "When he was a child Mooks saw them lynch Mr. Otis' son. He was hidin behind some bushes and saw the whole thing. A scared kid seein another kid get hung. It's stayed with him his whole life."

And I knew for sure that the day I saw that same dreadful chestnut oak, with its three branches sticking out—the same day I ran to get help for Grover Peek—was going to stay with me, too. Back then I thought going for help was the right thing to do, but I wasn't so sure anymore. Figuring out what's right and wrong seemed as hard as holding on to water.

Deputy Willard came in the front door and marched to our table, breathing like a fat man who'd just walked up a mountain. "Sheriff, we need your assistance."

"I'm in the middle of something here."

"No, please, Luther, go." Mama looked around the room. Then she yelled, "The show's over. And what the hell are you all lookin at, anyway?" She looked back at him. "Sorry, but I'd appreciate it if we finished this conversation in private. Take care of Deputy Willard's needs, and if it suits your schedule, when you're finished, maybe you can stop by the house. Or, Jason Lee and I can go into your office tomorrow."

"I'll come by your place after supper this evening, around seven."

Mama stood up. "But, I'll have no talk about the Otis boy in front of Mooks."

As Sheriff Videlle retrieved his hat and walked out, I couldn't stop thinking about poor Mr. Otis alone in his shack with no wife, no son, and no barn. No barn because of me, and no son because of the man I helped.

"Did Grover Peek ever die?" I asked Mama.

"I'm afraid not. But the good news is, when he leaves the Sisters of Mercy Nursing Home, he'll be in a coffin inside a hearse that's travelin past our house to the graveyard. Your uncle's lookin forward to that day."

On the drive home, storm clouds threatened in the distance. I looked out my side window and let myself imagine at least one boy hanging from every tree we passed along the road, sometimes two. They were only colored boys, like Emmet Till and the Johnson boys. Good boys, bad boys, from everywhere. After the shock of finding out about Mr. Otis' son, my head ached at the thought of what else Sheriff Videlle might have to say when he came out to our house.

Then I thought about how the efforts of people like J.L. had changed such things, and how so much more needed to be done by people like me. My headache finally eased.

"Mama, I forgot what Mr. Otis' son's name was."

"Jessie."

I wondered what I would have done if I'd been the boy who saw what Uncle Mooks saw back then.

"Jessie Otis," I said. "I'm gonna name somethin after him someday."

*

The storm finally made its way to Hadlee. We were stuck inside playing Chinese checkers on the dining room table when Sheriff Videlle drove up in his personal truck. He brushed the rain off his denim shirt and came inside.

"We'll sit in the living room," Mama said.

She had four separate bowls of popcorn prepared. When we got settled Mama handed Uncle Mooks a can of Falstaff. The rest of us had Coca-Cola.

"Sorry you had to drive all the way out here," she said, "but I'm not fond of other people listenin to my conversations. Tonight I'd rather stay clear of that aggravatin tribe of busybodies at the cafe."

Mama put herself above all that gossip that went on in town, but the truth be told, she really wasn't much different, being as she got her weekly doses of hearsay from Miss Therese over the phone.

"No problem," Sheriff Videlle said. I expected him to continue his account where he had left off that morning, with Mr. Otis in his office. Instead, he said, "The Marines and law enforcement are challenging careers, and I've spent all of my life as an aggressor, but thinking about the way I—"

"I reckon," Uncle Mooks leaned forward and cut him off, "you're havin a conflict."

I already figured what would come next. *Conflicts are for talkin out.*

Instead, Uncle Mooks said, "How about you stop talkin 'bout yourself and tell us what happened?" He sat back again.

"Sure enough," Sheriff Videlle said. He grabbed his glass and took a long drink. His fingernails were cleaned and clipped all the same size.

"Like I said this morning, old man Otis was in bad shape, but after a while he came out of his crazy spell. With proper interrogation techniques he finally realized it was Samson, not Noah, who picked up the corn that day.

"Deputy Willard and I thought it best to drop him off at the hospital so they could watch over him, and then we drove out to the Johnsons' house to investigate some of the things Otis talked about.

"The folks were at a church meeting with the younger boy. Your friend was alone. He cooperated at first, about picking up the hiker and about you being with him. Then he claimed he didn't know anything about the fire, so we cuffed him and took him to the office to jog his memory."

"Prick," I said under my breath.

"To scare him, same as we did with you."

Uncle Mooks clenched his teeth. "Scare a boy?"

"You get more out of them if they're scared." Sheriff Videlle looked at me. "It's good for boys your age to get a scare."

I waited for Mama to say something, but nothing came.

"What happened to Samson?" I asked.

"We drove him back to the office and put him in a cell. We left him with Boudreaux and headed out to your place."

"Who's Boudreaux?" Mama asked.

"Our night man. I told him to watch the boy until

we got hold of his folks. I made it clear he wasn't under arrest and the cell wouldn't be locked. My intention was to scare seven shades out of him."

A sudden downpour bombarded the tin roof. Sheriff Videlle studied the popcorn in his bowl until the noise died down. "If only I'd been more thorough." He shook his head like he couldn't believe what he was about to say. "Turns out he had the knife on him."

"Who had the knife on him?" Mama asked.

"The Johnson boy. The coroner found a harness made of rope under his pant leg, strapped to his shin."

"You sure?" I said.

"Sure as I'm sitting here. We didn't check for weapons because we didn't really suspect him of anything. We just wanted to get to the bottom of Otis' barn burning." He cleared his throat. "What happened next is more speculative than I'd like."

"What's speculative mean?" I asked.

"We're not a hundred percent sure, because no one saw it."

"So it's like guessin?"

"It's a whole hell of a lot more than that, boy."

A bolt of lightning lit the room.

"The night man," Mama said. "You said the night man was there."

"Turns out he wasn't there." Sheriff Videlle rested his head on the back of the chair and closed his eyes. In unhurried words, as if he was working it out in his head, he said, "What we do have are eyewitnesses. They spotted the drifter in town with both of the Chubb twins about the same time we drove the boy in. We speculate they saw him in the cruiser."

It seemed he used the word "we" when speculating.

"Where was this man Boudreaux?" Mama asked.

"After Deputy Willard and I left, Boudreaux went out back for a smoke. I don't allow smoking inside. It was his last cigarette, so he decided to mosey down to the Clark station for a new pack. Waynette Nelson worked the counter that night. She can talk the ear off a deaf man.

"It just so happens she had some moonshine behind the counter and offered a cup to Boudreaux. When pressed about it later," his voice turned cold, "she said she thought it was Johnson's Thunder."

"Good Lord," Mama said.

"Ironic, huh?"

I thought I'd been through every emotion possible, but that news brought another one—numbness.

Sheriff Videlle kept going. "When he finally got back to the station he checked the boy's cell and discovered it was empty. He went into the front office." Sheriff Videlle's shoulders actually slumped when he said, "The place looked like a God damn slaughterhouse. Blood smeared all over the floor and walls. They'd definitely fought hard to the death."

"Luther, please," Mama said. "This is difficult enough."

Sheriff Videlle cleared his throat. "Boudreaux found the hiker on the floor, his head cracked open like a coconut from being slammed against the brick wall."

He said it so matter-of-fact it took a minute for me to realize I'd seen some of it myself, the blood pooling around his head, working its way to the tattoo on his forearm.

"It's all my fault," I said.

Sheriff Videlle looked up. "Rest assured, you couldn't have changed anything."

But he didn't know.

"And Samson?" Mama said.

"Boudreaux found him in the reception area, on the floor, propped against the wall like a rag doll, bleeding from his gut. The knife was still in him."

My stomach tightened as if his knife had gone through me, too.

"The three of them must have pulled him out of the cell, not knowing he had the knife on him. I figure the boy killed the hiker, and the twins killed him. Like I said before, there was one hell of a battle."

"Did you get 'em?" I asked.

He looked down to check his fingernails. "They're both on the lam, long gone."

Dusk threw a pastel dimness over the living room. I went to the side lamp and twisted the knob one click. Shadows darkened the stubble across Sheriff Videlle's face.

Uncle Mooks stood up and said, "Best you be goin. It ain't right to scare a boy."

31

1985

My sixteenth birthday meant a great deal to Mama. "A milestone, a cause for celebration," she proclaimed.

She fussed behind a closed kitchen door all day and wouldn't allow me near. "It's bad luck to see the cake before lightin the candles."

"Never mattered before. Did the birthday rules change when I wasn't lookin?"

"Just shoo-fly, don't bother me," she said, with a giggle at the end.

I went outside to sit with Uncle Mooks. It wasn't long before a brand new 1985 Ford Ranger we'd never seen before, drove up our drive.

"Who's that?" he said.

The truck finally got close enough we saw it was Wally.

When it had become clear Darla was gone for good, Wally started coming out to our place on a regular basis. Little by little, he managed to help peel away the darkness around our hearts. He brought his green La-Z-Boy and placed it next to the porch couch. He also brought something hard to define, something as vital as the clasp that transforms a simple chain into a complete circle.

Mama's wounds, the ones on the inside, the ones she'd carried since the Vietnam conflict, began to heal. Her smiles came more freely, and she served our weekend flapjacks in the shape of animals and stars. She took up humming Loretta Lynn songs when getting the house straightened up for Wally's visits.

He walked to the porch with a smile big as a slice of watermelon.

"Nice truck," Uncle Mooks said.

"Thanks." Wally sat in his La-Z-Boy. His chest puffed out like a bullfrog's. "Whaddya think, Jason Lee? Had a hard time deciding between Sand Beige and Desert Tan but settled on the Desert Tan."

"Looks good," I said.

Uncle Mooks nodded, like he thought so, too.

"Where's Cassie?" Wally said.

"Locked herself in the kitchen, cookin up somethin special for my birthday.

"Big day." He rubbed his hands like there was sweat on his palms. "I'll go see if she needs help."

Even though Wally and I had talked plenty over the years, I hadn't allowed myself to get too close to him until we busted Mama out of Delta Community. The truth is, I began to feel closer to him than I did to Mama or Uncle Mooks. I let myself think to the future and to the hope that Wally'd be there for them when the time came for me to move on.

*

After a supper of fried chicken so juicy we needed three napkins each, Mama brought out the cake she'd worked on all day. A beauty in the shape of a heart, covered with chocolate cream icing and twice as many candles as a sixteen-year-old boy would need to blow out.

To see her that happy changed a regular old birthday into the one I'll never forget. As soon as I blew out the candles Wally raised his fork. "Time to open the presents."

"Before eatin cake?" I looked at Mama. She shrugged and smiled. "Why not?"

Uncle Mooks looked surprised too. Cake always came before presents. But he was quick to reach under his chair and pass me a hand-decorated paper bag secured shut with a rubber band. "Okay then, open mine first."

I pulled off the band and shook out twenty-four hand-made checker pieces onto the table, half whittled from white pine, the other half, red cedar. Each one was sanded smooth and buffed with wax. My initials, JLR, were carved on every one of them.

"Thanks," I said, my chest full of genuine appreciation. "I believe this is your best whittlin job yet." He gave me his big old Uncle Mooks grin.

"Mine next," Mama said and handed me a small box wrapped with silver paper.

I just about burst with excitement. "How'd you know I wanted a watch?"

"It's not just a watch, son. It's a water-resistant

Timex Triathlon, with a brown leather band and a sixteen-hour stopwatch." She said it like she'd memorized the instruction sheet. "Brand new on the market."

"Look, Uncle Mooks."

He leaned forward to take a look. "It's about time," he said and pulled his head back, laughing like it was the best joke of all jokes, of all time.

As I buckled it onto my wrist Wally slid an old fashioned accordion envelope in front of me. I figured it might contain a history lesson of some sort or old pictures of him and J.L., but when I unwound the string from the paper button and looked inside, a set of keys was in the front fold.

"What're these for?"

"My old truck."

I gave out a shout, jumped up from my chair and bounced in a circle like there were springs under my shoes. When I finally settled down, Wally said, "It's seen better days and the air conditioner's shot, but when those S.O.B.s at the dealership told me how much they'd give me for a trade-in, I suggested they take a flying leap off the bridge of their choosin. That truck'll do more for you than it will for them."

I wiped the moisture out of my eyes.

32

Dried magnolia pods rolled along the highway in the breeze and the smell of autumn leaves burning in the distance crawled up my nose, reminding me the season was about to turn. It was the first day after getting my license, and I lingered out front after school waiting for Elijah to come out.

I would've put off making things right with him a while longer, except my shame began to get in the way of everything. We needed to talk. I'd tell him everything I knew, with one exception. There would be no mention of Waynette Nelson's moonshine.

He spotted me and turned in the other direction.

"Elijah," I hollered. He circled around and looked me in the eye for the first time since school started. "Give you a lift?" I nodded toward my truck.

"Nope. I'm walkin." He picked up a pebble and pitched it across the lunch area, but he didn't walk away. I reached into my pocket and rubbed the two slugs I'd taken off Samson's eyes. They'd been with me every day since.

"I learned what happened. About Samson."

"How'd you learn that?"

"Let's talk in the truck."

"Ain't that Wally's truck?"

"Yep. He got a new one. Take a look inside."

Elijah opened the door and climbed into the passenger seat. I slid behind the steering wheel but didn't stick the key in the ignition. And I didn't look at Elijah.

"Remember what you said to me before, about needin to know what happened?" My voice cracked.

"Uh-huh."

"Sheriff Videlle came out to the house and told us."

"Never came to our house. Never said nothin to us."

"Figures," I said, thinking about how he didn't seem to care about anyone but himself and his investigation. "He's a prick."

"A dick prick," Elijah said.

"Whose mama was beat with an ugly stick." I smiled, looked at him, and went for another one. "Whose papa has a sleepy dick."

It took awhile, but he finally smiled. "Whose sister ain't worth a lick."

And the tension loosened.

"So," I said. "You want me to tell you what the sick, sleepy dick prick said?"

He nodded. "Beats wonderin."

We both stared out the windshield, as if not looking at each other would lessen the pain of it all. It was hard to get the first few sentences out, but soon the whole story gushed from my mouth like a river of relief. I told him about Mr. Otis' barn burning down and Boudreaux leaving to buy smokes. Then I had to tell him about the hitchhiker being with the Chubb twins and about the slaughterhouse.

Talking about it was worse than remembering it. When I came to the end, the part about the gurney with Samson's green high-tops sticking out from under the sheet, I steadied my hands on the steering wheel.

Elijah let out a breath that turned into smaller, faster gasps for air. I found the nerve to look at him. Tears fell down his face. The space between us was so full of grief I rolled my window down and started the truck.

We drove past the many places Samson and I had spent time together, past the streams and bridges where we shared secrets and laughter, and past chunks of myself that'd broken off when he died.

I stopped the truck at the edge of Wilders Grove pond. It looked different to me, more like a pool of guilt.

The truth is I'd told Elijah what happened, but not why.

We got out of the truck and walked toward the water, our emotions stretched, and as jittered as the lizards scurrying out of our way. I grabbed my head, fingers rubbing my temples, and there was no controlling what came out.

"It's my fault he's dead. Might as well have stabbed him with the knife myself." My voice sounded tired, and my eyes burned like sand had flown into them.

"What're you talkin about, Jason Lee? I know you'd never do nothin to hurt him. Never."

"I told him to pick up the hiker. Samson's dead

'cause of me." My feelings grew too heavy for me to stand under the weight. I sat in the dirt and crossed my legs. Elijah joined me. I put my hand to my mouth. "I was selfish, and he's dead."

"Don't do that, Jason Lee." Elijah stared across the pond toward the trees. I followed his gaze. Leaves dropped onto the shoreline. "Don't do that."

"He was my best friend." I caught myself rocking forward and back, like Uncle Mooks sometimes did, and stopped. "He taught me how to put my worries away and to try anything, and he showed me how to be strong enough to ignore what wasn't important. And that dreaming was only the first step." I pinched the snot from my nose. "Things I wouldn't have known without him. Samson knew all my secrets."

I felt lighter having confessed.

Elijah put his hand on my shoulder. "You were his best friend, too."

33

"It's up there."

I pointed to the flat boulder and led the way, offering Reba my hand, pointing out the places sturdy enough to hold our weight. Once on top we stood, overlooking the river as it rushed past. Shadows stretched over the water bringing about a patchwork of sun and shade. I brushed away the acorns that'd dropped onto the rock, and we sat next to each other, knees to our chests.

Being up there again brought a flood of thoughts about Samson, especially of our drinkin meetins. I had to say something fast to shoo away those memories.

"You know what I like about this place?" I said.

"What?"

"The river noise. It's different every time. Sometimes it's quiet and don't want any attention. Other times, like today, it's loud and pushy."

I looked over at Reba, her hair was pulled back in a single braid secured with a blue band, the same color as her sweater. Her cheeks and the tip of her nose had reddened from the chilly breeze coming off the water.

She leaned back on her elbows and studied the clouds. "I like the way it smells here. The dirt smell and the moss on the trees. And the wet leaves. Wet leaves smell like peppercorns to me. I can see why this is your favorite place."

I never noticed the separate smells before, so inhaled to see if I could recognize them. I couldn't.

Since I'd already told Reba about it, I brought J.L.'s journal along in case I worked up the nerve to share it with her. I had cleaned the front and back covers with a soft brush and replaced the brittle masking tape with new, clean strips. It was in my jacket pocket, along with the two Falstaffs I'd swiped from Uncle Mooks.

I handed Reba a beer. "Well, J.L. Rainey," she said with a grin, "don't mind if I do."

The beer was warm and tasted stale. I tried to think of something funny to say to make up for it, but no matter how hard I tried, my mind was an empty space. It must have happened to her, too. The more time that passed, the more the quiet wrapped over us and then over the river and out toward Hadlee and beyond.

The harsh caw of a crow interrupted the serenity. We both brought our hands to our foreheads to shield our eyes from the sun, but we couldn't spot the bird.

Reba said, "I read somewhere that if you hear a crow squawk before settin out on a task, whatever you're doin will turn out awful. You think it's true?"

"No." The word jumped from my mouth and echoed back with an unexpected snap. "I know for *sure* they'll help you out when you need it, like guardian angels do, or fairy godmothers or somethin." To make my point I told her about the time Samson, Noah, and I had our run-in with the Chubb boys and how the crows next to saved us from a beating that would've landed at least one of us in the hospital, for sure.

She looked at me like she had trouble believing crows would be helpful.

The beer helped me feel comfortable enough to say, "This ain't really my rock we're sittin on."

"What? Thought it was your special place?"

"It's special, all right. But Samson found it. We were the only two who knew about it until now."

I told her about our first meeting, when I learned to drink Mr. J's Black Thunder. And more importantly, I told her about the day I found J.L's journal and how Samson and I read it over and over together. "Right here. Right here on this rock's where Samson decided to become a lawyer for the NAACP. I've been thinkin about that a lot. Since he can't do it anymore, I think I will."

"Be a lawyer?"

"For the NAACP."

"You think they allow white people?"

"Course they do. It was mostly white people who started it."

"I'll be. I sure have a lot to learn." She looked back up at the clouds and then at me again. "I'd like to read that journal sometime."

"You would?" I couldn't have felt happier. "How 'bout now?"

"Really? Right now's good."

"Close your eyes and put your hands out." I pulled it from my pocket and placed the most important thing

I owned into her hands.

She opened her eyes. "This is it?" She turned it over. "Not much to it. I thought it'd look more important."

Had I been prepared, my chest wouldn't have caved in, and I wouldn't have flushed with rejection.

"Oh, Jason Lee," she said, her voice full of remorse. "Please forgive me. I didn't say that—dear Lord, tell me I didn't say that." She slammed the palm of her hand on her thigh.

"Sounded like you."

"No, no, it was my ma." She looked at me like she expected me to understand, then exhaled a gasp of frustration. "I'm tryin real hard not to be like her, but sometimes it just slips out with no warnin."

In a different mood I could have laughed at the idea. I wanted to be the kind of person J.L. had been, and she didn't want to be anything like her ma. I reached to take the book back.

"I mean it. I am truly sorry. Please let me read it. Pretty please?"

"Long as it's *you* readin and not your ma."

I knew it would take about an hour for her to get through it and tried not to look at her, but I snuck a peek. Her brows pinched right before she said, "Oh, my God, they beat on him." She continued to read.

I turned my gaze to the river. The sun had dropped, leaving shimmers of light that bounced on the water, and the faint scent of crushed pepper was all around me.

When Reba folded up the last newspaper clipping,

the one of J.L. standing next to the priest, I knew she'd finished. She tucked the clipping inside the back page, closed the book, and held it against her chest. She looked like she would burst from the inside when she handed it back to me. "Thank you."

She stayed quiet for a minute then said, "I have an idea."

"What's that?"

"Got it when I first started readin, and it grew stronger with each page. A real good idea, I think."

I tucked the journal into my pocket. "What?"

A lightning bolt might as well have hit the rock we were on when she said, "You need to find Spam."

"That's the best idea I've ever heard. Wouldn't it be somethin?" I couldn't believe I hadn't thought of it. "But how would I find him?"

"How many Arnold Jefferson Monroes do you think there are in this world?"

"Don't know."

"Me neither." She clicked her tongue. "So let's figure out what we do know. We know he lived in Selma in nineteen sixty-five."

"In the Washington Carver housing project," I said.

"And he was friends with Eddie who owned Walker's Cafe." She stood up, clenched her fists, and raised them to the sky. "We'll write letters."

"We?" I stood up, too. "You in on this?"

"Who came up with the idea?"

"You did."

"Then I'm in."

She took hold of my hands. "We'll write to your future boss, the NAACP." She squeezed tight and began to talk faster. "In Alabama and Mississippi. Maybe they'll know where he is. We can even write to the national headquarters."

Her enthusiasm got hold of me, and I moved closer to her. My jacket brushed her sweater. "And how about the newspaper in Selma? If he still lives there, maybe they'll know somethin about him."

"We can send one to every editor they have," she said. "We can write to Brown Chapel, too."

When Reba leaned in and kissed me I might as well have been drunk on Mr. J's Black Thunder. My eyes automatically closed. Her lips were soft against mine and fit perfectly. I let go of her hands and wrapped my arms around her like it was the most natural thing I'd ever done. Our mouths opened and the air above Mosquito River turned hot.

*

After that first kiss, being with Reba felt as natural as breathing in the morning air—and as necessary. For the better part of a week we were at the kitchen table every evening, deciding who to send our letters to and what they should say. Mama helped some but mostly left us to our mission.

My initial hope of one day meeting Mr. Arnold Jefferson Monroe grew into a full-blown delusion. I fantasized about the two of us on the porch sipping sweet tea or, better yet, drinking beer. We'd have long talks about J.L., and he'd tell me about "the greatest march on any capitol there has ever been in the South." He'd fill me in on the stories that weren't in the journal. He'd look like the actor with the big voice, James Earl Jones, and sound like him, too. I'd call him Spam, and he'd call me J.L.

I wanted to tell Reba about these fantasies but thought better of it because she wasn't with us in the daydream, and I had mixed feelings about sharing Spam with her.

When the last flap of the last envelope was licked and sealed, Reba held it above her head like it was a first-place trophy. "The Selma Public Library," she said. "Letter number fifteen." She set the envelope on top of the others and ran her hand across them. "Wonder how long it'll take to get an answer back?" She put her elbows on the table and clasped her hands under her chin. "What do you think, a week?"

"Maybe two."

"You ever wonder what he looks like?" Her eyes swept the room as if Spam might walk through the kitchen door right then.

"What he looks like?" I laughed. "Big. He looks big. With a big voice."

"What makes you think that?"

"Not sure," I mumbled.

*

After three weeks had passed I began to have doubts about getting any answers. Reba felt even worse than I did. One day I checked the mailbox twice, knowing it was foolish, but I needed to double-check just the same. No matter how many bills and advertisements were stuffed inside, for me it was as empty as last year's bird nests. I took to kicking the damn thing whenever I went by, and after a few more weeks had passed with no word, I stopped going out to check altogether.

Finally, one day when I got home from school Mama was waiting out on the porch with a smile on her face and an envelope in her hand. It was from the Selma Public Library—number fifteen. I called Reba, thinking she should be there when we opened it. While waiting for her, I held the envelope up to the light trying to make out any of the words inside.

Reba and Mama were across from me at the kitchen table, fingers crossed, as I slid a knife under the flap. My hopes were bouncing on the ceiling, and then they crashed to the floor when I read the form letter.

"Dear Patron, Staff cannot do genealogical research or obituary searches for patrons; however, a list of researchers for hire is available." I turned the letter over. "What's this about?" I said.

"Read the rest," Mama said. "Maybe his name's on the list."

"Library staff can perform searches of city directories and/or telephone directories for a fee. There is a three dollar charge per search, plus a twenty-five cent charge for photocopies. For example, if patron asks for five different names in one directory, that is a fifteen dollar charge; if one name, in six different years, there is an eighteen dollar charge plus photocopy costs.

Requests for directory searches must be made in writing and paid in advance."

I dropped the letter on the table.

"That's it?" Reba said.

"No, it goes on to tell us where to send the damn checks."

"How brainless can they be?" Reba's face flushed and her voice rose. "Are they idiots? Did they even *read* the letter we sent? Did they even *open* it?"

"Don't look like it," I said, deflated.

"Don't worry, you two," Mama said. "You'll get your answer."

"Not if they don't read our letters," I said.

"Son, there's fourteen more out there waitin to be opened. Give it time."

*

At the Grinnin' Catfish, Reba and I shared a platter of biscuits and gravy. After a while she stabbed her fork into one of the biscuits. "I guess the man's dead."

"Who?"

"Mr. Monroe," she said, studying how the fork stayed upright, prongs held firm in the gravy. "I wanted to meet him. Had my heart set on it. Even had dreams about it."

"Not as much as me."

Miss Therese came over. "What're y'all talkin about so serious?" That day her hair color looked more like beets than rust.

"We're talkin 'bout my daddy's friend from Selma. The one we're tryin to find."

"How long's it been?" Miss Therese took the fork out of the biscuit, wiped it off with a paper napkin, and set it back on the table next to Reba's plate.

"It's been too long. Reba thinks he might be dead."

"Chances are," Miss Therese said.

*

Missing Samson was never far from my mind, and I'd have long, one-sided talks with him most every day. The other conversations I had, the imaginary visits with Spam soon became little more than a feather's tickle in the back of my mind.

With that gone I had more time to think about a man I'd only laid eyes on once, but it was on the one day in my life I'd never forget. I began to fixate on him. Someone who didn't trust me for the sole reason of my skin color. I kept thinking about what happened to his son, and I couldn't get the image of the tree on Grover Peeks land out of my head.

Poor Clarence Otis—still alone in his shack with no wife, no son, and no barn.

34

At nine-thirty in the morning Uncle Mooks went outside and paced across the porch, occasionally whistling *"Taps."* He had on his biggest smile and his finest red and black flannel shirt, tucked in to show off his silver, soaring-eagle belt buckle. The black boots on his feet had a fresh coat of polish. It was the day he'd waited for. The day of Grover Peek's funeral parade.

Mama laid out a spread of fried chicken drummettes, corn fritters, and cabbage slaw, and around eleven both Miss Therese and Wally showed up to join in the festivities. Miss Therese brought a stack of silver julep cups, a bag of fresh mint, and a bottle of bourbon.

"Come to the kitchen with me Jason Lee," she said as she came up the steps. "It's time you learn how to make mint juleps."

She set everything on the sink counter. "The only good thing my pa ever taught me was how to make these. I call 'em Mississippi juleps 'cause I hold strong to the notion that the first julep ever sipped was concocted on our soil."

"I know it's a drink, but what's the big deal?" I said.

"Tradition. That's all you need to know, and there's four steps to makin a proper one. Step one: soak the mint in three jiggers of bourbon. One jigger for faith, one for hope and, 'course, you can't forget charity. My pa stuck a fourth in for the devil, but I think that's just askin for trouble. If you can do that I'll take care of step two, the simple syrup."

She pulled a pan from the cupboard. "Tell you what, Jason Lee, I'll just go ahead with step three by myself. It'll take less time and we can get to drinkin sooner. You get started on step four, which is the most important ingredient of the drink, the ice." She had me put cubes from our freezer in the canvas bag the mint had been in and smack it with the wooden end of a hammer.

We all settled on the porch, drank from our silver cups, and waited. The first sip of julep tasted like a rotten batch of spearmint cough syrup. The second sip went down easier. Everyone's lightheartedness and good humor was contagious.

"Whaddya think old Grover Peeks final days looked like, there in that nursing home?" Miss Therese said.

"Drool and dirty diapers," Wally said.

Mama raised her glass. "Sounds about right to me."

The squirrels across the way were especially active that day, like a new season was approaching.

As the procession—two cars and the hearse—drove past our house on its way to the graveyard from the Faith Deliverance Holy Church, Uncle Mooks hooted and hollered loud enough to be heard across the whole town of Hadlee.

I felt a huge sense of satisfaction that the likes of Grover Peek were a dying breed.

"Here, here," Wally said. "I'd like to make a toast to the smallest funeral parade Dunlap County's ever seen." We all raised our cups and laughed.

At first I thought my eyes were playing tricks on me because it seemed Samson's old truck come through the dust. It barreled down the road to catch up with the parade. It was Dicey, sure as eggs is eggs.

"Look at that," I yelled.

Dicey tailgated the last car and didn't back off.

"Okay," Wally said. "With that addition, now it's tied for the smallest parade."

I didn't find out until a year later it was Mr. Johnson and Mr. Otis. They followed the procession to Peek's burial spot in the whites-only cemetery. Peek had no family and the only people attending, other than the two of them, were nuns from the Sister of Mercy Nursing Home. Mr. Johnson and Mr. Otis followed the sisters deep into the graveyard, and under a canopy of oak trees and singing cicadas, along with the sisters, they both threw down a fist of dirt.

They left and went off for a Sunday drive to celebrate with a jug of Thunder. When the pressure in their bladders reached full capacity they circled back to the spot they'd been earlier, and under that same canopy of oak trees and singing cicadas, they pissed out two rivers of scorn.

35

Two weeks after I tasted my first mint julep and sixteen years after Uncle Mooks had returned from Vietnam, the shrapnel in his head made its final move. On that sunny afternoon while I studied the colonization of America at Cobb's Creek School, and Mama transcribed a deposition in her office, the metal fragments sliced through a blood vessel as he sat on his couch whittling. Mama found him with his head slumped and a see-no-evil monkey in his hand.

She thought better than to bury him in the cemetery. "Melvin won't find peace up there. We'll lay him to rest on our own land."

The spot she picked sat toward the back of the property, high on a ridge next to our biggest cypress.

Mama asked Wally to find her some heaven tree wood, a piece big enough for a headstone. He drove all the way to Pontotoc to get it. She asked me to do the carving. When I asked what she wanted it to say, she said, "It's entirely up to you."

I came up with something he'd like.

    Melvin Orville Oswald Kaster
    March 25, 1950—June 8, 1985
    The Best Brother And Uncle
    Of All Time

Wally helped me set up picnic tables under the tree next to his resting place. The ladies from the Diversity Coalition of Legal Assistance League cooked up casseroles, and Miss Therese brought Mississippi Mud Pies, compliments of the Grinnin' Catfish.

The temperature soared well past eighty-five degrees that day, and the coarse wool of my one-pocket pants gnawed on my legs. I didn't sit for fear it would get worse. My only hope was that all the people there would think I stood out of respect.

As those things go, the man who was always on the lookout for funeral parades didn't have one of his own—or a proper service. We just ate, drank and told stories about the timeless wisdom Uncle Mooks put forth in his uncomplicated way.

After everyone left and Mama and Wally went inside, I stayed out by the gravestone with his pocket watch in my hand. I looked into the watch face he had rubbed so often and tried to imagine all the things he could have accomplished and what kind of a man he might have been if not for the Vietnam conflict. I closed the watch and put it in my jacket pocket, and looked up at the wind spinners overhead.

I'd had a horrible year, but despite myself I thought about the good. About finding Reba and getting close to Wally and about Mama finally being normal again.

I remembered back to a time I'd asked Uncle Mooks why he only whittled monkeys. He got up from the couch, went into his room, and brought back a piece of paper wrapped around a dowel. A rubber band held it tight.

"What is it?"

"A poem," he said, handing it to me. "Read it."

I took off the bands and unwound the paper.

> *Over the door of the Sacred Temple*
> *They sit in their wisdom of three*
> *The little deaf monkey,*
> *The little dumb monkey,*
> *The monkey who could not see.*
> *With their eyes closed to evil*
> *Their ears that hear only right*
> *Lips that are closed to scandal,*
> *They sit in their silent might.*
> *Anonymous*

36

After Uncle Mooks died, thoughts of poor Mr. Otis pecked at my conscience so often they turned into a nagging ache. My selfish mistake caused his troubles. I owed the man something but knew firsthand he wouldn't trust me. Considering all the tragedies he'd suffered, I didn't blame him. The biggest thing holding me back from standing in front of him eye-to-eye, telling him the truth, was the dread of confessing one more time. *Buck, buck, chicken cluck.*

Instead of rising to the occasion whenever thoughts of what I could do for him tapped at my conscience I wrote it in my pocket notebook.

Put a coat of paint on his house.

"Hey, Wally, you think the leftover paint we used on the chicken coop's still good?"

"Sure, why."

"Just wonderin."

Take him food from our garden.

"Hey, Mama, what do we do with the leftover tomatoes?"

"Can 'em. Why?"

"Just wonderin."

Some of the things on the list were easy, like *read to him*. I had plenty of books for that. *Bake him a cake*. I was certain I could do better than the last time I made one. *Chop wood for his furnace.* We had three toppled trees on our property alone. *Build him a new barn.* I didn't know the first thing about how to build one, but my intentions were so true I knew somehow it would get done.

Instead of writing down *Mend his fences,* I wrote *Mending fences,* and when I realized the mistake I decided to share my struggle with Reba and showed her the list. Without so much as a pause she said, "Most likely his chimney needs cleanin. It's a nasty job, but I'll help you. I'm good at chimney cleanin. His roof might need patchin, too, and his garden probably needs weedin. How about fishin for him. I'll bet he doesn't do too much of that no more. Why don't you catch him a catfish or two?"

"Catfish?" I smiled. "Did I tell you about the night Samson and me got liquored up and decided to go midnight knuckle fishin?"

"No. Is that the same as hand fishin?"

"Yep."

She grinned and let out a puff of air.

"The moon was close to full, and we thought we saw somethin big swim past. We climbed off the rock and tiptoed to the side of the river to get a better look. We held on to each other for balance. Wasn't long before the dark shadow in the water slinked past again. Samson yelled, 'Catfish.'

"I saw it, too, a beast as big as Felix, hangin in the cafe. Maybe bigger. 'Get him,' I hollered. We both jumped in, tryin to grab the hawg and win braggin rights. Course there wasn't nothin there."

"Don't suppose," she said and gave me a poke with her elbow.

"Wait 'til you hear the rest." I couldn't help but laugh, remembering back. I grabbed Reba's arm, pulled her closer, and smelled her hair. "We were sure he was real and certain we'd have more luck if we sat in the water and waited for him to turn around and come back. Then we'd grab him."

"Smart." She nodded. "How much shine did you drink?"

"So much we figured it'd be an even better idea to float downstream so he'd think we were part of his family, his sons or cousins. You know, really fool him."

Reba laughed like crazy. "Someday I'd like to have a taste of Mr. J's Black Thunder."

My mind flashed, for the hundredth time, to the idea that Boudreaux's return to the jail was delayed by the brew, and I pushed it back as fast as it came.

"Wouldn't mind havin more myself."

*

The next day I pulled Elijah aside after school and asked if he'd pinch off some of his pa's Thunder for me.

"No, I ain't gonna do that." He frowned and crossed his arms to show he meant what he'd said.

"Why?"

"It's the devil's brew."

"Devil's brew?"

"My pa only sells the stuff 'cause he has to make a

livin, but look where it got Samson, gettin liquored up all the time."

"Shine didn't have nothin to do with what happened." I said with false conviction.

"It sure did. He was deliverin it when he picked up the hiker. I won't have nothin else to do with it and neither should you."

"You still collect corn from old Mr. Otis? How's he doin?"

"Wouldn't know," Elijah said and uncrossed his arms. "Pa don't buy from him no more. He stopped tendin to his crops and they're all but dead."

"Poor Mr. Otis." I actually said it out loud. "I been thinkin about helpin him."

"What for?"

I didn't look up. "He probably needs help."

Elijah shook his head. "He won't take no help from you. Won't even let you on his land."

*

Instead of going into Hadlee with Mama on Saturday morning, I stayed home and baked an Amalgamation cake.

"What's that for?" Mama asked when she got back.

"For Mr. Otis."

"Probably best to leave him alone, son."

"I gotta try, Mama. For Samson."

A dried-up cedar elm had fallen across the narrow road just beyond the creek bridge entering the Otis place. I couldn't go any further so I threw the gearshift into park, grabbed the Amalgamation cake off the passenger seat, and walked it in, not sure what to expect aside from a patch of scorched land where his barn used to sit.

The old wash pot balanced on the porch rail, no different than the first time I'd been there. A drying rag hung next to it. I heard a noise coming from the front porch and stopped dead in my tracks when I saw Mr. Otis sitting on a wooden bench against the front wall. His pink-rimmed eyes examined me through a pinched face. My heart revved.

"Mr. Otis," I said in a timid voice. There was no answer. The frail man, not much more than a thin black skeleton, got off the bench and tucked his threadbare T-shirt into trousers held up by a rope strung through the pant loops. The look on his face reminded me of a scared dog that'd suffered one too many beatings. He grabbed hold of the shotgun propped next to the bench. I guessed it was loaded and ready for intruders this time, and I stood still as a fencepost holding a cake. "You don't know me, but I'm Samson Johnson's friend."

He shook his head no, cocked the gun, and took aim.

"Mr. Otis, please don't shoot." My voice sounded high, like it'd been launched through a tin can. "I'm J. L. Rainey. I thought you might have a taste for some cake. It's my mama's recipe. Well, it's really her mama's recipe. But this cake here, I made myself. From scratch. Used pecans for this one. From our tree."

"Off my land," he yelled and squeezed the trigger.

The shot whizzed past my left ear. I flinched and went numb.

"Okay, okay, Mr. Otis, I'll be—"

"I said off."

The old man began to cough—and cough—and cough. He heaved forward with an attack of retching hacks. He dropped the gun and beat on his breastbone with his hand curled in a fist. He spit up blood that splattered on the wooden floor planks at his feet, and then he tried to sit back on the bench but missed it.

I placed the cake on the ground, rushed up the steps and took hold of him by the arms. Dribbles of blood stained the front of his shirt. He felt as light as a moth as I helped him back to the bench.

"You okay, Mr. Otis?"

He nodded, out of breath. I dunked the drying rag into the wash pot and wiped his mouth, then forehead. He began to relax.

"Much obliged, son." His eyes had gone all red. "Now, leave. Ain't no whites welcome here."

"I can't do that." I took a step back. "Hear me out, Mr. Otis. I came here 'cause—" I couldn't figure what to say next.

He drew a breath that whistled deep in his chest. "Who're you?"

"J. L. Rainey, sir."

His bloodshot eyes widened.

"Rainey?"

"Yes, sir."

"What you want?"

I pointed to the yard. "I brought cake for you."

"Donkey shit." He leaned his head against the wall and took in some deep breaths.

"Sir." I stood straight, my eyes locked on his dried-up face.

"Save yur breath."

"Mr. Otis, I'm having a conflict of the heart."

"More donkey shit," he said so low it could have been a whisper.

"And I've been taught that conflicts are for talkin out. It's why I'm here. To talk. And to lend a hand." I took the notepad out of my back pocket and opened it. "See? I made a list."

"We ain't got nothin to talk about." He gave a laugh that turned into a cough. "What kinda hand could you lend?" He shook his head. "Know what that list's worth? A bucket a spit."

His eyes didn't leave mine, like he wanted a full-blown stare-down. I lowered mine to let him know he'd already won and put the pad back into my pocket.

He brought his hands to his waistband and hitched his thumbs behind the rope holding up his pants. "What kinda cake?"

"Amalgamation, sir." I sprang off the porch to fetch it. "Made with raisins and pecans and blackberry jam."

He smacked his lips and wiped his mouth on his shirt sleeve, then he reached in his pocket and pulled out a jack-knife. "Hand it here."

I put the plate on the bench next to him. He cut a mountain-sized wedge, pulled it out with both his hands, and bit into it, barely chewing between bites. When he finished his second slice he sat back and let out a belch of approval.

"Ain't no one ever brought me no cake before. Reckon you can say your piece."

"Mr. Otis, sir, you don't know nothin about me."

"I heard the name." He stared at me, almost through me. "You the freedom fighter. Sure I heard a you. Say your piece."

Being confused for J.L. gave me a moment of panic. It felt like my tongue had swollen up. I took a breath and declared, "Sir, it was my fault your barn burned down."

His eyebrows shot up as if to say, *"How so?"*

My stomach did a slow roll as I worked up the courage to talk about what happened the day we picked up the hiker: the Bowie knife, the game of stretch, never knowing the hiker was a Chubb or had doubled back to Mr. Otis' place, and, of course, seeing the gurney with Samson's shoes rolling past my jail cell.

Mr. Otis' forehead turned into a field of wrinkles. He fiddled with his pants pocket and pulled out a hand-rolled cigarette. Fast as a thought, he struck a match against the bench and lit it. I looked at the blood on his shirt and wondered how soon it would be before he spit up more.

"You been holdin all this inside?" he said, with an exhale that sent a stream of smoke to the porch ceiling.

I nodded.

"Have a seat." He slid the Amalgamation cake

closer to himself. I sat down. "You was friends, huh?"

"Better than that. Me and him were blood brothers."

Before another word fell from my mouth I burst out crying into my hands. I cried for myself because I missed Samson and for poor Mr. Otis next to me because he didn't have a barn. But mostly I cried for him because I knew about the day he had to cut his dead son down from a tree.

Mr. Otis tapped out his cigarette.

"Keep goin, son. 'Til you get it all out. Best to get it all out."

I told him about my Uncle Mooks, who did his best, but could have been so much more if it weren't for those bastards who didn't have the balls to send their own kin to Vietnam. And I told him about being cheated out of a father, and that made me cry even more.

I wasn't sure if I'd be able to stop, but eventually the last tear dropped, and a sense of relief broke through. Instead of sorrow, my emotions took a turn, and soon the things I said were instinctive, critical for me to say, and they bounced out of my mouth.

"I want to make things right, Mr. Otis. To make people realize there ain't no difference between you and me. You and me, we both cry and laugh and bleed the same. Things gotta change, Mr. Otis." Hope washed over me. "Not just in Hadlee, but everywhere."

He shook his head. "I been 'round these parts all my life. It's a fool's game to imagine what can't be."

"But someone's gotta imagine. And try. You know,

Mr. Otis, there was a time I wanted to build skyscrapers 'cause I thought it would be an important thing to do, but now I've got a fire inside me to build somethin a whole lot bigger than that. I'm gonna lawyer for the NAACP."

"You be careful."

I went back to his house the next day. When I got there, he picked up his shotgun and threatened to run me off again. "Damn it, pest. I had enough of you yesterday, blubberin all over my porch. Take your skinny ass home."

I gave him my best smile and held up the basket of food from our garden. He let out a sigh, set the gun down and came off the porch to take a look.

"Them green beans?"

"And a lot more."

"Much obliged," he said. A wheeze came from his chest. "Much obliged."

That day I chopped logs from the cedar elm blocking the entrance to his property, split some for kindling, and stacked the rest.

Each time I paid a visit, Mr. Otis objected to the intrusion with the threat of the shotgun until I offered up my basket of food. It became our greeting ceremony.

Since his garden had all but withered away, I asked Wally to donate any seed packets on the shelves with ripped wrappers or splits in the seams. He came through in true Wally style, with a shoebox full of brand new Ferry Morse vegetable packs straight off the delivery truck.

*

I was on my knees planting carrots. Mr. Otis limped out to the garden. He steadied himself with a garden shovel instead of a cane and stood next to me. Had he been six inches taller, his head would have blocked the sun.

"Want another row, Mr. Otis?"

"No, that's more than 'nough. Much obliged."

"You sure?"

"Sure as piss rolls down tree trunks."

"It's easy enough. I got plenty."

He rubbed his chin and grinned. "Came out here to see if you was hungry."

"Whaddya mean?"

"Could you use a bite? Food? Grub?"

"Reckon."

He wobbled on the shovel. "Made some possum stew and cracklin bread. Like to share it."

"Yes sir, my pleasure."

We washed up on the porch. Mr. Otis led the way into the house, through a tight passageway bordered with stacks of bulging bags, boxes, plastic containers, and foil wrap, to the kitchen.

Two bowls of possum stew waited on either side of the pine table. A candle burned in the neck of a bottle between them.

"Grateful," I said and sat down.

"It ain't much."

"Means the world to me."

Over that summer Mr. Otis and I crossed off a good part of my list and accomplished things that weren't even on it. We planted a new cornfield, and when the crop grew to full height I convinced Mr. Johnson that Mr. Otis was ready for business and should be given a second chance.

His belly was full, his sweet tooth had been honored and satisfied, and his fear of one white person had become less.

But the time I read to him from my daddy's journal remains in my head forever. On that day, he cried.

37

The porch had turned too quiet and too empty without Uncle Mooks, but I forced myself to spend time there, alone, to learn how to welcome the silence.

With my eyes closed there were no squirrels to study or wind spinners to watch. If I relaxed and enjoyed the breeze as it passed, I could feel J.L.'s presence run through me the way it sometimes had in times of need.

Reba came by one evening when Mama and Wally were in town for a meeting. We drank sweet tea and watched the fireflies glimmer in the yard just before the sun set.

"The thing with J.L. happened again. This morning when I was out here."

She smiled at my news. "What's it feel like?"

"Hard to explain. There's times he takes over when I have to do things more suited to him than me. Other times he's no more than a thought that fills me with strength. A power within."

Reba said, "Maybe if we hold hands and both close our eyes, and if it happens to happen again, I'll be able to feel him, too." She took my hand, ready and eager to welcome him.

I wasn't ready to share it with her yet, the vibration

no stronger than an ant's heartbeat, the faint shadow of awareness I'd come to recognize. I hoped it wouldn't come, and I only pretended to close my eyes.

Twilight moved quickly through the yard and the fireflies seemed to be everywhere. A breeze rustled the cypresses causing the wind spinners to hum their hushed rattle, and the sound of a car interrupted the moment. Through the shades of dusk, a black Lincoln Continental with a colored man behind the wheel came up the drive.

I got up from the couch and walked down the steps to help him with directions. The car door swung open. The man sprang out, smoothed his tie, and offered his hand, a firm shake.

"Are you J. L. Rainey?"

"Yes."

He smiled and squeezed my hand even stronger. "My name's A.J. Monroe."

I found it hard to let go. The man J.L. had walked beside in a fight more important than the one he died for was shaking my hand. If Elvis Presley himself had left his grave and driven from Memphis to see me, I couldn't have been more bowled over.

I finally loosened my grip. "We figured you were dead, Mr. Monroe. Come inside. Mama's not home." It felt like happiness was tumbling out of my mouth. "This is Reba, I said as we went back up the porch steps. I opened the screen door to let him pass through, Reba following behind him. "We gave up on the notion of ever meetin you."

I turned the lamp on. The glow of light washed over us. "Please, have a seat."

He sat on the chair. I took the spot on the couch directly across, to look in his eyes, study his face, make sure he was the real thing.

He didn't look like James Earl Jones at all. He had a thin face, spotted with freckles. His ears were settled a little low on his head and could have passed for mushroom caps.

"A glass of sweet tea, Mr. Monroe?" Reba asked, taking on the role of hostess. Before he answered, she was halfway to the kitchen to fetch it.

"J.L. Rainey," he said with astonishment in his voice. "I didn't even know you existed."

I edged forward in my seat, wanting to tell him I didn't know he existed either until I read the journal, but I didn't say anything, just waited for his low, musical voice to keep going.

"I knew he got hitched a couple months after Selma, and I knew he'd been drafted, but we lost track of each other after that. I figured the worst when I never heard from him again."

Reba brought in three glasses of tea on Mama's favorite yellow tray. She set it on the table between Mr. Monroe and I, then reached to shake his hand.

"Pleased to meet you, Mr. Monroe." Her face glowed with triumph. "I helped J.L. write the letters." She sat down on the couch next to me. Despite myself, I wished she hadn't been there. She'd never been in my made-up talks with him.

"Thank you for this fine-tasting glass of tea," Mr. Monroe said. "But most of all, thank you for helping with the letter." Reba's fingers absentmindedly trailed the side of my leg. "I was just telling young J.L. here, I never knew his father had a son. Imagine my surprise when I got your letter."

"We sent fifteen," Reba said, excited.

"That don't matter," I said.

"I'm just—"

I interrupted her. "Which one got to you, Mr. Monroe?"

"Call me A.J. The letter sent to the national headquarters in Maryland finally made its way to me."

"The NAACP?"

Reba's leg nudged mine. "It's been more than six months since we sent 'em. We couldn't figure out why it was takin so long to get any answers."

"I haven't worked there for three years. It was by the grace of God my old secretary spotted it after her latest boss left. It'd been in his in-basket for all this time and only got to me this morning."

"Where's that?" I asked.

"I'm back in Alabama, lending a hand at the Southern Poverty Law Center. After I opened your letter I drove straight here from my office."

Reba crossed her legs and cupped her knee with her palms. She looked over at me. "You're never gonna believe this, Mr. Monroe, but J.L. wants to be a lawyer."

"Oh, I believe it. He'll be a damn good lawyer if he's anything like his father."

"He is," she said. "A lot like him."

Mr. Monroe looked up at the ceiling, then he looked directly at me and let out a sigh as if a long lost memory had dropped on his head. "Meeting your father changed my life. The kind of man he was, so sure and dedicated, helped me in my commitment to the cause. It was J.L. who steered my direction."

I thought about the article I had found in the journal. *White man marches alongside Negros on the certain road to integration.*

"It's been twenty years since I laid eyes on him. And over all that time I've held him in my heart."

I reached into my pocket and rubbed on the slugs from Samson's settin-up.

"I hear him, too."

"After getting your letter and now sitting across from you in your own living room, I have no doubt he somehow arranged the whole thing."

That was the moment I felt my past and my future meet, and it was perfectly clear to me, with a lot of help from him, I had become my father's son.

"I have no doubt either, sir."

ACKNOWLEDGMENTS:

In recent years I've been fortunate to hook up with many remarkable people who have given me untellable amounts of support and help.

I'm grateful for the San Diego writing community, which bestowed several awards on me — now that's encouragement. And, I'm especially grateful for my cohorts in our weekly critique group. We never came up with a name that stuck, but my favorite was Acme Read and Critique—*beep beep*.

I'm grateful for the writing family at the Santa Barbara Writers Conference where I was first accepted with open arms, as a writer.

I'm grateful to the brave ones who endured early drafts and whose input guided my story.

And I am especially grateful for Google.

*

To all my friends who thought this would never be finished . . . *Ta Dah!*

Made in the USA
Columbia, SC
21 May 2017